A TERRIBLE THING

CB555-07: A Terrible Thing
ISBN: 978-0-9962768-8-7

Carrion Blue 555
Chicopee MA / Lambertville NJ
carrionblue555@gmail.com

Atlantean Publishing
4 Pierrot Steps
71 Kursaal Way
Southend-on-Sea
Essex, SS1 2UY, UK
atlanteanpublishing@hotmail.com

"This is Heaven alright, but there's a man outside with a gun."
—Cardiacs, "What Paradise is Like"

TABLE OF CONTENTS

III: ...INTO THE HANDS OF A LIVING GOD

I:
YELLOW EPHEMERA

NOT ON THE RECOMMENDED READING LIST

DJ Tyrer

What great vistas of prehistory are yet concealed from us? What facets of the past are steadfastly denied discussion in the halls of academia? Who was it that dwelt in that Nameless City visited by the Mad Arab all those centuries ago? Just why is it that archaeological expeditions are forbidden to enter the Gobi, despite rumours of cyclopean ruins beside that long-dead seabed? What truth is but vaguely remembered in legends of sunken cities such as Plato's Atlantis?

No such topics will be covered in textbooks, nor the classroom, nor in reputable journals. Indeed, even the less reputable tabloids are disinclined to discuss some of the stranger stories that circulate amongst the tomb-raiders and fringe archaeologists. Such as the tale of the codices secretly brought out of Communist China that lent a surprising veracity to a certain banned play that circulated amongst the more decadent coteries of bohemia. Talk of other worlds and unknown cities of the distant past hardly fitted in with the accepted establishment dogma.

A name redolent of French Carcassonne was not out of place in a French text, but translate the setting to the depths of ancient Asia and it suddenly seems fantastical. Can there be any truth in the connection? Maybe the name was mutated to fit the author's native tongue? Or, is it all an amazing coincidence? Was there any connection to the Gobi ruins? Or, were those romantics who sought it in the Empty Quarter of Arabia correct in their assertions?

Perhaps we should follow the lead of the opium-smokers and lotus-eaters and seek that fabled city in the domain of dreams? Does dream have greater truth than our waking reality? I am inclined to accept that our world is but the shadow or distorted reflection of the true Platonic Ideal and that our dreams are a means of escape from this gross fallacy into the sublime truth. Maybe reality, as we term it, is the dream?

Banish all doubts and accept the truth, for the King is calling. Clothed in tatters, His rags belie His status, yet King He is. *They* might want to deny the truth, but He will not be denied. The play in which He reigns might not be on the recommended reading list, but there is more truth in one of its verses than in an entire volume of that stuffy lore. All I ask is that you read it and experience it for yourself. Cast off the shackles of orthodoxy and join me in His eternal embrace...

AN INVESTIGATION INTO
THE KING IN YELLOW
Simon Brake

Introduction

Sometimes, a story becomes more than just the territory of its creator. Sometimes, it outlives and outgrows its author. In the case of Lovecraft, and many of the authors associated with him, the combined stories have evolved into an entangled mythology that has become more than the sum of its parts. And the creations evolve beyond the original stories, the various mythologies expanded upon by other authors, even to the point of self-reference. The more effort put into setting these stories in a realistic setting (and, the more complex levels writers try to act on), the more self-reference appears within these tales.

Are these authors writing about the real world? You'd assume they aren't, of course, but how might you react if you found yourself in a situation where the only point of reference you have is a work of fiction (or, what you assumed to be fiction)? This itself suggests a further question: how have these writers been allowed to spread these stories, showing us "the truth," if there really is a terrible conspiracy of dark cultists and evil alien horrors lurking behind the scenes?

This stems from two possible misconceptions. Firstly, what if the reverse is true, that the authors of such stories are trying to cover their trail, to make rumours and "urban myths" appear to originate from a work of fiction? This might not make any sense at first glance. After all, you'd assume that these authors are trying to warn us of these dangers. They're not "bad guys" aiming to keep us in the dark about these evil forces, are they? However, if people were confronted with "facts" that sound so fantastic as to appear ridiculous or insane, is it any wonder then that the more cunning writers would want to veil their knowledge in the guise of a literary work? Not only will most fiction avoid the scrutiny of most aliens and cultists (who probably aren't reading fantasy novels in their spare time), but also most literature, as "art", enjoys a longer shelf-life than works of fact. The emotional and social elements of stories are often just as relevant as in the day they were written, whereas textbooks, particularly scientific ones, are either regularly updated or quickly outdated.

Also, consider the words of Lovecraft, of how small an island we live on in a vast universe beyond our comprehension. Then, you might start to realise that, if people were to accept these stories as fiction, we're not going to adopt the same panic-ridden anxiety that we would if it were presented to us as genuine fact. In these days of internet and mobile phone, where tabloid news takes mere hours to turn around and TVs show us live footage that inspire panicked reactions, we can imagine just what the results of such "news" might bring nowadays. That in presenting us the proof through works of fiction, we have a buffer between our minds and a cruel reality. And that, perhaps, if we do finally discover the "truth," it won't send us completely over the edge.

The second misconception is that the followers of alien gods want to keep such things secret. Perhaps it actually helps their cause that these well-meaning authors seeking to warn other people are actually spreading the word. Perhaps it has brought the idea so much into the mainstream as to be more familiar a concept to modern society.

The King In Yellow was unleashed upon the world at the end of the nineteenth century, both in terms of the book written by Robert W. Chambers and the Play he mentions within his stories. Of course, the Play is, of the two, the more dangerous work of literature. But, what if Chambers wrote his book to serve as some sort of misdirection for those seeking the Play? By presenting the Play as a work of fiction, at a time that the actual publication was being banned and taken off the shelves, the truth is hidden within the context of a series of stories. Anyone trying to find the notorious publication instead comes across the book of short stories by Chambers, with the merest snatches of dialogue and descriptions, and realises that perhaps it isn't really a notorious play after all. Furthermore, the individual stories might also cover up specific instances where people have suffered as a result of reading this play.

It is in this context that this document follows the trail of *The King In Yellow*, in the belief that perhaps both the original play and Chambers' book of short stories about it co-exist...

The King In Yellow Mythology – An Analysis

Mythology is more than a collection of old stories. The stories are the creative backdrops to many ancient religions, in much the same way as today's religions have their own stories and lessons. Still, if you look closely at any myth, particularly one that has been told many times by many people, you'll find inconsistencies amongst the parables and divine dynasties. Often it is the lessons that are important, not the specific relationship between different figures. As trends and beliefs change, and certain figures become more popular than others, myth has a tendency to contradict itself, to evolve into an acceptable form (rather than stagnate and die). History may be written by the victor, with religion and philosophy often written by the enduring scholar, adapting the old tales into the new world.

If we were to approach the mythology of the King In Yellow with as much hesitancy and uncertainty as we do classical (and historical) myths, we might accept that certain ideas and beliefs are malleable and defy definition because they mean different things to different people, at different times. It makes it hard for us to pin down exactly what is hinted at and referred to, and maybe that is how the mythology is best presented. Certainly, all the people in the short stories by Chambers who have been influenced by the Play seem to have their own spin on how it affects their lives, echoing how religious belief and understanding can be intensely personal and intimate. Likewise, readers of the various stories have different (and contradictory) ideas about what different re-occurring references and symbols of the mythology mean. This can be said to be true of any religion—in these times, we know only too well how the modern face of religion is often fractured into various factions, constantly squabbling and fighting (and killing) over "the Truth."

Still, there is a point where the King In Yellow mythology dramatically diverges from traditional myth to religion. We have the benefit of familiarity with the settings and characters of the short stories—through which we, in return, see the Play. Furthermore, we, the humble reader, know that we are reading fiction, and not some sacred text or legend. Whether it be Robert W. Chambers or the anonymous playwright he quotes, both authors must have had some sort of plan or agenda for the tales, surely? Even if this is not the case, we know that, from what has been put down on paper, details of the mythology can be fleshed out later. As, indeed, other writers have attempted to do (with varying degrees of success).

One of the points in favour of the King In Yellow mythology is that, by its very nature, it prompts insanity and chaos. It may be that the King In Yellow represents some form of chaos or entropy, either in his own right or as a herald or avatar of "Hastur" (Hastur is frequently referred to in the mythology of the King, usually as an overshadowing factor in the King's mythology–however, whether the name refers to some sort of deity, force of nature, or place is never really made clear). Regardless, this means that the jigsaw puzzle inevitably has pieces that do not fit, or even pieces that might exist one minute and not the next. There is no reason to the rhyme and the patterns seem elusive. This, in effect, means that the pattern may, at times, seem contradictory, as it weaves to and fro, attracted towards certain elements and truths whilst repelled by others. Bear in mind that what we see, in the course of what is little more than a handful of stories, are just scratches on the surface of a much larger unknown quantity. When examined in this light, it begins to dawn on you how immense a task it is to effectively map the territory and influence covered by the King.

And, yet, it is hard to shake off the feeling of the mythology as a simple, rigid religion. In particular, the backdrop to the story "In the Court of the Dragon," particularly with the passage quoted from the Bible at the end, being whispered by the King: "It is a fearful thing to fall into the hands of the living God!" (Hebrews 10:31). Does this place the King's mythology within the realms of established religion, or does it, instead, relate a mockery of this religion? Is it simply the exploitation and perversion of the narrator's religious beliefs? Given the subjective and individual attention each protagonist seems to suffer in these stories, it would most likely fall into the realms of a perversion of established belief.

Still, without any true followers of the faith, a religion has the capacity to fall backwards into existing as simply a structure of mythology. Examining the stories, there does seem to be the basis for some sort of the following: both Chambers and Lovecraft hint at followers of the King in their stories. Chambers mentions, in the first story of the collection, "The Repairer of Reputations," the thousand men who "had received the Yellow Sign, which no living human being dare disregard," whose names all appear on Mr. Wilde's list. Yet the narrator of this story may very well be delusional. If both he and Mr. Wilde are acknowledged to be insane, how much can we expect them to be telling the truth? How can we expect them to even re-cognise it? And, yet, maybe through the lens of their insanity, they are able to recognise it more clearly than anyone else. Secondly, the watchman in "The Yellow Sign," a figure which appears human, but, apparently, is not, that comes to claim the Yellow Sign from the narrator, possibly assuming the form of the King as he does so. Is "he" a lone manifestation, or are there others like him? In the play transcribed by Blish in his story "More Light," we are led to believe that such "people" are heralds of the King, but is this "fact," or just artistic licence on behalf of Blish or whoever originally penned the Play? Obviously, in a play written prior to publication of the Chambers book, we'd imagine it a more reliable observation than if it had been penned later, as if based on the watchman in "The Yellow Sign."

Lovecraft takes the idea of an actual following one step further. His addition appears in "The Whisp-erer in Darkness," where there is mention of a secret cult: "A whole secret cult of evil men (a man of your mystical erudition will understand me when I link them with Hastur and the Yellow Sign) devoted to the purpose of tracking them [the *mi-go* of the story] down and injuring them on behalf of monstrous powers from other dimensions." Here, strangely, the followers seem to be working against the story's antagonists, though we later find our information may have come from an untrustworthy source.

It's worth pondering this cult and their link to the Sign (other correspondents have referred to this cult as "The Brothers of the Yellow Sign," but I have been unable to pin down where this title came from).

Perhaps their goals coincide with the King's. Perhaps the Brothers and the King have a mutual enemy in the cold and emotionless mi-go, with no time for the creativity or decadence that seem to draw the King. Or, possibly, the Sign heralds from a time long before the Play, and the King is just a new avatar for an older evil. Certainly, the Brotherhood and the Sign appear to be aligned, perhaps predating the nineteenth-century publication of the Play. But, then, the King himself may well be independent of the Play that bears his name.

There is one more person that bears consideration: the organ player in "In the Court of the Dragon." Is he genuinely evil, a manifestation of the King's malevolence, or does he appear to be a threat as the result of the narrator's dream? The narrator of "The Yellow Sign" also considers the organist at his nearby church a "fiend in human shape." Is it the same person? Given the parallels here and a similar description of the priest and his sermons, we are led to believe they are, but is the organist a true manifestation of evil, or does he serve as a focus for the narrator's madness? Admittedly, Mr. Scott (from "The Yellow Sign") has his opinions of the organist before contact with either the Play or the Sign, and the church is also the "haunt" of the watchman. Maybe the organist and watchman are linked somehow, simply through contact with the church? The stories never touch on this, but it's certainly a possibility.

Despite these numerous hints and allusions, we never quite find out about the exact scope of any cult or following of the King. The observations of the narrators are all in a very personal context. Perhaps that is what makes the feeling of dread impossible to escape...

The Play...

Of course, you cannot consider the mythology without taking into account the Play. If the mythology of the King is considered to be something of a religion, then the Play is undoubtedly its holy book. The story told by it becomes a parable, a lesson, as demonstrated, perhaps, by James Blish's version in "More Light." Of course, as with any holy book, this doesn't mean the story is grounded in an imaginary world, with no basis in reality. Whilst none of the people from the short stories we read seem to encounter the characters from the Play, we do get echoes from that other world–dreams, nightmares, visions, and visitations.

If we take the original book by Chambers as an example, we have several stories that mention the Play, but each present different encounters with the King. "The Yellow Sign" is the only one with any tangible proof of some sort of physical manifestation of the King (or, some otherworldly presence) in our mundane world. "The Mask" has its protagonist falling ill and having feverish nightmares, though he recovers; the horror of this story concerns other, apparently un-related factors. The victim trapped in "In the Court of the Dragon" suffers a nightmare, too, albeit a very lucid one, only to end up facing an unholy vision of the King's domain–or, is he ultimately drawn into it? Finally, "The Repairer of Reputations" seems to be the narration of one man's delusion, and has no fantastic intrusions at all, bar the then-futuristic backdrop. The truth of even this reality is debatable. Is it the "real" world or the "perceived" world'? The story is the story of a madman, after all.

If we look a little further, at the stories of other writers, we see other people's additions. Some seek to add quotes from the Play, with James Blish going as far to attempt to write most of it. "More Light," however, fails to account for all the scenes hinted at by Chambers. For example, the following recollection–"I remembered Camilla's agonized scream and the awful words echoing through the streets of Carcosa. They were the last lines in the first act"–is notably absent from Blish's script. Also, the unmasking that takes place in the Blish story, towards the end of Act Two, is part of Act One, Scene Two according to Chambers, possibly occurring just before Camilla's "agonized scream" and the intermission before the terrible second act. Chambers adds, "Indeed, nobody ever ventured to discuss the second part aloud."

In terms of actual wording of the Play, we are presented only with samples, and, so, any conclusions we reach about the nature of the Play are those we reach ourselves, having decided what seems most likely. My own personal thoughts concerning the Play, and the frequently inconsistent references, stretch between two possible truths, either of which could be true, or, indeed, completely false. This all assumes the idea that there is some sort of single truthful mythology–whilst I doubt Chambers had any such "truth" in mind, it's possible that other authors, including the anonymous writer of the Play, may have.

The first idea concerning the Play is a practical one: that there are multiple copies of the Play, possibly multiple authors. If we consider all the related stories to be part of the mythology and not incidental fiction based upon it, consider Blish's version of the Play. It is suggested that Chambers had written the manuscript. Although it would have had to have been an edited version of the Play, condensing two acts into two scenes, it still doesn't account for some of the–apparently–missing scenes. This suggests it wasn't written by Chambers and, furthermore, was *not* a version he was familiar with. However, there is mention of "notes at the back that evidently were intended to be put into a later draft" that might explain some of the inconsistencies.

In "The Repairer of Reputations" there is mention of the initial response of the Play when "translated copies" arrived in Paris, before carrying on to London, then "continent to continent." Whilst many sources assume the original to be in French, Castaigne's story hints otherwise. If we are to believe Castaigne, we don't even know who the original author was, where he was from, nor how many translations (or adaptations) there might have been since. Some have suggested that Castaigne is the author himself. I'm not sure where this idea springs from—possibly the use of the phrase "the awful tragedy of young Castaigne" in "The Yellow Sign." In the context of the passage, it seems to refer to Castaigne's fate (or perhaps delusions), but might it actually refer to his *tragedy*, his written work?

It is almost as if the Play denies us the right to track down its mysterious past, its anonymous author. Which ties in neatly with the whole ambiguous nature of the King's mythology.

The second idea concerning the nature of the Play deals with the fact that, with *The King In Yellow* —and with all it entails—there is no certainty, no absolute. As the mythology interacts with different characters in different ways, so might the Play, the words themselves, not only on a subconscious level, but in a way that transcends and bends reality. Passages from one section might move to elsewhere in the story, all the better to shock a particular reader. Again, using Blish's story as an example, isn't it a little odd (as the narrator points out) that he should find the *Dramatis Personae* only after reading the First Act? Would the narrator's host have purposefully misplaced this page? Discovering the actors are all to be black (bar the masked Stranger and King, whose features are unlikely to be seen anyway) would throw most people off guard. It seems particularly out-of-place for a play supposedly written towards the end of the nineteenth century.

One thing worth noting about the play is that by the end of the twentieth century, much of it will have become dated. How shocking would the Play be if we saw it today, with our diet of violence fed to us daily through news reports and films that constantly push at boundaries that are traditional taboo? Would the Play shock us at all?

Maybe that's the point? Maybe it's *not* the shock we should worry about? If we become so desensitised as to not recognise the warnings of *The King In Yellow*, we will surely succumb to the same fates of previous readers and viewers of the Play. Perhaps we are already all the King's subjects, all in the hands of the Living God. And we don't even know it...

Tracing the Sign

If the Play represents a sacred text, then the Sign is paralleled with a religious icon. It is the crucifix to the King's Bible. A nice metaphor, but does it work? What *use* does the Sign have in the stories?

The Sign is, in its initial description to us (in the story of the same name), in the form of a symbol or letter, usually reproduced in yellow or gold, that is "neither Arabic nor Chinese, nor [...] did it belong to any human script." From the attempts artists have made to reproduce the symbol on paper, I am reminded of the Indian Om, used as a focus for contemplation and meditation and representing the name of the Deity. It has been adopted by many as a sign of absolute truth, purity. and good. In a perverse way, the Yellow Sign brings about a type of introspection, but whilst it might bring understanding, it doesn't bring peace. It has also been compared with the swastika, again of Indian origin, but the hard-edged iconic features of this symbol do not—for me, at least—conjure up the chaotic swirling "dance" of the Yellow Sign. Though, perhaps, the understated menace is the same.

In the story "The Yellow Sign," the Sign seems to fall into the hands of the narrator quite by chance, a gift from his model, after she has been unable to trace its original owner. The Sign is only "recovered" in the end by a figure originally identified as the watchman, and then, later, as the King In Yellow. This only occurs after the two central characters have read the Play and recognised the Sign for what it is. Whether the reading of the Play is a catalyst that draws in the King or whether He would have come to claim His Sign anyway is immaterial to the two doomed characters, but, in the over-all picture, it is of interest to us. Perhaps the understanding of the Sign works to focus their attention, unintentionally summoning the watchman/ King. This seems to be the idea formed by the narrator in his fevered recollection of the Play and how, in the midst of this terrible understanding, he knew that the King would be coming to reclaim the Sign.

This version of the Sign, gold on onyx, seems to be more important to the King than, say, those in "The Repairer of Reputations." Castaigne, at least as far as he is aware, has a "silken robe embroidered with the Yellow Sign." Castaigne also has a scroll "marked with the Yellow Sign," which he reveals to his cousin, who fails to recognise it altogether: "Oh, that's it, is it?" Indeed, the appearance of the Sign seems not to inspire dread or result in the tragic consequences evident in "The Yellow Sign," despite Castaigne's earlier claim that it was a sign that "no living human being dared disregard."

Towards the end of the story, Castaigne hands a Sign to a homeless person begging for money. "I had a blank bit of paper in my pocket, on which was traced the Yellow Sign, and I handed it to him. He looked at it stupidly for a moment and, then, with an uncertain glance at me, folded it with what seemed to me exaggerated care and placed it in his bosom." Of course, "traced" might mean that it was traced invisibly by finger, perhaps as some sort of imagined ritual. Does the homeless man see anything? We don't quite know, but we may have our suspicions, as Castaigne seems to. Again, within the context of the story, it simply leaves us in the dark. Which, whilst a good story device for installing a sense of dread, doesn't help us understand the Sign any better.

Maybe the Sign is valuable when fashioned into a gold and onyx amulet. Maybe it has some undisclosed power that is of use to the King that he doesn't want to fall into the hands of others. It is, perhaps, a royal insignia, one which is both used by the King to denote His status and by heralds or followers to denote their allegiance. Or, it could be as simple as a secret symbol worn or shown in order to let fellow conspirators recognise each other.

These last two cases are both valid for groups such as the "thousand men" on Mr. Wilde's list (who had "received the Yellow Sign") and the Brotherhood of the Yellow Sign (despite a lack of evidence to link them directly to the King). In neither case would it be desirable for an outsider to get their hands on (or use) the Sign, unless, of course, their own mad schemes coincide with those of the cult (or the King). Of course, perhaps when the Sign is in the hands of those who work towards goals that coincide with the King's, He *does* simply turn a blind eye?

Finally, I'd like to ponder on the actual meaning of the Sign. Recognising it seems to give it power, particularly in "The Yellow Sign." The tramp given the piece of paper traced with the Sign in "The Repairer of Reputations" might recognise it (we never quite know), but, if he does, is it because he knows the Play and recognises its power? Or, does he perceive something more subtle in the swirls of the Sign? Can he perceive and appreciate its inherent madness? There is something about the Yellow Sign that even we can recognise, three lines twisting out from a central point, swirling around it (like tatters of a robe?), whilst the centre sits fixed... and, yet, sometimes, it seems to have its back at us...

To those within the fiction of the stories, what else might the Sign reveal?

To me, it suggests a number of things: not "chaos"–at least, not in that clichéd way in which chaos represents everything random and haphazard. This is a directed chaos, a very personal sense of chaos turned towards you and, then, focused, as if you were at the wrong end of the telescope, being watched. Madness, in some ways. A build-up of intense, wild, and—sometimes–dangerous energy. True, sometimes a creative energy, but, ultimately, a maddeningly self-destructive one. It also brings to mind the idea of a "downward spiral." The spinning of the Sign suggests any number of nature's spirals, either unravelling and unleashing its influence on you, or pulling you in and enveloping you within its heart.

The Yellow Sign is a chaos that repels *or* embraces.

Welcome to the fold...

HASTUR AND THE KING IN YELLOW
Introduction to the 2007 Edition
DJ Tyrer

The Hastur Mythos (also more specifically defined as the Carcosa or Yellow Mythos) comes in many insidious forms. Hastur and Carcosa, common yet nebulous recurring names, were first mentioned by Ambrose Bierce, of *The Devil's Dictionary* fame. In "An Inhabitant of Carcosa," the channelled spirit of Hoseib Alar Robardin speaks of a long-ruined city he once called home, perhaps modelled on the southern French city of Carcassonne; Hastur is a god of shepherds in the story "Haita the Shepherd," where he has vague similarities to the God of the Judaeo-Christian tradition.

From these seemingly insignificant and—probably–unconnected beginnings, R.W. Chambers moulded something new in his short story anthology-*cum*-novella, *The King In Yellow*, bringing Carcosa and Hastur together and introducing the eponymous King. (In terms of the fictional play, *The King In Yellow*, there are also roots in Poe's "Masque of the Red Death"–colourful terror attending a masked ball.) It was this corpus that H.P. Lovecraft and others would continue to play with to create an ever-changing and expanding mythos of eldritch lore. Not bad, when Hastur, Carcosa, and the King remain little more than vague allusions in Chambers' work! Yet something about these exotic names grabs hold of one's attention, demanding that they be acknowledged, pondered, examined, perhaps even explained.

The stories comprising *The King In Yellow* are not overtly, as might be thought, horror. While there *are* elements of psychological horror, some parts are quite mundane; others are by turns fantastic and surreal. For example, "The Repairer of Reputations" is something of a SF tale, a look at a fascistic future (as the 1920s then were) of awful war and suicide booths. Perhaps, if Lovecraft and his acolytes had not seized upon the hints contained within it, the entire mythos would have taken a totally different direction, unconnected to horror–after all, Marion Zimmer Bradley used the terms in her *Darkover* novels quite independently of Lovecraft! Perhaps future writers will take the mythos in an entirely new direction...

There is, however, one point, especially interesting in light of "Haita the Shepherd," that is often overlooked by both commentators and writers alike. In addition to the oft-alluded Yellow Sign, perhaps the most commonly referred to aspect of the mythos is the phrase, "It is a fearful [or terrible] thing to fall into the hands of the Living God." In the context of the theme of a blasphemous play culminating in the King's unmasking (or not), this would seem to refer to the fate of those at the masque with the King In Yellow. Yet this evocative phrase is no invention of Chambers' fertile imagination–it is a quote of Hebrews 10:31, where it refers to the Christian God.

If Hastur and the King In Yellow are identical deities, as most, but not all, commentators assume, we see that, as Hastur, He parallels the Old Testament God in traits, by being worshipped by shepherds and by a connection to a great flood, while Chambers seems to explicitly connect the King In Yellow with the New Testament God. Perhaps the fictional play was blasphemous not just for its immoral or disturbing content, or for sending readers insane, but in a very literal sense? Could it be that *The King In Yellow* presented a blasphemous, even inverted, form of Christian belief? Or, maybe, it represents an extreme, even twisted, version of millennial judgemental belief? (The coming judgement and the terrible fire consuming the earth being the predominant themes of Hebrews chapter 10, from which the quote is drawn.)

Perhaps... perhaps the many redactors of the

Hastur Mythos have got it wrong? Perhaps the King In Yellow is not an evil alien entity or entropic person-ification or madness-inspiring being, but something more benign? Perhaps the reason why Church and State are so worried about the play in these tales is that the King offers a glorious release? As Hebrews 10:39 says: "But, we are not those that turn back and are lost. We are people who have faith and are saved." Perhaps the power of faith is the thing that is feared the most...?

A TERRIBLE THING
Introduction to the 2016 Text
DJ Tyrer

Nobody has ever seen the Yellow Sign, not for certain, yet it has inspired the creation of depictions. The complete text of the play *The King In Yellow* remains a mystery, merely hinted at by a few fragments and vague allusions, yet that hasn't stopped numerous writers from attempting to reconstruct it.

Twelve decades ago, *The King In Yellow* by Robert W. Chambers was published. What is it about the King and His Sign, Hastur and Hali, Alar and Aldones that still fire the imagination today? Some aspects of the Yellow Mythos–the names Hastur, Hali, Hoseib Alar Robardin, and Carcosa–predate Chambers, being the inventions of Ambrose Bierce, while its best-known manifestation, as part of or as an adjunct to the Cthulhu Mythos, derives from those writers who followed Lovecraft's lead when he mentioned elements in his story, "The Whisperer In Darkness." But, the Yellow Mythos predates that of Cthulhu and, as many of the stories in this collection show, can stand alone, unique and fascinating.

The Yellow Mythos means something different to everyone who encounters it. Sometimes it is a dark and threatening yellow, sometimes it is the washed-out yellow of an old playbill or the faded tatters of formerly-green wallpaper, sometimes it is the bright warning yellow of a wasp or hornet, and at others it is the vibrant and beautiful colour of gorse and sunflowers. To some, the King appears to promise enslavement, to some salvation, and, to yet others, dissolution or madness.

It is this mutability, I think, that is its greatest strength. Certainly, it is why I love it so, especially as a writer. I do have a tendency, when I write, to try and make everything (bar the most comical pieces) fit together in a single canon. Which, obviously, becomes either a restrictive straitjacket or an impossibility, given that many stories demand to be incompatible if they are to reach their full potential. But, within the Yellow Mythos, all things are possible. Indeed, Chambers opened his collection of tales with "The Repairer of Reputations," which not only deviates from events as they subsequently occurred, but hints that the entire narrative may be the product of a diseased mind. Dreams and reality exchange places, truth and lies mingle, madness and insanity become impossible to disentangle, while different timelines entwine, separate, and merge, and characters step into and out of Carcosa or even the Play itself. Indeed, just as the true contents of that forbidden Play are never certain, neither is the very location of that mysterious city, nor its true nature. Even the identities and relationship of Hastur and the King In Yellow change with alarming frequency.

Any story in any style or genre could conceivably be told within the Yellow Mythos, as ably demonstrated within these very pages, and all are equally valid, even those that are contradictory and mutually exclusive, within the myriad tableaux that comprise it. Although there may be tales that seem more aesthetically suited to the Mythos or which have proven more important to its development, all stories are welcome within it, and it is perfectly possible to ignore any or all that have come before, even those that seem to define it. Which means that virtually every reader should be able to find a tale suited to their tastes, whatever they are, and every writer draw inspiration from the Yellow Mythos.

To which end, I would invite you to read on and enjoy a selection of Yellow fiction of all sorts...

PLAY FRAGMENT
Cardinal Cox

CAMILLA: How can you say such... such... such blasphemies? If they heard, they'd–

CASSILDA: What, have my tongue ripped from my mouth? Give me to the mercenaries for their pleasure?

CAMILLA: If you don't fear for yourself, fear for me! I could be punished for hearing your lies!

CASSILDA: They are not lies! They have been granted to me by the Phantom of Truth, He that wears the Pallid Mask.

II:
IT IS A TERRIBLE THING TO FALL...

FUTURE IMPERFECT
Glynn Owen Barrass

White sky, black stars, a moonless nighttime in negative above a horizon of twisted towers and minarets. The view was surreal–the closer scene, that of a grey, lichen-infested, cobbled square flanked by a squat, crumbling, granite wall?

Horrendous.

Crouched on their knees, their hands behind their backs and their heads bowed in supplication, were eight *things* lined in a row. Tall, bald, gangly humanoids, their naked yellow flesh was covered in scabrous patches. Not all were supplicants, however. A female specimen, bald like the males but with pendulous, flaccid breasts, looked in Campbell's direction with bulging grey eyes, licked her lips with a long, vein-filled black tongue.

A red dot appeared near the centre of her forehead, and the back of her head exploded in a cloud of atomised skull and brain matter. Campbell shuddered as if he'd heard the gunshot, but the video, now as it was at the beginning, was completely silent. Whoever held the camera shook a little, backed off as the dead female slumped forward. A momentary close-up returned. A gore-filled crater replaced the back of her head, a protuberant twist of spine poking up behind it. Her hands, tied with a black plastic cable tie, bore obscenely long, twisted fingers, the jagged nails thick with dirt.

The camera zoomed out. A male form dressed in black combat fatigues, a ski mask, and tactical vest replaced the corpse. He held a Glock 22 in his gloved hand. Kitted out for combat, and murder, he lifted a sheet of cardboard towards the camera.

Black letters read:

REVENGE IS SWEET

The man stepped away, and following that cold, clinical first kill came a barrage of gunshots that tore the defenceless things asunder, the shuddering bodies ripped to shreds while silently screaming faces blossomed with new orifices and screamed no more. The screen turned blank. Further darkness followed as Campbell closed his eyes, numb with disgust. *What the hell is going on here? A rival agency or some foreign power in competition with us?* He was sure Analysis would have a field day with the video, but had decided to keep this his secret.

Campbell opened his eyes and stared at the screen. It made no sense. He was accustomed to seeing the *things*, had been in the Carcosans' presence off and on for eighteen months now. But he never thought he would see them die; didn't think they *could* die. *Do I speak to The King about this?* His superior in the Bureau, Mr. King, would be suspicious as to why he'd kept this alien snuff film to himself. Two days earlier, Campbell had found the dirt-smeared, yellow object in his jacket pocket, and, considering its contents, he could only assume it had fallen there from the sack of offerings he'd carried from the summoning room after the last Carcosan Event. And his instinct told him to remain quiet.

He checked his watch and sighed. It was almost time. He pushed the chair back from his desk, pulled on his jacket, and, halfway to leaving the room, returned to his desk, removing the memory stick and pocketing it before powering the computer down.

***

Revenge is sweet. Campbell pictured the slaughter. Yellow corpses, dirty cobbles pooled with black blood—with difficulty, he shook the image away. Standing with Gibson, a short, female, blonde fellow agent, the tall, bald-headed King and two armed, buzz-cut blonde guards wearing khaki combat fatigues, a palpable fear filled the elevator's small confines. Whenever Campbell was in close proximity to the summoning device, he needed to be somewhere else, anywhere else. By the looks on the other men's faces and the sweat beading Gibson's brow, he guessed they suffered similar thoughts. He didn't envy The King's role in this, the man holding the black cloth-covered device with his arms outstretched as if it were a bomb. The device was an artefact from the Roswell Event, one rumour went. Another said it had been discovered in Egypt, stuffed inside a mummy. Whatever its origin, the device was bad company.

The elevator continued its descent, to a floor unused by anyone but the score of members belonging to Project Yellow Sign. Officially, The King's agents belonged to the FBI's Facilities and Logistics Services Division. That's what it said on paper.

Campbell grew lost in thought again, his mind drifting back to the blood, the death. The memory stick felt heavy in his jacket's inside pocket.

An almost unfelt shudder, the elevator touching the basement floor, returned him to the here and now. The doors parted and The King strode forward, flanked by the guards. Campbell followed them down a grey basement corridor lined with rusted pipes. As The King and his retinue walked, ceiling tubes flickered above their heads. The group turned left at an intersection, and–contrary to the unkempt state of the remainder of the floor–now faced a relatively new, reinforced steel door flanked by two armed guards. "They're in there," the guard on the left said, and tilted his head towards the door. While the rest paused, the petite Gibson stepped forward and, with quick movements, slid a card key past a reader at the door's midsection. A loud beep followed and the door fell forward a few inches. Gibson backed away, gave Campbell a nervous look as The King moved forward.

He nudged the door open with his shoe and revealed a familiar, frightening room.

Bare, dirt-smeared white plaster walls, a cracked concrete floor, fluorescent tubes starkly illuminated the room. The offerings flanked the door. Sedated, strapped to gurneys, two death row criminals awaited a doom far worse than death, and they deserved it. Campbell had read their sheets. One, a man named Devon "Dee" Dewitt, had supposedly been executed two days earlier, for the multiple rape and murders of eight women at Fort Bragg, North Carolina. The other—Allen Stuart, "executed" by lethal injection but instead retained and sedated by Campbell's team—had murdered four people during a robbery at a Chuck E. Cheese. The FBI procured them easily. Monsters, scum, Campbell had witnessed what the Carcosans did to their "subjects" for they occasionally dumped their leftovers when collecting fresh offerings. Why? Because they were evil, sadistic bastards.

"Okay, let's get this started," The King said, his pockmarked face betraying only a hint of nervousness. "Campbell, close the door. You two push the offerings towards the back wall." This was directed at the guards. They shouldered their rifles and reluctantly wheeled the squeaking gurneys to the rear of the room.

Campbell pushed the door closed and heard it click as it locked. The way he felt, utterly trapped, was mirrored by Gibson's strained expression, the woman's eyes wide with anticipation. Beyond Gibson the guards returned, passing The King who now crouched on the floor with the device uncovered. He shoved the cloth in his jacket pocket, stood, and backed away. The device, an amber, roughly triangular blob, released a mellow glow Campbell knew from experience would fill the room when the lights went down.

"Lights," The King said, and Gibson followed his instructions. Campbell placed his hands behind his back and clenched his fists. His throat dry, he swallowed loudly with fear and anticipation.

The device, now a yellow blob of fire, revealed an object embedded in its depths, a bulbous black cylinder surrounded by three twisted spokes. The King's body became a black silhouette before it. Within the device's apparently solid matter, the spokes moved with a sinuous life of their own.

"Here we go," Gibson whispered, and reality shifted.

Blasts of wind, accompanied by wild, animal roars, appeared as the walls and ceiling disintegrated, revealing a blurred white sky spotted with obsidian stars. A too familiar scene. The chaotic air buffeting Campbell smelled of cinnamon and overripe fruit. Everyone but The King ducked at the gusts pounding their bodies. He stood stolid, his arms folded as the gurneys rattled around him. Where the walls had stood, just beyond the concrete floor, a world of sandy desert surrounded the group. Although the air shimmered, the wind only assaulted those within the remains of the basement.

Campbell stood straight, tried composing himself to match The King's firm countenance. He shuddered when he saw they were no longer alone. As if from thin air they'd appeared, too many figures to count. The things, the Carcosans, were everywhere, spotting the sand dunes into the distance. Campbell shuddered, the guards stood alert, and Gibson turned and said something that was lost in the wind. Campbell was distracted anyway, for a tall, spindly male creature now stood facing The King, its ugly, elongated form matching those surrounding them, matching those things he had seen murdered on video.

Fingers reaching past its knees twitched on multiple joints as the Carcosan bowed before The King. Its face, small and withered within a bulbous head, bore a grin of huge black teeth, its eyes glazed and unfocused. It spoke and Campbell shivered, the ugly voice resembling scratches on a record. It didn't speak English, yet the words appeared in his brain as such.

"You bring things? Good things yes?"

The Carcosan raised its head and giggled like a child. Its voice filled the air as it looked to the sky, its chest convulsing at it laughed at some private, alien joke. It looked to The King and nodded. *"Good things."*

Movement in the corner of Campbell's eye shifted his gaze to the gurney on his right. Another Carcosan had stalked closer, now looming over Dewitt. Unlike the others, this one, a female, wore a diamond-shaped, bone-coloured mask over its face. It stared down from narrow eye slits, teasing its hands across Dewitt's prone form like a pianist. Then Dewitt awoke. His screams filled the air, louder than the chaotic wind as he rocked in his gurney, twisted against the straps. The female Carcosan pressed a spidery hand against his mouth and muffled his terror. More movement: to his left, Campbell saw another masked female interfering with the Stuart man.

"You return to your blue world now. Live blue lives," the male Carcosan said. The King looked small now, insignificant before the being, and was he shaking? *"Goodbye day,"* the Carcosan continued, and in an instant Campbell's world became a void of black silence. Lightheaded, his knees crumbled and he was on the floor, his quick reflexes saving him from injuring himself. The sight of his spread hands pressed against concrete replaced the darkness, and the room surrounding him stood whole again. Nearby, he heard one of the guards vomiting. Footsteps to his right followed, tender hands gripping him as Gibson helped him up from his knees. He looked around and found The King bent forward, pawing through a large burlap sack. The Carcosan had deposited this before dis-appearing: their payment for the offerings.

After he composed himself, Campbell ap-proached The King with slow hesitancy. The gifts from the Carcosans varied in usefulness: boxes of costume jewellery, crumbling maps to unknown continents... Once a map had been in French, titled *Carcosa: Chemins Le Fer*. The name had stuck for the aliens.

"Anything useful?" Campbell asked.

The King shook his head and snorted. "Uh, pieces of half-built technology. I don't know what, but Tech will have a field day. Nothing living, thank God." These words brought some measure of relief to Campbell. The living things were always the worst, especially when they consisted of the mutilated, mewling remains of past offerings. Sometimes, the Carcosans deposited the corpses of *future* offerings, condemned criminals still alive somewhere in America. At least in those cases, locating and procuring the subjects proved simpler.

It was a relief to everyone it was over, the feeling palpable within the room. Still, leaving it provided added relief, The King bearing the device before him with Campbell hauling the burlap sack over his shoulder. It was heavy, but still, not as heavy as the memory stick.

***

Campbell went home that night in a mental haze. Gibson had noted his disposition, even offered to drive him home but he'd refused. His fellow agent meant a lot to him, and he didn't want to show weakness before her. He drove to his apartment knowing that if he'd left his car at the Bureau, it would have meant her picking him up in the morning and more time alone with her.

He stepped into his apartment, flicked through the day's post, then slumped on the couch, drained of energy and, also, feeling poisoned. The Carcosans had that effect on him, every single time. A shower wouldn't clean the psychic stink from him, and neither would changing clothes.

A little later he plugged the memory stick into his computer, re-watched the movie, and was disgusted and confused all over again. Afterwards he put the offending object in his wall safe. The tiny object seemed offensive there, polluting the sanctity of his mother's heirloom jewellery, his safety cash.

He stripped, worked out on his treadmill for half an hour, then took a shower before going through a few glasses of Jim Bean, lay on the couch naked while watching television. At 11 p.m. he went to bed, masturbated, and fell into an uneasy sleep.

***

As with every day after a Carcosan Event, a 9 a.m. conference was held by Mr. King. Usually this was in regards to what the aliens had given them, and what they would do with information gleaned from their technology. Campbell was not looking forward to it. For a start, it would be the ideal time to admit to owning the memory stick. Secondly, he felt like shit. The night had been a long one, waking constantly from vivid dreams about Gibson intermingled with nightmares about the Carcosans. Still, he went through the motions of getting up at 7:30 a.m., showered and dressed. He was on the motorway and winding his way around slow moving traffic at 8:15, was in the offices with ten minutes to spare. When he left home he'd brought the memory stick with him. For some reason, he felt it was safer on his person.

When he stepped into the large, white-walled Conference Room B, sugar-loaded coffee in hand and his brain still foggy from last night's poor sleep, the tense atmosphere hit him like a sledgehammer, instantly clearing his head. Fellow agents were already seated at the circular, glass-topped table at the centre of the room. The King stood before the TV on the far wall, his scarred, stony face looking more cadaverous than usual. He turned to Campbell at his entry, as did the other agents. All looked worried, to a man. All men... Gibson wasn't present and this, for a start, seemed wrong–in Campbell's experience, she had never been late for anything. Then The King spoke.

"They've taken one of our own."

Those worried faces stared at him. Campbell wasn't partnered with Gibson, but he did spend a lot of time with her, had formed a friendship, of sorts.

"Gibson," he said quietly.

The King opened his mouth, stretching his pockmarked cheeks to reveal white, perfect teeth. "Sit down, Campbell," he said finally. "We have it on surveillance."

Campbell slumped into his seat, his coffee ignored as he watched The King fiddle around with a remote control.

"I just had this spliced together by the tech team," he said.

The screen came to life, revealing black and white surveillance footage of the reception room downstairs. The time code at the bottom right said 8:19 a.m. The King pressed fast forward, zooming two minutes ahead, and on the screen Gibson came walking through the doors into the reception.

Her hair in a ponytail, she wore a black trouser suit, her usual attire. For some reason she looked unusually flustered. Campbell, feeling a fluttering in his chest, looked around self-consciously before returning his gaze to the screen. Another scene followed, Gibson walking down a corridor on the first floor.

"No sound on these," The King said, "but the explosion was heard throughout the building.

"Explosion?" an agent whispered, and many nervous glances were shared. Campbell kept his eyes on the screen. Gibson entering an elevator, the next camera shot showing her standing inside the elevator. All looked normal, and then Gibson shuddered, spasming where she stood. This happened two further times, then she dropped her briefcase. Next, her head turned directly towards the camera. Her mouth opened wide, her head flicking back so brutally that Campbell flinched like he'd heard it snap. Gibson's eyes rolled back in her skull, leaving nothing but staring whites. She froze there, and the screen turned to static

Silence filled the room until a few agents muttered to one another across the table. The King switched the screen off and sat heavily in his chair. Campbell noted this peripherally as he continued staring at the screen. He watched his own dim reflection and screamed inside.

"She never left the elevator," The King said.

Tortured and violated. Mutilated for sadistic, insane needs.

"Forensics have been over it with a fine tooth comb."

They'll deposit the remains in front of us, with a smile.

"Nothing. The explosion had no natural source. We believe it was just some part of the abduction transition."

An agent said in a panicked voice, "This could be an attack!"

Another said, "Any of us could be next."

Campbell rose from his seat. All heads turned to him, but the only gaze he acknowledged was The King's. He said, "We have to get her back."

***

The King had flatly refused Campbell's request. It went completely against protocol. Campbell had argued that protocol had been broken as soon as they'd taken Gibson. The King still refused. Campbell had gotten angry, shouted. The King had ordered him from the room, or he'd face suspension.

Campbell sat in his office and brooded, fingering the memory stick.

Revenge is sweet.

He slipped off the end cap and examined the USB. It was still tarnished with black residue, despite multiple uses. With unconscious volition he brought it to his nose. *Sulphur, the stink of hell.* Campbell plugged the memory stick into his machine and found, as before, an .avi file. He clicked the link.

This movie was different. Impossible, but there it was.

Men in black combat boots and fatigues, their faces concealed behind black balaclavas, stepping over the Carcosan corpses. They were armed with MP5 machine guns, the preferred weapon of choice for the FBI's own Black Ops teams. The leader with the sign, for this was most certainly a continuation of the other footage, stood to the right, talking animatedly with another masked man.

Of those examining the dead, one nudged a corpse with his foot. The leader budged past him as he strode towards the camera's POV. The man he'd been talking to dropped his arms dramatically in resignation. The sign was dropped, and the leader signalled to the one holding the camera. The view changed to that of the leader's head, armoured shoulders, and the terrible Carcosan sky. The leader raised a gloved hand and started pulling his balaclava up. Campbell saw a stubbled chin, then the leader had the balaclava past his lips and up over his nose and eyes, leaving the head past a thick tangle of unkempt sandy brown hair. Campbell gasped at the face, for his own familiar visage stared back at him.

"How... What the hell?"

Impossible, it's impossible. No, not really, he realized, as offerings from the Carcosans had defied time's arrow before. Who was to say he couldn't do the same, at least if he was there, in their world?

He knew just what to do.

***

A betrayal, a betrayal of The King *and* the FBI, was required to retrieve Gibson. He couldn't just leave her there, suffering at the clammy hands of those terrible beings. *I can't*, he thought, sat in her office, a room already cleared of her personal belongings. It wasn't right. She had a family. What if he was next? What if The King was next? Would a retrieval be in order for *him*?

Campbell looked at the only remaining object on Gibson's desk: her telephone. He picked it up and dialled a little-used in-house number connected to Project Yellow Sign.

"Yes?" answered a male voice.

"This is Agent Campbell. We need a small team for a Black Operation. I know this is out of the blue, but The King ordered it. Yes, of course I have proof. Just get a team together. We're going through the incursion."

A barrage of expletives followed, giving Campbell pause. He bit his lip then said, "We're going through, armed. We're going to retrieve a lost agent. Be ready in twenty." More arguments followed, then Campbell added, "Bring a camera."

He checked his watch. *One-fifteen, The King should be out.* Campbell rose from the desk, looked around the bare room wistfully, and steeled himself for the next part of his unsanctioned operation.

The King's office stood two floors above Gibson's, and after popping to his own office to collect a few folders, Campbell headed there while trying to hide his nerves from those he passed in the corridors. As soon as he reached his destination, he was forced to deal with The King's secretary, Mrs. Bell, a small red-headed woman with a stern demeanour who told him flatly to come back when Mr. King returned from lunch.

"He needs these files on his desk when he comes back," Campbell lied, waving his props in the woman's face. He ignored her further protestations and walked past her desk, into The King's office.

What could she do after all? Complain to The King when he returned? All going well, Campbell would be long gone.

The King's office was cream, with dark brown carpet tiles underfoot. A large pine desk stood against the north wall, against which stood a large cabinet stroke bookshelf filled with books and files. The one window, upon the east wall, was shuttered with a blind. He looked around briefly, then stepped around the desk. Campbell sent the office door a look, but the secretary didn't appear to interfere with him. He slapped the files onto the desk, sneered at the framed family photos there, then moved The King's chair, leaning down to reach the safe beneath the desk.

Five, seven, nine, two, he thought as he typed the numbers into the safe's keypad. All the agents connected to the project knew the code, just in case something happened to The King. No one would have thought of using it for this. The door unlocked, Campbell opened it and found sealed letters, a few files, a Glock 22 (he took this, pocketing it), and the device, wrapped in its black cloth. He hesitated over touching it, briefly, then he was barging from the office, past the shocked Mrs. Bell and towards either his doom or his destiny. He didn't know which.

It took taking the elevator to the basement, walking down those cold corridors, then entering the currently unguarded summoning room before everything finally hit home.

Fuck, I'm going into their world. Their hellish

world. And what if I'm already too late?

Campbell scraped his shoes across the concrete and stared at the reinforced door, left ajar for his team. The device was tucked under his right armpit, its presence not a comforting one. The Glock 22 in his left hand was. After a few minutes standing in indecision, the idea of backing out was taken away from him as he heard footsteps marching down the corridor towards the room. A quick check of his wristwatch told Campbell they were right on time.

Yes, of course I have proof, he'd said, and hoped the object under his arm was proof enough.

The footsteps paused at the door, followed by silence, then the door burst open.

The King entered the room, his face red with rage. This unforeseen sight made Campbell gasp. The Black Ops team, their weapons trained on him to a man, followed The King, and his shock became fear.

***

He awoke from a dreamless void, his mind hazy, his sensations padded in cotton wool like he'd just come around on a dentist's chair. The comparison was apt, for Campbell found a plastic mask strapped tightly over his face. Laid flat, he blinked at the bright, nebulous vision above. Gentle noise surrounded him, distant waves crashing against a shore. Then his vision cleared, his mind cleared, and he saw a looming nighttime sky in negative.

Campbell screamed into his mask. Fear overcame his numbed body with an impetus to move. He struggled but found himself strapped tightly down against... he knew what.

A gurney. The ritual. The Carcosan Event.

He twisted his head to the right; saw The King, other agents, standing solemnly in the desert. They *could* hear him. One of the agents, Barnes, had his head bowed in shame.

Campbell screamed himself hoarse, begging, the foam from his pleading mouth soaking his lips. He froze in his struggles as a thin shadow fell atop him, a shadow sourced by a cadaverous, Carcosan female. She was naked but for a diamond-shaped, bone-coloured mask with slits for eyes, a slit for a mouth. Long fingered hands stroked Campbell's chest and he voided his bladder in fear. The Carcosan laughed and said something in their twisted alien tongue. Campbell didn't hear the translation. The fear growing too much for him, he started to hyperventilate, shuddering uncontrollably.

The Carcosan touched his crotch, stroked it intimately, then lifted her hand towards the mask. Unattached by anything visible, the mask came up easily. The shrunken face revealed, too small for the surrounding, swollen yellow head, it looked down and smiled. The thing wore Gibson's face.

YELLOW TRIPTYCH
DS Davidson

Yellow Art

All that could be seen was the colour yellow. Row upon row of canvasses dripped with yellow paint. *Just* yellow paint, and not a vibrant yellow, either, but a sickly colour like that of pus. The paint oozed and ran, dribbling obscenely, and dripping down easels and onto the floor where it pooled with rubbery skins that resembled half-healed scabs. The artist sat in the middle of the room, amongst the strange yellow art, picking at a paint-scab in absent-minded repose. His clothes were dirty and splattered with the same yellow paint. Even his eyes, with their distant and unfocused gaze, seemed to reflect the yellow that was all around him.

The critics had written accolades about Tom Berridge and his art, hailing him the next great thing. His first exhibition had led to his being lionised, as being at "the cutting-edge of art." His second exhibition had been a critical success. Since then— nothing. The critics had been perplexed and wrote puzzled pieces in art journals about his surprising seclusion. At the height of his powers, Tom Berridge had effectively disappeared. Even his close friends and family had found themselves cut off from him; growing more and more concerned at his hermit-like ways and his curious fixation with the colour yellow, they, too, had been unable to elicit any meaningful response from him.

Now, he barely even painted, just sat staring at the canvasses, staring at an infinity of yellow.

No one was certain as to when his obsession commenced. It might have been when Tracy had left him. Or, it might have been when his cousin Charles brought him a slim volume of poems back from Paris.

Either way, he had developed obsessive-compulsive traits of the most alarming sort, and had become a recluse. The paintings, if you could really call them that, were all he had now. Even the poems were gone, their pages torn out and used as makeshift canvasses coated in dribbling yellow. But the words still haunted his mind, repeating again and again like an unholy mantra whispered in his ears. Despite the paint, the words still seemed visible to him.

There was a hammering at the front door of his house; the raps came with staccato urgency and, yet, barely penetrated into his consciousness. His head tilted quizzically, maybe due to the sound of knocking, maybe due to the words repeating within his head. Still, he sat there, staring. Tom did not even move when he heard the splintering of wood as someone kicked his front door in.

"Mr. Berridge?" a voice asked. "Tom Berridge?"

A blue figure loomed into his field of vision, blotting out the field of yellow like a horrendous storm cloud. Still, he didn't react.

"Mr. Berridge?" the policeman asked, shaking him slightly.

Tom shifted his head a fraction, but didn't really look at the policeman, his eyes remaining un-focused.

"In here," the policeman called to his partner, a note of urgency in his voice. Tom was emaciated and obviously severely dehydrated. "Call an ambulance!"

Slowly, his gaze still unfocused, Tom's dry lips moved as if he were trying to say something. He swayed as a vortex of yellow whirled around him.

"It is a terrible thing," he managed to gasp, "to fall into the hands of the Living God." And, with that, he tumbled backwards onto the floor, knocking over a can of paint, which flowed across the room like a haemorrhage of yellow blood. The policeman leant forward to check for signs of life: there were none.

Yellow Death

The yellow glow of the gas lamps excited something deep within Orson Wantage, causing him to quicken his step. A wave of nausea and dizziness swept over him, making him wish for his opium; he needed something to calm his nerves. The chill air burnt his throat and he wished he were back in his garret: it was not much, but it was not quite that of the starving poet of myth. With a well-stocked stove, it was quite warm and snug, and far preferable to being out in a harsh Parisian winter.

"You look sick, Orson," Louis said as he went inside the doss-house.

"Just need a good night's sleep."

He climbed the stairs to his room, grateful not to be crowded in with others, and went inside, locking the door behind him. Looking in the mirror, he could see why Louis had said he looked sick: he rarely looked too well–late nights and copious amounts of opium left him pallid and with dark-ringed eyes–but now his skin had an unhealthy yellow sheen, as if he had some liver disease. No wonder he felt ill!

Opening the small cabinet in the corner of the room, he fished out a tincture of morphine and swigged some down. The effect seemed almost instantaneous: his throat ceased hurting, his head seemed to clear, and all his aches and pains faded away, as if his body were some place far away from him. Lying back on the bed, he felt much better. He reached out and picked up his notebook and began to scribble notes for poems: he had a new volume to complete, to satisfy his publisher's demands.

But the muse seemed to have abandoned him recently, leaving him uninspired, a dry well of ideas. So, he did what he had done more and more often recently and turned to his copy of *The King In Yellow* for inspiration. He wasn't sure why, but the new and controversial play seemed to unleash his artistic skills and erase his lingering doubts that he was no more than a poetaster scrabbling for crumbs of recognition. Ever since he had first been given a copy by a friend, he had found that it helped inspire him–his poems had begun to more and more reflect the surreal and alien worlds hinted at in its obscure soliloquies.

"So many moons," he mumbled to himself as he gazed out the window at scenes no one else could see. He tried to write down the vision before his eyes, but could not gather the words he needed.

A hammering on the door called his attention back to reality. It was his landlady demanding the rent. How could she think of such paltry banalities? He pulled the pillow about his ears to drown out the noise and, eventually, the knocking ceased and he could return to his curious reverie.

"O! My Jaunetic Muse!" he cried in desperation, praying that the words would come to him. "Bring me the words to describe Your majesty!"

But still, the well was dry. In frustration, he threw pen and paper aside and tossed the play out of the window in disgust. Throwing himself off of the bed, he stormed across the room in a temper and slammed his fists against the wall. Plaster scattered to the floor and a great sob escaped his lips as he finally accepted defeat.

A moment later, the knocking at the door began again, Mme Gilbert yelling at him at the top of her lungs. But he didn't hear her. He was staring in a terrified trance at the mirror on the wall. A pallid mask was staring impassively back at him.

A final sob hiccoughed around the room as his landlady forced the flimsy bolt on the door and barged in. Slowly, he slid to the floor in a foetal curl on the threadbare rug.

Mme Gilbert screamed in horror as she stared down at him. Orson's flesh was a horrible wan yellow colour with a waxy sheen, and bile-coloured pus ran from his eyes like vile tears, and from his nose and ears, dripping to the floor to pool in an obscene curl.

Yellow Peril

Charles Berridge sat in business class, the slim volume clasped tightly in his hands, which were stained with yellow nicotine. When he had spotted it, a collection of American poet Orson Wantage's verse published shortly after his death in Paris—which was where he had found it—he just had to buy it. His work took him all around the world and he would always bring his artist cousin something back from the places he visited: paintings, books, sculptures. This book, in particular, had caught his eye; in fact, it was almost as if the mustard-coloured book called to him.

He had plugged his laptop into the socket provided and begun searching the net for data on Wantage. The poet's name had been vaguely familiar to him; he must have read something by him before, somewhere. The collection had also had a very brief, and even vaguer, note on his life that described his birth in Illinois and his short poetic career in New York, London, and Paris. The search engine popped up a mixed bag of hits: a Wantage Town Council site, a Michael Wantage genealogical entry, and others equally unrelated. But there was one entry that looked promising: a listing of *fin de siècle* poets.

Charles clicked the site open and began to read. The site commenced with a précis of Wantage's life, not much more than he already knew. There was also a list of his published work—this posthumous collection, *Jaunetic Muse*, wasn't mentioned. That made him raise an eyebrow—a very rare collection, then. All the better a present for his cousin.

Suddenly, the screen froze in mid-scroll.

"Dammit!" he exclaimed as he futilely clicked

and pressed control-alt-delete to no effect.

Slowly, yellow began to fill the screen, flowing down it like yellow blood or paint. Before the screen grew totally yellow, a message briefly flared, yellow on black: **IT IS A TERRIBLE THING TO FALL INTO THE HANDS OF THE LIVING GOD**. Then, the words disappeared under a mustard deluge.

"Damn viruses!" He slammed the screen of the laptop down in frustration, then turned it off.

"So much for technology," said the man beside him.

Charles grunted his agreement, picked up the book and began to read.

Beside him, his neighbour smiled a knowing smile.

THE DEVIL'S MUSTARD
David W. Barbee

The walls here are tan, but that's yellow enough. He's watching.

To you it may appear that I'm sitting alone in this cramped motel room, the sort of room that's seen plenty of unsavory acts. It may even appear that I'm sitting on the ratty green bedspread, staring at the tan wallpaper just a foot away from my face. But these are just appearances, they certainly aren't really happening.

Certainly it appears to be happening, though. It looks exactly like I'm sitting on that bedspread for hours, silent and staring, never moving a muscle, holding a revolver in my lap. Sure, it looks ominous, but I figured all of this out already. There is no motel room and no revolver. The hours that I spend sitting there aren't real, as even the passage of time is an illusion here. The space I occupy and the things I observe are all tricks. What I am experiencing is not reality but some vague simulation of it, something that I exist within that, over time, I've been able to detach myself from. Now I am torturously aware.

The motel room doesn't last long. The simulation... *he*... would have me believe that I spent two days there. But it was never there. The simulation blinks away and is replaced by new stimuli with new context.

I am sitting at a table in my underwear. The revolver is replaced by a spoon. I bring a bite of cold cereal up to my mouth but stop at the last second. The bowl is painted bright yellow. I spit the food onto the pale linoleum at my feet. Since I became aware I prefer to never touch things that are yellow. Whenever I blink into a new scenario to find myself touching something yellow, I react badly. In this case I throw the yellow-painted bowl down where it shatters across the floor with a splash of milk and cereal.

My policy on touching yellow things is the one thing about the simulations that I try to control. It is my one form of resistance, since I know it is through the yellow that he watches me. I can sense him in the shards of painted ceramic all around my feet. I call him the Yellow Man. He exists in the colors, the vast imagery of every landscape I see. He hides his face behind the colors but through the yellow, the bright blinding yellow to the sickly brown yellow, he can be seen. I've caught glimpses of him before. The Yellow Man is like a dragon the size of the moon. No matter how artificial my reality has become, he above all is real. Through the yellow, the great creature watches me in this dimension he's trapped me in.

I don't know how long I stand there staring down at the broken bowl. Perhaps the Yellow Man is taunting me by setting the bowl in my hands for this simulation. Thankfully, the scenery blinks away and I don't have to think about it anymore. In this place of shifting dreams, nothing is permanent.

I find myself in a car, the color yellow absent from my clothing or anything I'm touching. I realize that I am driving across a bridge, flowing with the traffic. The more aware of my driving I become, the more recklessly I handle the wheel. A few yards ahead in the next lane I can see a big yellow box truck. I actually find it comforting that he's still there. I push the gas pedal and the car sprints down the bridge, faster and faster. I pass the box truck but see other yellow things as I zoom along. I'm curious if I'll crash before this dream stops and the next one begins.

The vast majority of these dreams are what amount to ordinary experiences. Day-to-day moments that could be a part of anyone's life. Other times I find myself flying through space or running like a cat through savage jungles. I used to wonder if something was wrong with my mind. I was terrified by the dreams, and secretly hoped that I'd had brain damage, like I was in coma. I wished they were dreams because then they could be ignored.

But no one's watching you in a dream.

Instead it's a simulation. A trick. I try not to interact with it unless I absolutely must. Perhaps this would make me appear strange and lonely. In an unreal world where I can do anything, I make it a point to do nothing, because the more time I've spent being watched by the Yellow Man, the more certain I am that these virtual experiences must have a purpose. And the purpose must serve him somehow.

The Yellow Man could be an alien creature watching me as some form of entertainment, like a bug in a jar. Or he could be a participant in the simulation, though he hasn't interacted with me yet. The Yellow Man could be an enemy or ally I'm meant to confront in order to make some sort of progress. Worse yet, he might be controlling all of my actions and thoughts in these simulations. I could very easily be his unthinking pawn, an avatar he directs by remote control. Even my free will could be just an illusion.

In this state I can neither control nor validate my very existence. I admit that all of this knowledge has come with repercussions for me, but for the most part this realization has been liberating. I'm actually glad I've given up on reality. There's freedom in knowing for certain that nothing matters.

I never crash the car, but instead find myself on a subway platform, squeezed into a huge crowd of people. The subway comes to a stop in front of the crowd and I close my eyes as a hundred people flow around me, bumping into me and brushing against my clothes. If I see a single stitch of yellow come into contact with me I know I'll lose my mind, so I tell myself to breathe and remain calm. Soon I hear the subway start moving again and I know that I'm alone on the platform. When I open my eyes I see the yellow lines traced along the concrete floor. Perhaps I was truly alone when my eyes were closed, before I could see the color.

I close my eyes again and wish that in the next dream I am swimming like a fish or making beautiful music on an instrument I don't know how to play. Instead I wake up lying in a puddle. It's raining and I'm bleeding from my eyebrow. There's a golden street lamp glowing high above me. Through the rain and the throbbing in my head it looks like an evil eye.

The street lamp and the storm all blink away as the next scenario creates itself before me. I am in a booth at a fast food restaurant. A single hamburger sits before me, wrapped in red and white wax paper. I suddenly realize how famished I am. I unwrap the burger and study it for a moment. My hunger is joined by suspicion. The burger looks plain, free of ketchup or cheese. I take a quick bite and it tastes so good that I devour the entire thing.

It's not until I have the entire thing in my mouth that I notice the taste.

Mustard.

My mouth is too full of burger and bun to speak. The mustard's mild spiciness coats my tongue and it refuses to push the food out of my mouth. I'm forced to continue chewing, whimpering pathetically through my mustard-flavored burger. I begin to swallow the food, bit by bit, and dry heave as the last of it settles into my stomach. The mustard taste coats my tongue and throat. He's inside me now. My rule against touching yellow was specifically to prevent this from happening, and yet I've been trapped. I know that this is his doing. I know I have no chance of vomiting up the burger and freeing myself. I leave the fast food restaurant and run into the street. The last thing I see is the bumper of a small black car tackling me at the knees.

A sane man would expect to wake up in the

hospital, but I know that I can wake up literally any-where.

I wake up on a mountaintop, surrounded only by sky and stone and clouds. For once I believe that I have seen the last shade of yellow. Perhaps ingesting the yellow man's mustard has brought me into a new phase of our game. I gawk at the endless majesty of God's creation, but while the color is missing, I can still feel his presence. He is inside me now. The Yellow Man got inside me through the mustard. I toss myself off the mountaintop, arms spread to embrace the crags below.

I wake up at a picnic table. The people around me are all wearing pink shirts advertising their family reunion. Several men are cooking at grills. The picnic table is covered in a red and white checkerboard cloth. I hear the buzz of conversation and the thick scent of barbeque. I gaze around and pat my hands against the tabletop. Perhaps the dreams aren't the only things that aren't real. Maybe the Yellow Man isn't real, either. The black car that hit me couldn't have been real, but both of my knees are swollen and ache.

Then a woman walks by and places two bottles on the table. I grin up at her but she ignores me, heading off to the next table to put more bottles there. When I look at the bottles she's placed before me, my heart sinks. One of them is a glass container of hot sauce. The other is a fat plastic bottle of mustard.

I can't stop glaring at it. I carefully reach forward and take the bottle into my hand. It feels full and heavy. The clear plastic is bulging with bright yellow paste. I pop open the lid's cap and squirt a small dot of mustard onto the table. I must have expected something sinister, because I am elated when the blob of yellow just sits there. I squeeze the mustard again and draw a big yellow circle on the tablecloth. I give it eyes and a happy smile, little zigzags for hair and finally a big glob for a nose.

It's strange. In all the places I've seen him, in

the walls and on my skin and shining in the rays of sunlight, I've never seen him as clearly as he was in that mustard face. I find myself smiling at it, and before I know it the mustard bottle is being crushed between my reddening hands. The plastic folds and whines and the mustard forcefully squirts itself into a wet pile on the table before me. I toss the bottle and smooth the mustard with my fingers until it's an even disc of yellow. I finally realize how perfectly yellow mustard is, how pure. I bend my face down to the table until my nose is an inch from it. I suck its stout aroma into my nostrils and stare deep into an endless void of yellow.

"Listen to me," I say to the mustard in an even baritone. "Look at me. Talk to me. I know you're there. I've always known." My voice rises in volume as my muscles in my neck turn tight. "And I don't care!" I growl. "I don't want anything from you. I don't care what happens here. I don't give a *shit!*"

Things go fuzzy for a moment and I'm being dragged away from the picnic table by very large men. They disappear and suddenly I'm at Woodstock, my pupils dilated and my yellowed teeth chewing on my knuckles. I'm on the planet Doob, subjugating the pale-skinned barbarian hordes. I'm reading, and even the color of the paper seems off.

DREAMS OF THE YELLOW KING
Dirk Holland

I had the dream again last night.

It's the one with the city with the empty streets. I'm all alone, walking down mist-sheathed, cobbled streets. Pus-yellow tendrils of choking smog slither about my limbs, as if seeking a purchase on my flesh or clothing with their clammy tips so as to pull me down into some abyssal deep. I pull on through.

I find myself in a park, overgrown and uncared for. Trees and shrubs and grass all withered and dying, as if the night, here in my dream, were unyielding in its grips, their leaves crisp and yellowed.

Approaching a mound, I begin to slow in fear. There is something not quite right about it. It looks like the outline of a sleeper beneath a sheet. I knew what it was and recoiled from it in disgust. The sheet moved, *undulated*; I dared look no closer.

And then, the Yellow King is standing before me, mouthing blasphemies through his waxy lips. His tattered robes flutter lightly in a breeze I cannot feel and he speaks to me of my innermost hopes and fears. Slowly, his make-like countenance moves closer to mine...

That's when I awake.

***

The Doctor taps his pen on his notebook as I finish my description, then scribbles some sort of comment down. He asks me questions. He wants to know what blasphemies the figure is mouthing. He wants to know what my hopes and fears are. I hate his probing.

"Hildred," he says, "how can I help you if you won't help yourself?"

***

DIRK HOLLAND

I had the dream again last night.

Now, I know what it is that the figure demands. The figure represents me: that explains why it knows so much about me... It is my kingship, my sovereignty. It demands that I take up my rightful throne. This I must do. I cannot deny it.

***

I have arrayed my forces and rallied my troops. With the armies, none shall stand in my way as I re-establish the rule of my dynasty, a rule so long denied.

***

I killed Doctor Krycek today. He refused to believe me. Refused to acknowledge my right to rule. I will show him. I will rule again—master of all I survey. I shall become the Yellow King, master of the worlds of man. I shall triumph.

***

The patient expired last night in his sleep. While I cannot know for certain, it is interesting to speculate as to the identity of the thing that the mound concealed beneath a blanket of bugs: could it be that he finally dared to look closely and discovered that it was he himself lying there? Could the culmination of such a dream have killed him?

I can never know, but I can be sure that the criminally insane patient who called himself Hildred Castaigne is finally dead.

Signed, Dr. Robert Krycek

THE SWELLING
David Conyers

For five violent days, the unrelenting storm battered the *Daintree*, threatening to submerge her at any moment, but it was the unravelling of Greg Wright's mind that disturbed Tracy more than any elemental assault.

As the weather worsened, so did his delusions. First he claimed to see mermaids, then fish-demons. Both, he said, were plaguing the angry waves, clawing at their yacht. Tracy never witnessed these fanciful creatures herself, even when he pointed them out. After his fifth day of peculiar behaviour, Greg calmly explained to Tracy that he'd finally read the truth in a book. It told him what to do and he had done what he was told. He had just murdered their daughter Matilda. How? A revolver pressed against her temple had splattered her brains all over the cabin walls.

Unwilling to witness his wife's shock and grief, Greg threw himself into the crashing waves, becoming lost within seconds. Perhaps this was his only appeasement.

Not long after, the weather finally beat her. Tracy knew she had lost her mind, and then didn't know who or what she was.

That was the beginning.

As for the end, she didn't know when that day might come, and if it did, would she even recognize it...

***

The *Vestibule* churned over the swelling ocean. Salty foam broke at its bow as the steamer fought back and ploughed towards its unknown destination. Overcast and grey, the clouds above filled the sky, never relenting in spitting rain. The chill captured in the wind ran straight from Antarctica itself.

Wrapped in a blanket while the tears on her cheeks vanished in the spray, she lost her thoughts towards the horizon where the water and clouds merged into one. Their unnamed destination was somewhere out there and it seemed to her to be so far away, unreachable, as if it did not exist except inside her mind.

She understood that her current emotional state was shaky and weak. Her thoughts had been disjointed these last days or weeks–exactly how long, she could not remember. To compensate, she tried to recall pleasant memories and found that she had lost all that she might once have known. A loss which served only to catapult her into deeper depression.

No birds in the sky, no fish in the sea, and the colour of the water always a decisive grey, textured like spoilt meat. What survived in this place? Herself, obviously, and the crew, but what the crew were was not exactly what she would call "living."

Despite her misgivings, the fresh air did somewhat relieve her nausea. In the last few hours, the swelling had grown worse, and she wasn't sure why. So, she had slipped outside, hoping to escape her sickness. With the fresh air came the cold and wet, which, in minutes, became a worse misery. Yet again, there was no simple solution.

In the end, she returned to her cabin, found her daughter wrapped in blankets as she had left her. The little girl's smile was faint and grey. Her face pasty and dry like cardboard.

"Where are we?" her daughter asked sombrely.

"Safe," she answered. A mother's response, spoken while she ran her fingers gently through the young girl's auburn hair. Ever since the accident, the strands had tangled in knots and stayed that way. Neither mother nor daughter had been able to straighten them again, even with persistence and their only comb.

"Where's Daddy?"

"Daddy's gone away for a while."

"When's he coming back?"

"Soon," she whispered. "We'll be with him soon."

One day, she'd have to tell her daughter the truth, but to do so, she would first have to be honest with herself.

Running out of time, she didn't know if that day would ever come.

***

During the passing weeks, her daughter had become infected with a lasting illness that was more than just a cold or flu. Confined to her bunk and this cabin, her little girl had remained here since their rescue. All fates considered, it had been a miracle that they had been discovered at all. Floating alone, thousands of kilometers off the east coast of Australia, fighting to stay alive in a cold, frigid, and tumultuous ocean. What had begun as a luxury yachting cruise from Sydney to the tropical Pacific atolls had ended in nightmare. She wasn't sure that her torment would ever end.

Always, they were hungry. Always, the food was unpalatable, its taste nothing more than wet cardboard or soggy paper. Yet they must eat, especially her little girl, whose health was not improving. As a mother, she instinctively knew that she must again seek medical help. Unfortunately, she didn't trust any of the crew, so again, she was forced to take on the role of examining doctor herself. The cause was easy: they needed to eat proper food; and to find proper food, she would have to overcome her loathing towards venturing beyond their cabin. She would once more have to explore the interior of the *Vestibule* in hope of discovering the elusive kitchens.

Like a memory that was a dream turned inside out, she recalled their third day when the mother first wandered into the lower levels on a similar quest. In no time at all, she became hopelessly lost in the labyrinthine turns and dead ends that made no sense. There had been no doors or portals down there either, only stairs and corridors that echoed endlessly. As she foolishly descended to each successive level, they progressively became darker and colder than the one above, and the half-heard noises muffled through the walls became harder to disbelieve. A part of her knew that if she descended too far, she might actually hear what they were saying, and what they had to say would not be pleasant.

The one location on this ship that she could easily find at any time was the bridge.

From all points on the decks, it could be seen, high and lofty like a lighthouse upon a cliff, a beacon of rationality. At night, when the ocean was pitch-black and restless, it seemed that the bridge and her cabin held the only light in the entire world, that everyone elsewhere on this ship did not require electricity. After this realization, she ceased to venture out at night.

It was the middle of the day now, not that the sun was ever seen. Climbing the metal stairs, drenched by the incessant salty spray and convinced that she was always wet, the mother stumbled inside the bridge. She sensed the pronounced effects of the swelling now that she was up high, looking down on the *Vestibule* as if it were a map. The nausea returned, but if she threw up again, her subconscious reminded her that she would probably drown by doing so.

At the wheel stood the Captain, positioned in the only place she had ever seen him. He was staring forward, towards the vanishing point that was a never-ending merger of a violent ocean and a tumultuous sky. He turned when she sealed the porthole behind her, and nodded delicately to acknowledge her presence.

Wrapped in a dark grey coat, his feet and hands were covered in their entirety by leather boots and gloves. The woolen scarf about his neck was wound tight, and that large pirate hat on his head didn't really seem all that odd, despite its misplaced historical context. What numbed her most was his mask: World War One flying goggles and the scarf, wrapped around his face so she could never see what he really looked like. There was flesh in there, glimpsed only occasionally when he let his mask slip. Nothing more had ever been revealed.

"Ma'am," he nodded ever so slightly. His voice was lyrical, even familiar, and disturbingly feminine. He was her height exactly, so she didn't need to chink her neck to look up at him, as she had to do when conversing with any of the strange crew.

"Captain," she shivered then dripped. Now that she had joined him on the bridge, words were lost to her. He said nothing in response. He would wait indefinitely until she had a question to ask of him.

Concluding that she had not come here to talk, the Captain returned to the wheel. Feeling awkward, she glanced at the charts pinned to the back wall, hoping to discover a topic of conversation. She quickly found one, when she was surprised that the charts displayed no continents or even islands, as if the sea was all there ever was and ever could be. "What's our destination?" she asked, knowing that she had asked before, only she could never fully remember his previous answers, and that she would forget again what he was about to tell her now. Still, he never seemed to mind her repetition.

"Carcosa," his words were soft.

Whimsically, she said, "I've heard of that place, but just can't seem to remember where?" She searched for it on the map and failed to find it. "Will I find what I'm looking for there?"

The Captain nodded slowly. "If you can create happiness, Carcosa is the one place that I know of that can manifest it in you."

"And if I can't?"

"That is the normal state of affairs, for most that arrive there. That is how it will be."

"So, then, why is that our destination?"

He did not answer. A part of her knew she didn't want to hear the answer, anyway. It was as if the Captain understood her very mind, had probed the very insanity festering inside, and knew what must not be said to keep the insanity locked inside.

"Is it far? I can't see it anywhere." She pointed to the blank charts.

The Captain appeared unconcerned and shook his head. "Not far." His reflective goggles turned to the swelling seas while a gloved hand pointed toward the horizon. "I've seen the signs."

She followed his finger and saw nothing unusual. "What signs?"

"You don't see them? Then watch the horizon."

Doing what she was told, she spied nothing out of the ordinary, or what passed as ordinary in this place. Then the sign appeared, as if the distance to the horizon had suddenly shrunk, as if the circumference of the earth had diminished to almost nothing. A moment later, the horror of what she witnessed overcame her, and she understood that it was neither of these things. Rather, it was a wall of water, a tidal wave a hundred meters high, rolling straight for them.

"Oh, my God!" she exclaimed. There was nowhere to escape, for it grew from every horizon, roaring like the thunder that follows impressive lightning.

The Captain turned to her. She saw her fear reflected in his goggles. "There is no concern," he spoke calmly. She expected his lips to move behind the scarf when he explained such things to her, but they never did. "This is the eighth tidal wave today. It will pass without effect."

"Eighth?" He was so calm she almost believed him.

Almost.

What was she to do? The crest was advancing so rapidly it would be upon them in minutes. Not even enough time to run back to her daughter, to be with her at the end. Dumbfounded, she could only stand calmly by the Captain, tasting sea water in her mouth, ready to drown again.

But when the wall of water finally caught their vessel, she saw that it was wide, and they rode right over the top without incident. She compared it to the rising and falling of her daughter on a swing, and suddenly, an explanation for today's peculiar nausea was revealed.

"See," said the captain once the ocean settled again. "No danger."

"No...?"

Even to herself, her voice sounded distant. Unreal.

She knew she should have been worried about the wave. But she just wasn't, couldn't afford to be, not while she was still pretending.

***

Still hungry, always hungry, her drive for food again overcame her distrust of the ship's interior, and she ventured into the one place she dreaded more than any other. She told herself to trust her instincts and that her nose would smell the food, lead her to the kitchen and then all would be right in the world again. They both needed to eat. If they did not eat, then her daughter would never recover.

Progressing into the depths, the interior seemed to grow darker at every turn. Grey walls, fashioned from old timber supported by heavy iron struts, vanished into the shadows. The swell seemed more pronounced without portholes to watch the ocean, and the taste and wetness of sea water in her hair and clothes would not leave her. The corridors carried dampness. It was no better than standing on the deck, and she wondered if the *Vestibule* were not rotting from the inside out.

Again, despite the whispering voices in the walls and the distant sounds of portals opening and closing, she failed to find any doors apart from the one that had led her down here.

Vestibule... The thought occurred that this was a strange name and that maybe it held meaning. A clue, perhaps, which might reveal her purpose in her being in this place, this nightmare. All this time, she had been thinking "vestibule" was a French word, and it probably was, but it was also commonly used in English. "Vestibule" meant an entrance hall, a reception area, somewhere to wait. Were they waiting to get somewhere? Was the Captain waiting for something to happen? Did a decision need to be made first? But to get where they wanted to go, well, they'd have to first step outside of the "vestibule" to get there. She wondered how to do that.

She remembered bobbing in the ocean, crests threatening to crash down upon her time and time again, while the reciprocal troughs promised to drag her into the depths at any moment. The nightmare never seemed to end. The sea spray kept her cold and filled her mouth with the salty water taste that lingered with her today. Her only hope was rescue... For a moment, she was back, really in the ocean, really drowning.

For a moment, she scared herself half to death.

"Ma'am?"

A steward had found her, dressed in his fine, three-piece suit cut entirely from paper. His face was hidden behind one of the paper masquerade masks that all the crew insisted upon wearing at all times. He was stuffing something into his sleeve, and she noticed it was more paper, crunching into tiny balls. Memories came back to her, of a scarecrow on her parent's farm in Adelaide, an effigy fashioned from her old clothes, filled with yellow straw.

"Hello," she stuttered, surprised that the servant managed to sneak up on her unannounced, even unheard. "I'm looking for the kitchens. I'm lost."

"I'm sure you are." Like the Captain, his answer was matter-the-fact and useless.

Annoyed that he had not properly answered her, she straightened her back and raised her pitch. "Well, then, would you be able to show me where they are?"

He said nothing. Did nothing. The silence grew more uncomfortable as each second passed, but only for her.

"Are you going to answer me?"

As if snapping out of a hypnotic trance, the crewmember's head flicked towards her, the motion reminiscent of a mechanical doll controlled by external powers. "Sorry, ma'am, I cannot. It is not possible to reach the lower decks from the upper decks."

"What do you mean? I mean, that's ridiculous."

"Yes, it is," he said, without modifying his pitch or tone. "But I can arrange to have food brought to your cabin, if you like."

She didn't know whether to feel relieved or angered further. In the end, her daughter's wellbeing had to be her first priority. She could never take any course of action that would harm her daughter. Besides, picking a fight just to win a point didn't seem worthwhile, not if there was any chance they could eat again. "Yes, for me and my daughter, both. And please be hasty about it—my daughter is not at all well."

"Certainly, Ma'am." He gave a curt bow, spun on his toes and vanished down a corridor as if he were gliding on wheels.

***

The yacht was lost and so was her family. Tracy cried, giving to the ocean more water than it would ever need or even notice. Moments before the *Daintree* splintered and crumbled, she had dared to peer inside the cabin. Tracy was sure she had, for the image of the blood and skull fragments splattered on the wall was too powerful a nightmare to easily forget, burning into her mind and tearing apart her soul. Her only child... For the life of her, Tracy could not recall why her husband chose to murder their only creation together.

Much later, while the crashing waves and the storm's unrelenting downpour threatened to drown her again at any moment, she heard a ship, its foghorn reverberating through the sleeting rain. They might all still be rescued, she hoped. They might all become a family again. All she had to do was believe.

Anything was better than believing she'd lost everything and that the only path lying ahead was a lonely death at the bottom of the Pacific Ocean.

So, she clung to Greg's book, his sole purchase on their last port stop at Rarotonga. It was *The King In Yellow*, with its waterlogged pages and disintegrating cover. What did it say about that place on the shores of the Lake of Hali? What did that book mention about hope and the futility of it all? What did it say about distant, fabled Carcosa, where one could lose one's mind and, in doing so, perhaps rediscover happiness?

She didn't know, but she knew her husband had discovered the truth. She recalled that it said something about them all being together again, perhaps.

So she kept reading.

***

Somehow, she found her way back from the

endless corridors and up onto the deck again. Here, her nausea lessened and so, she took a moment to study the waves, all the time ensuring that she didn't drown from vomiting. The massive surges of water were like big angry slugs shaken inside a bowl, fighting each other to crawl to the top of the chaotic collection of their own kind. The ocean was rising higher and higher by the minute. The spray was hard on her face, tasted again in her mouth, and stung at her eyes. She fought against the salt water sloshing inside her stomach, expecting at any moment that the *Vestibule* would be overrun with breakwaters.

On the distant deck, she spied two of the masked, paper-wrapped crew, struggling to tie down several loose crates, wooden boxes large enough to hide elephants. She had failed to notice these crates before and wondered why, as if she perhaps had just made them up and placed them into this picture.

As if sensing her awareness, the two men stopped dead in midpoint of their frantic work then pointed together back towards the ocean. Theirs was not a command, but she had the sense that if she did not look, she would miss an important aspect in the deeper symbolism of this exotic ship, where she was nothing more than one of the lost.

Heeding their advice and returning to the rails, she gazed out into the churning waters and spotted what she thought must be a human head. Then she noticed arms attached to that head, pushing through the waves. It was a young woman without garb, swimming in the frigid waters. Next to her was a man, then another figure. Soon, she became aware of dozens of humans, naked and cold, powering through the water. The heavy waves kept taking them down, pounding them with their foamy swells, but they kept rising up, kept swimming. They had hope when really, they had none. They believed in the impossible.

As the next wave subsided, the new vision

presented before her forced her to draw breath. Not a dozen, not even hundreds, but thousands upon thousands of pale, naked humans were swimming these seas. None screamed, none called for help, not even in this cold water, where they should have all died from hypothermia. Uncaring, the *Vestibule* ploughed right through them, crushing swimmers who were too slow to get out of the way, or too preoccupied to care. Yet none of this shocked her. She knew their fate was hopeless, and yet, they blindly continued to pretend otherwise.

But what did tear at her soul was the fact that each and every man, woman, and child was swimming in the same direction, swimming in her direction, towards Carcosa. Did they, too, believe salvation might find them in such a distant and exotic land? Was she perhaps not one of those swimmers herself?

Unsure both of whom she was and what her eyes now witnessed, she fled to her cabin, sealing the portal behind her. Somehow, the darkness seemed inviting. She drew a breath, then another, and tried to forget.

"Mummy, are you okay?"

It took a moment to remember where she was, that there was a shape in the far corner, wrapped in blankets like a swaddled baby. The only bulb overhead swung with the ocean roll, casting sharp shadows over the shape that she remembered now must be her only daughter.

"I made you something," spoke the child.

Fear returned to the mother. She looked at her daughter for moving lips, or perhaps for fidgeting, anything, something to indicate that her child was real.

"Something for me?"

"Yes... Mother."

A chill stung at her heart. That was not her daughter's voice. It wasn't even a human voice. Rather, it was something artificial like the voices that all the crew shared. For the briefest of moments, she was back in the ocean, lost in the storm, recalling what had really been left behind inside their crumbling yacht.

"That's really nice. How sweet."

She sat by the dark, speaking shape. An arm extended, wrapped in papery cloth so tightly that no skin showed. At the end of the appendage was a white-gloved hand holding forth folded paper. Tentatively, with more than a hint of trepidation, she withdrew this gift from the icy-cold grip. "I'm so lucky to have you," her words forced themselves, spoken through whispers and trembles.

The paper unfolded easily into white cut-outs of mother and daughter, hand-in-hand, foot-to-foot, unravelling in a chain. Like two mirrors that forever reflected occupants trapped between their panes, so, too, the paper continued to unfold. She almost cried at the thought of its symbolism, of being bound to her only child forever. That nothing would take her away again, that everything distant Carcosa promised her was here for her now.

She kept unfolding.

The paper stretched deeper, into her daughter's arm and then on through into the sleeve. In moments, she had hundreds of the mother-daughter folds spilling out of her hands. And then, without warning, the arm vanished under the weight of paper and now, the very sheets themselves were unfolding, cut and shaped into the same pattern: mother-and-daughter, mother-and-daughter, mother-and-daughter...

She kept unfolding.

Paper lay everywhere. Soon, her undoing smothered the entire floor until the bunk itself was lost under a mass of folded pulp. The paper became wet and it was no longer pure white, for words were etched in the cuttings. She read some of the lines. It was a play, the characters speaking nonsense she could not read. The play's characters were her daughter and herself, or that was how she interpreted the passages. Characters were discussing their loss, but they were unwilling to accept the truth. They focused their minds on discovering lost Carcosa on the shores of Lake Hali where Hastur lies. Carcosa was a mystical land–the words kept telling her–where answers and loved-ones would always be rediscovered, even when they weren't real.

She kept unfolding.

How long she unravelled she could not recall. To her, one moment, this had been her cabin. In another, it was a mass of pulpy, wet paper filling all the space that was possible to fill in such cramped quarters. A chain of the larger-then-smaller women repeated endlessly, cut from the pages of a waterlogged book that she had so desperately clutched in her hands for so long, reading it for hope.

"Where are you?" she asked, pushing through the walls of paper. Its mass was too thick, so she had to tear at it, shred her way through like some Victorian explorer braving the thick jungles of Africa. "Where are you?" she cried wildly. She sobbed the same words again, sensing now her pathetic loss.

"Where are you?" she could only whisper.

Eventually, the weight of paper was pushed aside and the bunk re-emerged, only for her to discover that it was empty.

Empty except for a cut-out masquerade mask. Like all the other masks worn on this ship, it was fashioned entirely from paper.

It was the mask that her daughter had worn.

It was all her daughter's face had ever been.

***

Exhausted and terrified, red-eyed and wide-eyed, she ran across the decks, screaming inside, hoping for any kind of release.

THE SWELLING

While she sprinted across the deck, a wave of salty water gushed around her. Ahead, it grew large, collected the two crew and their huge boxes, tossing them into the water like dust flicked from an emptying dustpan. As the ocean took the crew, they crumbled and folded, as if they, too, were made of paper and the spines of old, water-logged books. Neither cried nor struggled to hold onto life. Both accepted their fate as readily as she accepted the sun or moon, or that her daughter and husband had once loved her. She was struck dumb as they promptly vanished, then felt sick at the thought that death was so easy and so casual. She didn't want to die like that. She'd do anything to ensure that never happened to her and her family.

A second wave, not as crushing as the first, managed to wipe the decks, drenching her further, filling her mouth with its putrid tastes. She clung to the railing, feeling its pull grow ever stronger, threatening to take her, too, or, failing that, drown her on these very decks themselves. She held on. She knew that she was drowning. Very soon, it would all be over.

And then, at the last moment, the waters subsided and she was cold and wet and drenched on the decks as she had always been. Now, the *Vestibule* was rising out of the water, still floating, still powering ever onwards to hopeful Carcosa. She stared out. Beyond her immediate surroundings, it was impossible to see much beyond the rising waves and the grey spray of the mist. Of the horizon, nothing at all could be seen. The world was shrinking inwards, trapping the *Vestibule* inside what must seem to some to be an enormous glass bottle, forever shaken by an angry owner.

Darkness was settling, readying the world for the night.

She took to the stairs, climbing higher to where the only light shone, to the only place that might provide answers... or relief.

At the portal, she wrenched open the latch and threw herself inside. Everything was as before. The sole captain wrapped in his coat, scarf, and flying goggles, diligent at the wheel, fighting the angry ocean. Lightning flashed outside and he lit up like a black-and-white photograph before he had time to notice his visitor.

She ran up to him, pulled him by his arm so he had to look upon her. "My daughter, someone has taken my daughter."

The expressionless face, always concealed, gave nothing away concerning any emotions that it might feel. "Daughter?" he asked in that strangely familiar voice. "You have a daughter?"

"Of course I have a daughter."

The Captain shrugged. "Oh? Well, that is strange, because I was well-informed that your daughter had been dismantled."

"What?" Her voice became hysterical. She needed answers. She needed them fast; otherwise, she knew she would really lose her mind, or find it. "I want to know what you and your crew did with my daughter."

Another shrug. "We did nothing."

"Then who did?"

"Oh, I thought that would have been obvious, too."

She tried to speak, but his words were just confusing her. She wanted to be angry, wanted someone else to take the blame for her hopeless predicament. She wanted the Captain to take control, to bring her back and restore everything that she had lost these last weeks. "Who dismantled her?" she finally demanded, even though a part of her already knew, a part of her that knew a lot of things that the rest of her mind pretended not to.

When the Captain finally answered her, all he said was, "You did."

"I did?"

Her mind flashed to that moment, the unravelling of the mother-and-daughter paper chain. Only now did she see what she had done. Her daughter had been made of paper, always had been. From the beginning, her only child had been nothing more than the mother-and-daughter chain. Her heart turned cold at the very thought of what she had created.

"I pulled her apart, didn't I?"

"Yes, but you made her, first. Don't ever forget that."

More lightning as deep shadows threw themselves onto the wall of charts behind them.

"We just assumed that you no longer required her. But don't concern yourself. My crew are clearing the mess away as we speak." Again, that voice, it was almost female. And he was her height exactly, even the same build.

"You mean, she's gone?"

"Yes. You no longer need her, now that we are nearly there."

Her anger flared, built upon an ever-foreboding thought that in reality, all was lost, and all that she had hung onto was nothing more than fantasy. She didn't want to think that, didn't want to remember.

"Who are you?"

Once more, the face was as silent as stone, the goggles reflecting her own eyes. Or were they? She looked again and saw that they were not reflections, rather, real eyes behind the mask, so similar to her own. "Who are you?" she asked again.

"I thought you already knew."

Her hand flashed to her open mouth, because suddenly, she did know.

How easy it was for the human mind to deceive, especially to deceive oneself. So, she unravelled the scarf, pulled away the World War One flying goggles and drew from his head the pirate hat. He was her height, of the same build—these should have been clue enough. The familiar voice, like the familiar human face that looked back at her now, she was looking at herself.

Who was the only living person in this entire ocean who was willing to do anything to find fabled Carcosa?

Only her.

***

Tracy Wright came up from the ocean for what was probably the hundredth time. It could have been her thousandth for all she cared, or remembered. Down there, in those moments trapped in the murky, dark waters, it was calm, it was just water. Down there, she couldn't breathe either. Up here on the surface were the swelling waves, the eerie lightning and angry thunder. They would eventually claim her and send her back down again. That final moment now could be no more than hours away at most. Probably sooner, considering how exhausted her muscles had become treading water.

The wreckage of the *Daintree* had long dispersed. Her daughter with her splattered brains was somewhere down there, many miles under the angry sea. Her husband might still be alive, but she doubted it. He was never as strong a swimmer as she.

All she had left was his book, that dreadful *King In Yellow*. She'd held onto it this long, so she might as well keep reading until the very bitter end. Only that book offered any semblance of hope, no matter how futile that hope had ever been.

She laughed at the irony. Her wish would finally come true. All she had to do now was to decide how to make it so. Down there, at the ocean's end where the dead are never found, she could still be reunited with her husband and daughter and it would be a silent, lifeless reunion.

Instead, if she wanted the madness, if she wanted to escape oblivion, to become lost in her own torment in a world where she would always believe her family could be made whole once again, all she had to do was keep reading.

It was the impossible dream. Oblivion with nothing, or madness with false hope?

The choice was so easy.

So, she kept reading and asked again of her captain to take her to the distant shores of Lake Hali, where fabled Carcosa lay.

HELL IN THESE LIPS
Zachary T. Owen

Helen Carmichel wasn't afraid to die—she was afraid of getting older. To die was to be surrendered from this endurance test into something easier: Heaven, Hell, or nothingness. She felt the arthritis beat its way further into her bones. It was a tiring game, getting old. Especially here in this place, this prison of elderly bodies rotting slowly into dust, preparing themselves for grave dirt. This wasn't a nursing home, it was a hospice.

She wanted nothing more than to be young again—not even young, really, so much as restored. She would give a limb to be forty. But, barring new youth, she wanted death. The problem was that she was too afraid and too physically weak to end herself. So she begrudgingly trudged forward even as the veins in her body screamed *here I am* and her skin became mottled and grey. She hated it, but at least she wasn't alone. Every other resident was going through the same thing—endless, prolonged death.

For the most part everybody left Helen alone. She preferred it that way. But she felt resentful despite her need for isolation. Didn't anybody care? How many times had the aides passed her by without saying hello? How many visitors had she had in the last five years? When was the last time her daughter Camille, who had put her here, had come in to see her?

Maybe she didn't *really* prefer to be alone. She had just taught herself it was what was best. Especially considering how many had died, how many nurses and aides had been replaced and replaced again. There was no reason to make friends here.

The only thing Helen had was the puzzle room. It wasn't actually a puzzle room, but a small lounge which rarely got used. Every day, whenever she had enough energy to pick herself up out of bed, Helen made her way down to the puzzle room to work on another of the many jigsaw puzzles. There were stacks and stacks of them inside the lounge. Once she started one she could usually leave it alone on the table in the lounge, come back later, and find it undisturbed.

So she toiled away her days with puzzles. Sometimes one over the course of a week. Sometimes several in just a matter of days. She built herself vistas of places she could never visit, except maybe in dreams (though, in Helen's opinion, you couldn't think of dreaming about places you knew you would never see as anything but nightmares). When a puzzle was finished she took it apart and put it away. Eventually, when she'd finished all of them, she could start over again.

Now she worked on a rather complex puzzle of a cozy scene—a couple, hands clasped together, standing in a field of white flowers. As Helen put the pieces together, one after another, sometimes having to hunt for the right piece or fearing she'd lost an essential bit of scenery, she longed for that human contact she no longer had. She remembered not just her husband, a decade dead, but all the men (and, though she'd never revealed it, women) she'd touched, held hands with, kissed, slept with, snuggled with in bed on rainy days.

The energy went out of Helen's legs. She pulled a chair from the table and sat before the puzzle and closed her eyes. In her mind pieces formed their own scene...

A friendly face. Howard. Helen held him close, the naked sky above her glinting with stars, the feel of dewy grass soothing on her skin.

She kissed him on the bridge of the nose, on each cheek, on his chin, his neck. "We should stay here forever," she said.

"I'd like that." He nuzzled her. Ran his rough hands through her hair, down her nape. They tangled against each other, breathed long, deep breaths.

The feel of his callused hands against her back made her feel secure...

"Helen, you didn't take your pills."

Looking up, stunned, she fought for words. The nurse held out a hand and Helen absently took it. "I'm sorry," she said to the nurse.

"It's okay. We'll just go to the nurse's station and get you fixed up."

"I don't think I want any pills," Helen said, sluggishly trailing behind the nurse.

"I strongly advise them. You're going to be in a lot of pain if you don't take them."

"I'm going to be in a lot of pain no matter what I do."

The nurse stopped walking and gave Helen a hard stare. "At least you can still walk. Honey, we don't want you to hurt more than you have to."

They were always calling her honey or sweetie. She couldn't stand it.

"Okay. Hurry up. I want to get back to my puzzle."

***

Afterward, Helen felt too tired to go back to the puzzle. It was incredible how much energy could leave her body just from standing around and taking pills. A walk down a long hallway and a little standing and it was enough to send her straight back to bed. She walked forward, slumped, and made her way toward her room. Stopping, she felt a panic surge in her. Which room was it? Helen gritted her teeth and tried to control her breathing. She looked back the direction she'd come and found the break in the hallway, where it was joined by another hall that went past the nurse's station and toward a set of double doors that led to another section of the building. She focused, for a moment, on the first room after the nurse's station, then counted the doors, turning back again, until she hit six. This was her method for finding her room. The day she forgot how many rooms to count was on the horizon, but she tried not to think about it.

On her way to her room, she passed an open door. Inside a resident was talking to the nicely dressed woman who always quizzed them to gauge their memory and mental health. Helen found these tests humiliating and degrading. She told herself it wasn't in her nature to pry, but found she couldn't quite move on after passing the door. Leaning against the wall, trying to disguise her out-of-breath pants, she listened to the conversation inside.

The nicely dressed woman always used a calm, slightly loud tone which grated on Helen's nerves. It was so fake, so condescending. Every time the woman spoke to a resident it sounded like she was talking to a child.

"You haven't been feeling suicidal at all?"

Johnny's voice hitched. "*No.*" He laughed. "I'm alright."

"Can you tell me what year it is, Johnny?"

"Uh, well... I think. I mean I know what it is, give me a second. I think, uh, well it's..."

"How about the month? Do you know what month it is?"

"Is it... um... it's July?"

"It's a fall month, Johnny. It starts with an O."

"October." Johnny's voice tremored nervously.

"Good, Johnny. It's October. Now can you tell me what day it is?"

"I... I would say that it's Friday."

"Hump day. Which day is hump day?"

"Wednesday. It's Wednesday."

"Very good, Johnny. Now I want you to remember those three words I told you at the beginning of this test. Do you think you can do that for me, Johnny? Just three words. I'll give you a hint, the first one was a color."

"Red?"

"No, try again."

"Yellow?"

"Good guess, Johnny. Now tell me the second word."

"Uh..."

"It's something you wear, an article of clothing."

"I don't..."

"You might wear it after getting out of the bath."

"A robe?"

"Good, Johnny. Can you remember the last word?"

"No... I don't seem to recall..."

This was enough for Helen. She stopped listening and pressed forward. She noticed the woman on the other side of the hallway, passed out—Alice maybe, or Evelyn. Alice or Evelyn couldn't talk and was severely immobile, permanently bound to a wheelchair. Helen wasn't exactly sure what was wrong with her, but was thankful she hadn't ended up like her—but also incredibly sorry that *anybody* had to end up like that.

Alice or Evelyn sat slack-jawed, her face pointing down. A faint snore wheezed out of her mouth. She'd thrown up on herself again. The vomit had begun to dry on her heavily stained shirt. Sometimes she would sit like this for hours before somebody cleaned her up.

***

Helen released a gigantic breath as her head settled into the stiff pillow on her bed. She pulled the thick comforter over herself and rubbed her hands against her chest, trying to warm her body. Sleep already tugged at her eyelids, made her lungs work rhythmically.

She turned, adjusted her body, her limbs full of aches. Her left arm wanted to be stretched out, then begged to be folded back against her chest again. Each leg cried in pain and Helen moved them periodically. This was standard procedure and, despite all of it, she headed toward sleep.

As the world dimmed a vague collection of thoughts crept lazily through her mind.

The smell of her room reminded her of disease... She wondered where they found all the new nurse's aides...? And what was the name of that dog they used to bring in to see the residents...? Colors were always getting dimmer, more muted... The building was old, like her, and falling apart, like her... Whatever happened to Howard...? The feeling of bubble wrap snapping under her fingers... "She loves you, yeah, yeah, yeah..." They should play more music in this place... If she could just keep sleeping... Who lived here before her?

...somebody said it was a strange lady with odd talents...

...a musician... a magician, something...
...she had...
...a...
...nickname...
The Old Priestess.

***

She dreamt she stood in a field of white flowers, their petals whiter than snow, with hearts vibrant and golden. In her hand was a jar full of blood so vivid with red that when she began pouring it on the white flowers, the contrast was stark and pleasing.

"I have killed what I love," she cried. "The world's thirsty, so let it drink." The jar never emptied and so she ran through the field, turning white to red, leaving her indelible, morbid mark and smiling, though somewhere inside she felt she was dying, wanted to fight against this act. It was like there were two of her. A surface and something more complicated, pushed below as she painted the world red.

***

Helen woke up, lips cracked, eyes stinging with fatigue, and lifted herself carefully upward. She rubbed her tired eyes and yawned, momentarily unaware of where she was. When it all came back, when she remembered it was the nursing home, a sob made her tremble. Every time Helen woke up she thought she might be home again, maybe at her daughter's house, somewhere familiar to her. It was never any of these places, of course.

She turned and lowered her feet off of the bed into her snug, fuzzy slippers. Absently, she put a hand on her nightstand. *I've never really used this thing,* she thought. Helen had very few possessions—mostly just clothes, a few knickknacks. Much of what she had was the nursing home's: her dresser, her pillows and bedspread, the television, the clock. Her daughter had promised to bring her more of her own things from home but never had.

The top drawer of the nightstand contained a stash of sugar packets, napkins, reading glasses, Christmas cards and other paraphernalia, but Helen had never opened the bottom compartment. What would she have put in it anyway? She had almost nothing to her name.

Curiosity coiled in her gut and then unfurled. She pinched the tiny handle of the small door and opened the bottom compartment of the nightstand. Inside there was a small black box.

It was heavy for its size and the darkly painted wood had a sheen to it. Setting it in her lap, she stared at it, searching for any indentations or signs of what could be inside. There was no visible latch or button. Instinctively, Helen placed her hands on either side and lifted gently upward, splitting the box in half horizontally. Inside was a pile of black puzzle pieces and a single piece of torn, moldy paper, which appeared to be from a play. Most of the lines were obscured—it seemed the woman who had owned the box and its contents (the one who lived in this room before her, Helen guessed) had spilled something on the paper, in addition to tearing it. What little she could read made no sense, characters rambling about names and places that had no meaning to her.

"Gobbledygook," Helen said. She threw the paper in her wastebasket. But the puzzle pieces intrigued her greatly.

***

With the pieces spread across the table, Helen worked diligently to put the puzzle together. Because there was no vista, no scene, no design of any kind to help guide her, it was difficult. Pressing her reading glasses tightly against her brow, Helen watched the pieces on the table as if they were alive. She searched the curves, the dips and angles of the pieces laid out before her, and assembled them slowly. She let her hands do most of the work once she was a third of the way to completing the task. Her fingers felt the edges of the pieces, slid them across the table, and pressed them into each other.

She never questioned why the jigsaw puzzle was nothing but a sheet of black fractured into dark shapes. To her it was a challenge, a strange change in method and complexity from the colorful puzzles she usually pieced together. And as she worked she began to feel those puzzles were inferior. They were sentimental, cheaply cheerful, cloying.

This puzzle was cold and emotionless. It didn't lie to her, didn't try to tell her about places she wouldn't see, to put hopes in her she wasn't allowed to have here in the nursing home.

This puzzle was reality.

An hour later and Helen was finished. The puzzle, despite coming from such a small box, spanned the entire table. The smooth blackness glimmered under the lounge's clean, dull lights. Bracing herself against the table, she leaned forward and examined the work. Darkness and more darkness. The seams of the pieces were completely invisible, allowing the puzzle the illusion of being a kind of void.

Then, something strange.

A faraway face appeared in the darkness. A pale face with shimmering eyes.

Helen, without another thought, reached her hand toward the face. Her hand went through the puzzle, not as if it penetrated anything, but as if there was nothing there to begin with—a vast, square-shaped abyss.

The face had become lost. It didn't matter. Something in this puzzle, this defiance to everything she had ever known, called to her. Helen was not afraid. If a creature lurked in the dark depths of another world she would have to face it. She would face whatever lay beyond and grin beautifully at it, knowing she had escaped the nursing home and discovered... *something else.* Something besides aging, pain, and bitterness.

It was almost impossible for Helen to jump in. The energy just wasn't there. So she pulled one of the table's chairs out, took a breath, and attempted to raise a leg. Once one foot was on the chair, the other came with more ease. Her balance began to go almost at once. Before flubbing the whole thing, falling to the floor and flailing like an idiot, bruising herself or even breaking a bone, she let herself fall face forward. No nurse was going to find her sprawled on the floor in a painful heap.

The journey from the world of dying elders to the land of darkness was the briefest transition in Helen's life. In moments, she was gone.

***

She stood somewhere in the darkness which ceased to be darkness, but was instead infinite light filled with faraway black stars. Not quite standing, actually, but not floating, either. Helen moved forward, propelled gently through the void. Her pain was slowly magnifying; every aching bone threatening to crack or crumble, every tender muscle shaking with spasms. She swore she could hear water lapping against a shore, somewhere, though there was no landscape visible in the light surrounding her.

The face she'd seen was visible again, off in the distance. As she moved toward it the pain enveloped her and she began to cry.

But she moved on, knowing that it was too late to turn back, that this face would either reward her or end her misery. That wasn't such a bad set of options, she thought.

I have nothing in my life to return to and, so, nothing to leave behind.

The face was not merely a face, but perhaps a mask made of wax or clay. As she watched it grow closer she saw that it possessed a body. It was tall and draped in billowing yellow tatters, slender wings rising gently behind it.

The being outstretched his arms in greeting, his face stoic but not frightening. Despite the pain, Helen felt a sense of comfort as she stared dazedly at the shimmering eyes of the nameless phantom. Something inside her told her she should be afraid, but she knew he had something to give her, and that kept her mind from reeling with horror.

A voice came from somewhere inside. It was a soft, almost sensuous voice. It was powerful and godly, but vaguely human.

"Helen Carmichel, you come to me in a time of great pain and need, do you not?"

Wiping away a tear, ignoring her muscles which grew tight and enflamed, ignoring her weeping, creaking, screaming bones, Helen nodded a yes.

"You wish to be young once more, yes?"

Again, a nod.

"Are the lives of others expendable? Would you kill to be youthful once more, would you do terrible deeds?"

Helen sucked in a nervous breath, hesitated, and began to nod. She stopped herself. "I don't know," she said. She had never thought of herself as a model citizen, but far from immoral. The thought of deliberately harming another person to get what she wanted was new to her, something she had never considered even as a young woman.

"Those who cannot choke a heart that pumps the blood of society are dead before they draw another breath," the voice said firmly. "No gift is given for free. The Old Priestess would have told you much the same."

Helen closed her eyes, the pain manipulating her, curling her fingers inward, pushing her teeth together, squeezing her heart with every beat, pushing more blood through her, faster and faster, the blood burning, spreading a poison in her body.

"You can have youth again, Helen. You can have it with a kiss. And you must spread the Sign. But there will be consequences. The power of a kiss is temporary. You must be ruthless. And you must never forget to leave the Sign. For far too long they have forgotten me. You will make them remember and be rewarded with youth. Do you accept?"

Movement was almost gone now. Helen attempted to nod her head. It was unmanageable. Every fraction of a movement was a thousand suns burrowing into her skin. Instead she forced a sound out of her throat. It did not become a word, did not evolve beyond anything other than a sound, but it was meant to be a yes, and so it was.

"Very well. I will take your pain away. Swallow my eyes, old woman, and awake with kisses to give and Signs to leave for those who dared to forget."

Then the pain peaked, reached an operatic height, and dulled into a terrifying numbness, a total lack of feeling more trying than any pain known before.

With great effort Helen held out her left hand and uncurled her fingers. The eyes snapped out of the white face like gems from a statue and fell gently into her palm.

Struggling, Helen moved the palm toward her mouth, opened wide, and choked them down her throat and into her empty, gurgling old belly.

And then she woke on the floor of the lounge, a nurse standing over her with a delirious look of concern.

***

For three days they did not allow her in her room by herself, did not let her stray far from their sight, and insisted they help her to bathe and use the restroom. And they forced her to choke down the pills, no matter how much she objected. Her dignity, the shreds she still clung to, fell away.

She was examined by several nurses, then a doctor. Her body had accumulated bruises but her bones remained unbroken, her innards intact.

For some time she felt too self-conscious to enter the puzzle room under supervision, but gave in, finally, and felt a flicker of hope at the thought of seeing her beloved black puzzle. Maybe she could escape again.

But it was gone, if it had ever existed in the first place. The pieces were not scattered or thrown about, but absent all together. The black box had disappeared. Of course she had thrown away the scrap of the strange play, so that even that could not be ruminated on.

It wasn't until, deep into the night and on the cusp of sleep, Helen fingered her comforter and found one, solitary piece of the black puzzle which she clutched against her heart and whispered to like a god who could fill her life with promises.

***

She dreamt of a great bridge. A throng of people waited outside of it, young and old. Helen watched them as they stood patiently, looking up at the imposing gate, staring upon the gatekeeper who was dressed in a garish black robe, his face sad and whiskered. He reminded her of Howard. And maybe a little of her husband, too.

The gatekeeper looked upon Helen, his eyes stern but somehow kind. "Pass!" he shouted.

"There is time," Helen said.

The gatekeeper decided to let a few others through. A selection of dreary, sickly-looking children with blood-red eyes and a woman much older than herself. Once they were through he stood silent. He looked upon Helen again. "You must pass," he said.

"There is time. I have time! I do not have to pass. I do not *want* to pass," she said.

"Very well. Are you certain?"

"I am. I'm staying here."

"It is not natural," the gatekeeper said. "But if you say there is time, though I do not understand it, then there must be time."

Helen watched as he let a family through the

gates. All of their faces were charred, their clothes reeking of fire. She smiled and stayed outside the gates, forever, watching the other people pass over the bridge.

***

The nicely dressed woman came to visit Helen as evening quickly fell. She shut the door gently and approached the bed. She sat down, her slight weight disturbing Helen's comfortable position. Though she had been awake for hours now, had eaten both breakfast and lunch, she felt as groggy as though she'd only just awoke. The sight of the woman only made her more tired.

"Maybe we should get you a roommate," the woman said. "It must be lonely in here by yourself."

"I don't want a roommate. She'll just end up dying and I'll be even more alone than I am now."

The woman pretended not to hear this remark, but instead shuffled through the papers on her small clipboard and cleared her throat. "Helen, why don't we have a nice little chat? I'm just going to ask you some questions."

"I don't want to have a chat," Helen said. Her breath came out hot and wet against her chapped lips. She shifted her arms, ever-aching, and turned away from the nicely dressed woman.

Again, the woman pretended not to hear Helen. "First, I'm going to tell you three words I want you to remember. A color, an article of clothing, and a name. I want you to repeat them to me at the end of the conversation. Let's practice. The first one, the color, is orange. The second, the article of clothing, is pants. The last one, the name, is Gertrude. Can you repeat those back to me?"

"Orange, pants, Gertrude," Helen said unenthusiastically.

"So, Helen, have you been having any pain?"

"I'm old. Of course I'm in pain," she said.

"Have you been feeling blue at all?"

"Of course."

"Have you been feeling suicidal? Anything like that?"

"I don't want to do this," Helen said sternly. "It's humiliating."

The woman repeated the question.

"Sometimes. Everybody entertains the thought of suicide."

"That's not the same thing, Helen, as being suicidal. Morbid curiosity and..."

Helen thought of the white-faced man in the tattered robe, his wings spread out behind him. She had begun to doubt any of what had occurred in the black puzzle. But as she sat there, doubting this, her left hand felt in its grip the small black puzzle piece and suddenly she was seized by an urge.

"Can you tell me...?"

Helen sat up tall in her bed, stared at the woman, and kissed her on the lips. The woman's eyes widened and she moved back, stunned, then stood up.

That's when the change happened.

The nicely dressed woman opened her mouth and her tongue lolled out before she could speak. Her skin hung loose, her eyes went bloodshot, her hair turned gray and stringy and she slumped over painfully, huffing. She collapsed onto the floor and beckoned toward Helen, confused, in need of help. Her hand shrivelled and shook with spasms, turning pale and liver-spotted, the fingernails rotting with fungus. Her teeth grew dark and crumbled. She attempted to stand and suddenly her bones were snapping through skin so old and worn it tore like parchment. A scream almost found its way to her lips before they were lost and then her face was oozing and aging, her body crumpling down, down to the floor where she aged decades and decades, became the oldest person alive for a few moments, then went to dust.

Helen bolted out of her bed, terrified, ran for the door.

I'm running, she thought. *I hurled myself out of bed. This terror has given me energy.*

She looked down at her hands, now youthful and full of color. She found her mirror and stared into it. What she saw made her cry—her youth had returned, like the winged man with the white face had told her it would. She could feel the eyes somewhere within her, warming her insides, sending energies through her.

She turned to the dust on the floor and expected to feel sadness and horror but, instead, felt liberation and triumph. She placed her hand absently against the wall, thinking of her next move. Her skin grew hot and sizzled and a slight burning smell crept into the air. Helen removed her hand from the wall and stared at where it had been. There was now a strange sign, a sort of glyph, etched into the wall. This was all she had to do? Remarkable. She stretched her rejuvenated limbs and sucked in a glorious breath.

The pain was gone. But how long would it last?

***

Not long. After a disappointingly short amount of time, she felt sharp aches traveling up her spine, re-sculpting her body, gnawing at her organs.

The pain, the dread, was indescribable. Helen limped pitifully toward the nurse's station, getting older by the minute, until she was her former self.

"Helen, you look like hell," the nurse said.

She reached out with her gnarled, hideous fingers, and grabbed onto the nurse's shirt, pulled herself closer, practically fell over the desk, and pressed her lips against the nurse's horrified expression.

"What's going on with you? Have you taken

your medication?" the nurse said. She backed away, trying to part with her attacker but gently, firmly, so as not to hurt her.

The nurse felt a sudden pain inching through her body. At first she tried to remain calm, told Helen to stop acting so strangely and have a seat while she looked at her. But flaring pain soon consumed all pretense of normalcy.

The nurse howled. Raked at her wrinkling, grey flesh. Gritted her teeth as she tried to keep her brittle fingers from curling against her palm. Soon she was like the nicely dressed lady—a pile of human ash.

Helen lay her hand across the desk and felt it burn with power. When she raised her small, healthy hand from the wood she saw there the same glyph she had left in her bedroom on the wall. How easy it was!

She felt so new, so vibrant and alive and beautiful. Helen knew she could no longer stay here, she had to have freedom. What was the point of being young again if she couldn't have freedom? She knew it would be easy to walk straight out the doors, straight into a new life.

But she would have to act fast. She would need to remain young long enough to leave undetected. And after an odd assortment of time she knew she would grow old again—it would be wise to steal as much youth and energy for herself as she could before making her exit.

Many of the residents were already asleep. She didn't want to hurt them, not at first. But then her perception of hurting others changed. Helen had an epiphany and she was comforted by the coming of night.

***

Johnny was awake. He sat in bed staring long-ingly out his window. There was nothing there, just patches of dead grass and the window of another resident's room on the opposite wing. That window remained dark, the curtains drawn. With evening slowly giving way to night, it was doubtful he could even see these things, as Helen could—though her eyesight was already beginning to waver, if only slightly. "Lord Almighty, it's so cold in here. When are they ever going to let me get home?" Johnny said. His hands moved restlessly. His roommate was once a source of constant headaches to the staff but, at least, a person for Johnny to talk to. Now the man was in a mostly vegetative state and offered Johnny no words of solace.

"I have to get home to my brother."

Helen knew Johnny's brother had been dead for almost three years. Something she hadn't remembered before, but with her youth came memories, facts, pieces of information that she'd lost.

"Do you miss him?"

Johnny turned and looked at Helen. He squinted, trying to put together how he knew her. "Of course I miss him. They won't let me out of here. I just want to get home."

"I might be able to help."

Johnny brightened. "Do I know you? Do you know how I can get out of here?"

"My name is Helen. I live here in White Haven Nursing Home, like you do."

"Nursing home?"

It was unclear just where Johnny thought he was and what he thought he was doing here, something which had always been obvious, but now seemed undeniably depressing to Helen. "Yes, Johnny. But I can help you end your pain."

He nodded and silently opened his mouth. Instead of talking, he closed his lips and looked at his feet. "I don't think I can walk. That's why they got me this chair."

"You won't need to walk." Helen approached his bed and sat down beside him. "Are you in pain?"

Johnny nodded again, his expression puzzled. "My hands hurt. My bones hurt. How did I end up like this?"

Helen hugged Johnny and felt him tremble under her touch, felt him quietly sob in her embrace. After a moment she pulled away from him, held his old face in her hands, and smiled. He smiled back. "Give me a kiss, handsome," she said.

He was gone, more quickly than the others. Before there was time for horror to strike, Johnny disintegrated. Helen sat on his bed, staring vacantly out his window, contemplating all she had done up until this moment. She left a glyph on the windowsill.

Then she made her way to Johnny's lifeless, painfully alive roommate, ready to kiss him out of existence.

***

Alice or Evelyn was even easier. Her name, Helen now remembered, was actually Amelia. She never woke up, but her twisted body, old and worn, combined with a face contorted by deep, hurtful nightmares made Helen's move to kiss her feel like the only option.

So many times Amelia had been left in a corner somewhere, vomit on her chin, her wheelchair seeping with urine or shit, neglected and alone. So many times people believed she could not hear them, couldn't be a part of society anymore. Her family had left her here to die. And so she had.

But quickly—as an act of mercy from one of the only people left who still noticed her.

***

With her temporary youth, Helen remembered the code to the next section of the building. She punched it in and walked straight through the doors. The main doors would be even easier; they were not locked but merely alarmed—this section of the building was for temporary residents of much more sound mind.

She didn't wish to give out any more kisses, only to escape. The eyes were burning inside of her again, a deep but pleasant heat that made her feel like a furnace. The main double doors, an entrance for many, but for her an exit, beckoned her. She did not know the code and, at this point, was not afraid of the alarm going off. She didn't look anything like a resident. To all staff members Helen would simply appear to be a visitor on her way out who'd forgotten the code.

She threw herself through the entrance, the alarm blaring loudly behind her as the doors slammed and the crisp night air greeted her skin. She thought of the man, Howard, she'd kissed so long ago, decades and decades. What she would give for a kiss like that again, a passionate and tender touching of lips. Now her kisses were nothing but death. It was going to be a lonely second life for Helen.

How would she ever make a life for herself even if she could stay young? Making a new identity seemed impossible. She would have to constantly rekindle her youth, find a way to make money, a place to stay. The effort needed weighed heavy on Helen. As she fled, with no idea where to go, she thought about the people she'd killed tonight.

Their names suddenly came to her, names she couldn't previously remember because they weren't far back enough into her past. Francine and Yvonne. To know the names of who she had killed, at least those who she hadn't acted as a merciful executioner to, seemed to make it more personal.

"This isn't what I wanted," Helen said, her stomach hot like a fireplace, her energy already waning. Suddenly all her feelings of triumph, her ability to remove herself from emotion in order to celebrate her new youngness, whatever the cost, began to crumble as quickly as she'd assembled it. Tears gushed from her eyes. She thought of the tall, pale-faced man in tatters, and then The Old Priestess. She wondered what ever became of the latter, if she was out there somewhere kissing herself young or if she had created the black puzzle only to amuse herself, just another magic toy inspired by the fragments of some lost play.

The black puzzle piece was in the front pocket of her cotton shirt. She hadn't even dressed correctly for her escape. The cold air began to sting. Helen grasped the puzzle piece and threw it aside angrily, making her way down a barren road.

In time, a car pulled up beside her. A window rolled down. A man inside looked out and smiled. "Need a ride?" he asked.

Helen wondered if she should travel to see her daughter, if somehow she could help. Then she imagined kissing her and the thought was unbearable, despite how unkind Camille had been, how she had left Helen abandoned at the nursing home.

"Sure," Helen said, with no idea where she was going.

She got in the car, glanced at herself in the rearview. She looked at least forty now. Not bad, but she would be older soon.

"Where you headed to?"

"Anywhere. Some place warm."

"Hotel?"

"Sure." Not that she had any money.

"What's wrong?" the man slowed the car, looked over at Helen with sympathy. He was handsome, his face smooth and pale and his hair dark and slicked back. His voice was soft and firm and he had kind eyes.

"What do you mean?"

"You're crying. Is there something I should know? Are you running from somebody?"

Helen shook her head, completely at a loss for words. She looked into the rearview again. She had aged. The changes were subtle, but they would be more obvious soon.

"Are you running from somebody?" the man said again.

She nodded.

"Maybe I can help. We could get the police. If you don't have any money I could pay for a hotel room. It's really no problem. I hate to see a person in trouble." The man stopped the car, put it in neutral, and waited.

Helen nodded mechanically.

"Say, what's your name? My name is..."

"Don't bother," Helen told him. *I don't want to know your name,* she thought. *Because soon you will be dead and I will be the murderer, I will be the one who took you away from your family, your friends, from a life you had every right to finish, all for the purpose of leaving behind a damned sign and keeping myself from the brink of my inevitable death.*

"Why? I should like to know your name. I just want to help, I..."

"This is not what I wanted, there's Hell in these lips," Helen said. She felt panicked. A dull pain travelled up her leg, into her knee. She stared at the dashboard, at the little dancing toy on it. It was yellow and nondescript, a plain sort of figure dancing for no reason. It reminded her, unsurprisingly, of the man in the black puzzle. Of her *master.* She cringed. *He doesn't have to be my master: if I only accept the natural end, if I only let myself go down the path all normal people must...*

Helen stared at the coffee mug in the cup holder. And the words—the words on the mug drew her eyes to them and she watched them, hoping they would disappear. *#1 Dad.*

"I don't understand. What's not what you wanted? And what do you mean there's Hell in your lips... are you sick?" For a while, it felt like the silence before these words was all there was. Now that it was over, Helen winced. She knew what she had to do.

Before the man could notice her changing, could start to glean something was wrong, Helen leaned over and kissed him.

When he was gone, she moved from the passenger seat to the driver's seat. She allowed her hand to burn that damned glyph onto the dashboard. She put the car in drive and began her endless journey forward. This wasn't what she wanted, but growing old was painful, getting closer to death was terrifying, and she still wasn't ready for it. She had fooled herself into thinking death was nothing to fear, but the taste of longevity and health revealed to her that death was *everything* she was afraid of, and holding onto youth (and thus, life) was her best weapon against it—and even that, a weapon against death, brought little relief. Her life had become a puzzle which was torn apart every time she put it back together, an infinite jigsaw that she scrambled to find all the pieces for, a play with no ending.

Helen cried as she made her way toward rows of houses, toward cities bustling with people of all kinds, toward a world brimming with human lives. She cried because she was selfish and she cried because she was guilt-ridden and afraid. She cried because she could feel the eyes of something insidious and god-like cooling in her gut. She cried at the thought of them growing hot again.

She cried, most of all, because she would just have go on kissing and kissing and spreading the Unholy Sign. She would have to kiss the world to death, one person at a time, always leaving a mark that

said *a terrible thing is on its way.*
    And it was her.

BITCH MUSE
Joseph Bouthiette Jr.

"You will beg for my recognition as a
disciple amongst the plague."
—*Pan*

We were running. Why were we running?

From a point somewhere above his body, Hugo does not watch the scene before him unfold, for to unfold implies a directional driving action—he simply observes the portrait of his unmoving surroundings.

Carina stands in such a way as her feet point away from Hugo, with her upper torso twisted to vaguely reveal the curve of her breast, and the profile of her face. Her pale legs merge seamlessly with the several inches of snow she stands in, as though she organically grew from the substance. The wind tousles the dark hair of her messy bun, snowflakes adhering to the flyaway strands.

Hugo's own posture is more natural, if also more tense. In contrast to Carina's nudity, he is wrapped in several layers of thick garment, a hide more reminiscent of reptilian scale than mammalian leather. His gloved right hand holds a palette; his left holds a small brush. The canvas on his easel is showing age—its amber drab against the snow like a wine stain on a virgin wedding gown.

Peering through his own eyes once more, Hugo mixes minute drops of red into a secluded smear of white paint, attempting to recreate the rosy complexion of Carina's wind-chilled buttocks. He continues, however, to be distracted by the distant landscape: thin spires of granite, curved like fangs. By all graces, they should not physically be able to stand.

"You haven't touched brush to canvas in several minutes, and I'm freezing." Carina's voice lilts as ever, but Hugo catches the stern undertones.

"I most certainly have. Speak not about which you know not."

"You forget I can see you clearly, you oaf. I'll not be called a liar."

"And I'll not be insulted by my bitch of a model, Carina. The longer you tantrum, the longer the snow has to bury you."

With his retorts, traces of green meddle with his pink, giving it a pallid hue of rot.

"Now look what you've done. I could paint a corpse of you."

Carina drops her arms from her pose as Hugo throws the palette onto a small wooden table. He looks into the fog, shadows undulating in the falling snow.

A black tower crumbles.

A rumbling passes through the earth, imperceptible through Hugo's thick boots but noticed by Carina as she dons her red woollen robe. The shadows shimmer with the quake.

And another.

She appears by Hugo's side as he prepares a new palette. She lays a hand on his arm. "It's getting pretty rough out here, why don't we call it a day?"

He shrugs her off. "Not enough progress." Flat, business-like. "The more we do now, the less later. I guarantee I can finish this session."

She tries touching him again, and he swings at her with the back of his gloveless palm. Skin to skin. Carina maintains her balance, but only just, as the ground shakes once more. Hugo spies the red of her brightening cheek. "At least that's not the visible side of your face. Get back into position."

A shrill burst of sound catches their attention, equal parts dragon roar and the piping of flutes. The shadows in the distance start to coalesce. Hugo sees the form of a man, impossibly tall, obscured by cloud and fog. Its gait is uneven, each limping step the pulse of a terran heart, each limping step carrying it infinitely closer. Carina and Hugo take their own steps back.

And another.

They turn to run, but the shape's impossible pace brings its next step right through Hugo's work table, the chipped hoof of a massive black goat. Above them, the satyr shrieks again, and easily clears them as it ambles forward. Within seconds, the form is gone.

*****

Shall we don a pretty dress?

Shall we weave our hair?

Shall we spritz our skin with cinnamon? With lavender and honey?

Shall we smell of the earth?

Shall we place our face in the grass?

Shall we inhale?

Shall we lie with the rats?

Shall we kiss their fur? Their tails?

Shall we kiss ourselves?

Shall we kiss at all?

Shall we burn the dim city to cinders?

Shall we discard our shoes?

Shall we lace our fingers together?

Shall we dance upon the shore? Bury our toes in the sand?

Shall we spritz our skin with salt and breeze?

Shall we wade into the lake?

Shall we scrub the stains from our dress?

Shall we keep the scent of rat upon our lips? The pleasant sting?

Shall we strip ourselves of these heavy garments?

Shall we lay them on the stones?

Shall we dry under the suns?

Shall we feel the pleasant sting of the light's kiss?

Shall we observe the skyline?
Shall we appreciate the towers?
Shall we turn away?
Shall we enter the city?
Shall we tread the streets?
Shall we mingle with the common folk?
Shall we accept their offers for coverings?
Shall we accept their modesty?
Shall we graze our skin upon the onyx bricks?
The lost foundation of a lost city?
Shall we infect the masonry with our plague?
Shall we smile as the towers crumble? As the walls lie flat?
Shall we wait for the torches to set the ruins ablaze?
Shall we hope that they do?
Shall we dance upon the rubble? Bury our toes in the ash?
Shall we don our crown?
Shall we kiss at all?

***

From a point somewhere to the left of his body, Hugo watches Carina. She stands in such a way as her feet point away from Hugo, with her upper torso twisted to vaguely reveal the curve of his breast, and the profile of her face. Her pale legs merge seamlessly with the several inches of snow she stands in, as though she organically grew from the substance. She picks snowflakes from the loose hair strands of her messy bun.

"The more you move, the more time this will take."

Hugo's own posture is more natural, more tense. In contrast to Carina's nudity, he is wrapped in several layers of thick garment, a hide of reptilian scale. His gloved right hand holds a palette; his left holds a small brush. The canvas on his easel is mostly painted gold.

An exercise in futility: Hugo paints Carina, but not as she is in the bleak winter wastes—he paints her in a pleasant field of wheat, a stark contrast to their stark surroundings.

"You haven't touched brush to canvas in several minutes, and I'm freezing."

"I most certainly have. Speak not about what you know not."

"You forget I can see you clearly, you oaf. I'll not be called a liar."

"And I'll not be insulted by my bitch of a model, Camilla. The—"

"Carina."

A pause. Annoyance stems from Hugo's confusion.

"What?"

"My name is Carina."

"Not important. Put your arms back up. We're making progress."

Hugo mixes minute drops of red into a secluded smear of white paint, attempting to recreate the rosy complexion of Carina's buttocks.

"By the graces, this is surely divine justice. I am a lauded model throughout the city, and for my devotion, I am landed with a bull who fancies himself a painter. Blessed be—"

The sound of Hugo's palette sinking into the snow cuts her short. He stomps towards her, snow dislodging from his boots in all directions. Fury hardens his face. Carina steals a glance at her red woollen robe, but the enraged artist proves too intimidating an obstacle. She takes a step backward.

And another.

She turns to run.

The reckoning. The summoning. The purge.

The frozen wastes are eternal beneath Carina's

bare feet, but she continues to run towards the distant landscape: thin spires of granite, curved like fangs. By all graces, they should not physically be able to stand. Hugo follows her pale limbs, obscured by shadows undulating in the falling snow.

The shadows start to coalesce. Carina trips at the edge of the snowfield, shards of stone piercing her heels. She lands hard, rolling in the gravel that surrounds a tower of black brick, crashing into it. Hugo does not hesitate. He clamps around her throat with both hands.

Fearful eyes watch from slits in the tower's wall—watch the little color in Carina's face ebb away, watch a few drifts of snow entreat onto the clearing.

"The longer you tantrum, the longer the snow has to bury you," Hugo gasps through clenched teeth. Each struggle of Carina's is a pulse of a terran heart, each squirm bringing her infinitely closer.

We will not turn away.

Hugo never lets her go. Even as the clouds clear and the tower spears the moon like a holy sword cleaving a field of wheat, he maintains his grip.

"Now look what you've done. I could paint a corpse of you."

Shall we hope that they do?

"Kneel before the One who wields eternity,
or fall to the remnants of a broken empire.
Give up your lives and set aside all your doubts."

—Pan

THE UNMASKING
Alexander Kreitner

You want to know how I did it, don't you? How I staged the greatest play mankind has ever produced. Of course you do, why wouldn't you?

Well, it wasn't easy. But then again, genius never is. I'm sure they even laughed at Castaigne when he declared that he was going to finish the play. I know they laughed at me. But I've done it. You've seen the result, haven't you? Now you want to know.

I admit: I had some trouble with the script. I wrote it out a couple times, and once when I lost the original copy and rewrote it, I found that I had written an almost completely different play. But the final version of the script was perfect; I know it was. I looked it over a hundred times.

No, a thousand.

I spent nights upon nights reading it aloud, crying; even drinking sometimes to shut out the voices of derision. But in the end, when they beheld what I had created, they all grew quiet.

The first step after the script was finalized was to start the casting. So I was forced to leave the stage that I had been working on and enter the world beyond the theatre doors. I needed to find my two darlings: Camilla and Cassilda. The catty aristocrats. I assumed that with the way things were going in the world today, they wouldn't be too hard to find.

I was half right. Almost as soon as my foot left the stoop of the theatre I found my Cassilda, the younger. I came across her talking on a phone, and I made my preposition with declarations of her unearthly beauty, and pitch-perfect, sweet voice, like that of the angels. I told her that I needed someone innocent but arrogant, and though she was sceptical at first, I could tell she was intrigued.

I did a reading with her right there, in the

street. After a quick explanation of my chosen scene, I played the part of the stranger, and as I revealed myself to her she showed such magnificent terror that I knew I had to have her for my performance. She was still unsure and skittish, but I managed to convince her of what she would be passing up, and she eventually agreed.

So I left her to practice her lines on stage while I went searching for my Camilla, the older.

Emboldened by my initial success, I eagerly searched the streets, but after a day and a half of wasted time I began to doubt myself. I know it's silly, but I began to wonder if what I was doing was worth it. Everything had seemed so easy and *right* at first, but now I found myself wandering the crowded streets looking desperately for one woman to fit my part, and while away from my artful womb the voices returned to taunt and mock me.

You'll never find her, they chortled in my ears. *The play will always remain unfinished. You aren't worthy of Castaigne's genius. You're just a hack.*

"A hack?" I screamed at them, which seemed to quiet them for a moment. I would show them who the hack was, and to that end I doubled my efforts.

Before half an hour passed I had already found her, which only reassured me that I was doing the right thing. The play would indeed be finished; the voices be damned.

When I saw the woman I knew at once that she was perfect and why no one else would do. She walked with such upright regality and with such poise and purpose. But you could see that underneath the surface of so much control and beauty was something awful and vicious. She was just what I needed.

Like my Cassilda, she was tentative at first. She claimed a prior engagement: a business meeting. But I politely insisted, and I showed her a copy of the script. I detailed her part, and I heaped upon her all the praise that was due to such an important character. Even though she wasn't entirely convinced, I sensed within her a burning urge towards fatality that I knew would secure her cooperation.

I was proved correct when after a few minutes of insistent debate she agreed to show up and try a reading with my Cassilda. And so I had my Camilla.

You should have seen how well they got along when I brought her back to the theatre. They veritably clung to each other, like a real mother and daughter. Seeing them together, I knew that everything would turn out just as I had imagined. Just as Castaigne had imagined, even.

I asked Cassilda if she had been practicing while I had been gone with the copy of the script I had left on the table. Regrettably, she told me that she hadn't gotten around to it. Too excited, I imagined. But I forgave her, because now her co-star was there to read with her.

By the time we were ready to start reading the first scene they were both more than dedicated. I then explained to them my vision for the play. I think, no, I *know*, that they could see it, even through the clumsy words I used to describe it.

The first reading went so well that I decided to try a scene from the second and last act. Again, I played the masked stranger, and they both reacted wonderfully when I revealed that I was in fact not wearing a mask at all. Their screams of terror and madness echoed through the hall with a music that would have made the author himself cry.

They were more than ready to play their parts. And as you saw, play them they did, and beautifully so. Wouldn't you say?

***

The officers responded to a strange emergency

call and showed up at the suspect's house. People were freely moving around the first couple of rooms, their faces pale, pointing and gasping. The officers had to escort everyone off the premises and seal the entrance with caution tape.

Then they re-entered what the suspect later called his "theatre." Both were on guard for anyone who might be hiding in the rooms; however, the primary suspect had all but turned himself in when they had first arrived. He was patiently waiting in the cruiser, after insisting that they observe his "play."

What the two officers found when they first entered the dwelling was relatively innocuous. Most of the rooms were made up like average living spaces, with a kitchen and bedroom, as well as a study room with hundreds or thousands of books lining the walls in rows of wooden shelving.

The study was clearly the most used room of the house. Next to the leather chair was a stack of books that appeared to be unread, next to some that looked more used. The fireplace showed indications of a recent fire.

It was only when the officers reached the back of the house that the surroundings became more extreme. The first door they reached was open, as the neighbours had already been through it. A small bronze plaque on the wall, at the level of the doorknob, read `Mother, Daughter`.

Both officers kept their handguns at the ready position as they stepped into the strange room. After a quick survey of the corners, they found that there was no one hiding. They lowered their weapons, but kept them ready at their sides while they both kept an eye on the closed door at the other end of the room.

The walls of the room they stood in were decorated with a giant mural of a fantastic castle and what appeared to be a ballroom filled with people. Some of the painted figures were so realistic that they had to look at them twice while they surveyed the room, but other than the officers there was nothing alive in the room. The only sign of life was a puddle in one corner where one of the neighbours had been sick after seeing the main attraction.

They knew a little of what to expect from what the callers had reported to the operator, but both were taken aback when they focused on the centrepiece of the room.

Huddled together were two women: one younger and most likely in her late teens, early twenties; the other in her late thirties. They were dressed in fancy ball-gowns which looked to be right out of another century. The older woman's arm was draped around the younger, protectively holding her close. Both faces looked towards the other door of the room, and their faces wore twin expressions of abject terror. Both of them were also quite clearly dead.

The pair of officers separately attested that in all their years on the force they had never seen an expression like that on any face, living or dead. It was after seeing the pair that they called for more backup, as well as an ambulance, though it became clear that it would not be useful.

After collecting themselves they took a closer look at the pair in the middle of the room. Closer inspection revealed details even stranger than before. The face of the older woman bore a set of clawed marks which raked down her cheek, leaving one length of skin hanging down in a tattered flap. When the younger one was examined it appeared that her nails had done the raking, as one was cracked, and all of them had bits of skin and flecks of blood underneath them.

What was more inexplicable was the razor-sharp dagger that the older woman had in her hand. Instead of being held out to defend against whatever terror she imagined from the other room, it was hidden in the hand that wrapped protectively around the young woman; as if she was planning to stab her "daughter" in the back.

***

I have been called insane. I'm sure that's what your psychiatrists will tell you after they talk to me as well. But you must keep in mind how close insanity is to creativity and genius. They called Castaigne insane, too, but the excruciating beauty of what he has written speaks loudly for itself.

When I first read it, I'll admit, I couldn't understand it. Like you, I thought it was madness itself, and not worthy of print. But on a compulsion I read it again, and then again. Before I knew what had happened, something opened within my head, and I understood what he was saying.

From that moment on I became dedicated to the play. Your psychiatrists might call it obsessed, but like madness and genius, it's all a matter of perspective.

Day and night I lived within the worlds of the play. I danced with the Queen in the halls of Yhtill. I stared out of the windows of the palace as the twilight fell upon the city, and my vision stretched towards the Lake of Hali. I watched as the moon illuminated a reflection upon its still surface and I stared at the reversed, watery image of the city across the lake, which no human being had built or inhabited.

I think at those moments I was closer to genius, or insanity, then I have ever been in my whole life. I would shiver in an ecstasy so blissful—one that your kind could never feel—despite the balmy night which pressed continually at my windows.

After I had read it until I knew every word, I read it again from back to front. Then I watched as the city of Yhtill repaired itself after the exit of the King, and the people of the court grew sane and whole once again. I watched as the masked man pulled away from the great door of the palace, and returned to the place of horror from whence he first came.

It was then, as I plodded word by word from the ending, and watched as everything returned slowly to ignorance, that I knew I had to direct my own version of the play. You see, it was the placid ignorance of the people in the story, and people like you outside of my doors, that drove me on. I had to make them, and you, understand.

I see the look in your eyes, and it makes me wonder if you've personally been to the theatre to see my work. I think you haven't.

But you still want to know how I did it, yes? What happened after I had found my leading ladies... I believe that's where I left it. Well, obviously the next step was to find my stranger.

I needed someone who could bring mine and Castaigne's truth out, and display it to an uncaring and unknowing world. Then after a brief search, I found him.

A conman.

Who better for my stranger than a conman? Someone who wears a mask to fool the masses, day after day. Who better to reveal that underneath his lying mask is nothing at all? That the mask he wears is truth itself.

Once he had determined that I was no ordinary mark, he dropped the act, and all that was left was the blankness I desperately needed. I explained what I was doing, and I tried to show him what he could be with my help. It was the ultimate scam, giving the masses the truth they didn't want to see. He was more than eager to help once he understood the angle, and so I took him back with me to the theatre.

I displayed for him, with the help of my two ladies, what I had of the play so far, and I could tell that he was impressed. The look on his face said more than his slack mouth could have ever told me. That part was perfect—now the next step was to make him into my stranger.

I showed him the mask that he would be wearing, which he approved of with wide-eyed appreciation. Though if my play was to mean anything, it had to become his new face. The last face he would ever wear. He needed some more convincing before I could get him to put on the mask and adhere it finally to his face. But once it was on he was transformed completely, and when he looked into the mirror and saw the Pallid Mask that was now his face, he understood that there was no turning back.

As all must understand once they see my work. There is no turning back for any of us.

***

The officers at the scene waited for the backup before entering the second room. Once the larger group had arrived, and the suspect in the cruiser was taken away to be interrogated at the station, a small group prepared to enter the second room.

One of them noted that a second bronze plaque was inset on the wall next to the doorknob. This one read **The Phantom of Truth.**

The lead officer turned the knob and pushed open the door, bringing his weapon up to protect himself. Blackness poured out the door, and the rest of the officers tightened their grips on their weapons, readying themselves for anything or anyone that might jump out at them.

A single light shot down from the ceiling of the room, illuminating a lone figure in the centre. The final officer through the door kept his weapon trained on the figure, who was not moving, but whose face was hidden behind a mask. The rest of the group fanned carefully out from the doorway, their flashlights turned on and sweeping around the room, illuminating the far corners.

What the sole light source revealed of the centre of the room suggested that the floor should have been blank and empty, but outside its circle the officer's flashlights exposed another intricate mural that extended onto the floor itself. Around the walls were more ballroom guests, except that their painted faces were showing some of the shocked terror that the women in the other room exhibited.

Twisted, demented faces popped up with every sweep of the police-issued flashlights, keeping the officers on edge; though no human figure except the one in the middle revealed itself. Only face after face and image after image painted onto the walls of terrified ballroom guests in the same antique dress as the pair of corpses in the last room.

The floor was painted to look like the floor of a castle's ballroom. It was coloured to look like polished wood with bits of streamers and other festive bits strewn across it. Except when one of the officers followed the painting of the room towards the centre he noticed that the image stopped exactly where the light fell.

Only once the officers had searched every corner of the dark room, found another door at one end, and were satisfied that no one was hiding in the darkness, did they approach the figure at the centre. The lead officer spoke to the man, in a continuously reassuring tone, until he was able to reach out and touch him, and found that he was cold and still. Further examination revealed that he was as dead as the women before him.

He wore clothing that was similar in fashion to the women; though it was more of an actor's puffy, multi-coloured suit. He was in an equally dramatic pose, one arm extended out and curled in a way that implied an unmasking, except that he was still masked.

The officers noticed that the mask that covered his face didn't seem to have any ties in the back, or any visible means of attachment. But when one of them looked closer he could see that the edges of the mask and the flesh around it were warped and distorted. After pulling his hands away with a jerk of revulsion, the officer realized that the mask was actually melted directly onto his face.

***

There comes a time for every great creator when they behold the formation of their masterpiece and a new doubt assails them. No longer is there the nagging feeling that they are attempting something that is impossible. No, it is a completely different feeling: more akin perhaps to a sort of terrified awe.

This is when the artist looks at its creation and wonders if the world itself is ready for its birth. The perfection of it all becomes staggering to one who is merely a man. But as I said before, there was no turning back for me, nor for the world. That didn't mean that I didn't spend a couple days completely ineffective and oppressed.

For those two days I spent most of my time wandering back and forth from one scene of my play to the other, all through the theatre. My mind was all but overwhelmed by the things which had come from my own hands and thoughts, propelled along as well, from the grave, by Castaigne himself. Of that I am sure.

Then I would go to the final place, and the final scene, and I would try to visualize it.

But I was unable to.

Can you imagine the horror I felt staring at all that empty space? I knew it was the finale, and it had to be perfect. I also knew that perfect didn't just come right away, it had to be teased out of all the worldly imperfection holding it back.

Oh, there was much imperfection in my mind, and I seemed to be unable to form it into the perfect scene which I knew would tie up the last of my magnificent work. It was then that I went back to the written words. Not even my script, which I didn't trust entirely, but the original itself.

Then for the next couple nights I poured over Castaigne's words, ignoring the first act entirely. While reading, however, I fell asleep. When I awoke, the dream I had began to slip from me, but before it did I knew what had to be done. I knew the mistake I was making.

I had assumed that the first couple scenes were done and had no impact on the finale of my piece. But it was those first two uninteresting scenes, written by the mundane genius of Christopher Marlowe, which held the key to the completion of my work. You see, it is the innocence and the simplicity of the first act which makes the whole so much more amazing. Without Marlowe's first act, the power of the play is lost completely.

What I realized when I woke up, which seems so simple to me now, is that the King is a child. Of course. Who better to be my avatar of Death than a young boy? You see, the doom of Yhtill must have come from the lips of an innocent.

Without further doubt or hesitation I went abroad to find my young King. It seemed that no sooner had I come to my realization of my need than it was fulfilled. Shortly after entering the city I found him, the perfect child: so pure and so horribly average.

He was exactly what I needed. A simple boy of moderate intelligence, with hair the shade of old wood, and eyes the colour of stagnant rainwater. There was absolutely nothing special about the young man in the least; which made him perfect for my King.

Unlike my older actors, I knew that the boy could never understand what I was trying to do. So I admit I had to use deception to get him into the theatre, but once he was there, and met my other players, I knew he was mine.

The robe I made for him was breath-taking, as you would know if you had seen it. It was a marvel of splendour and simplicity, a tattered yellow robe with fringes of the most subtle red for contrast. I had even debated adorning him with his own Pallid Mask, as I had envisioned in one version of the play, but I later decided against it. The mask would only take away from his visage.

And so my final act was ready, with just a few minor touches to add to the scene. Then it was done. I can't begin to describe to you the feelings that I had when I viewed my work as a whole. Each player playing the part he or she was born to play, to the hilt. It was beyond perfection. I knew that even if the world wasn't ready to view the masterpiece, it would have no choice. Because it speaks volumes to the world, and in turn the world is mirrored within it.

It was then that I alerted the people outside of my finished play, and bade them enter and view it. Which is what brought you folks to me.

And I absolutely must insist that you see it as well, dear Captain. I can sense that you are an intelligent man of taste. I think you of all people will appreciate it, for it is the embodiment of art and human achievement itself.

***

After my officers had finished searching the suspect's house, after the crime scene investigators had begun to go over it, and after I had gotten everything I could out of the suspect himself, I decided to take him up on his offer. I had had to listen to his egotistical ramblings for hours, and now it was time to face what he had done. I never felt qualified to judge the words of a suspect until I had seen the crime itself.

By the time I got there the house looked much

different than it would have if I had been one of the officers that answered the call. Every room was swarming with a combination of my detectives and the forensic guys. Even the very normal looking rooms like the kitchen and the sparse bedroom were occupied by employees of the state, going over everything with a depth and precision that I would never care to attempt.

The first two rooms of his "masterpiece" had their impact stripped off of them as groups of men crawled all around each tableaux, picking off hairs and dusting them for prints. Chalk marks around the bases of the corpses robbed them of everything that made them horrible to begin with. They no longer looked like fully realized images from the mind of a lunatic, but merely museum pieces being studied by callous scientists.

When I reached the second room I noticed that even the light from the ceiling which illuminated the masked man was turned off, and normal lights were installed to make it easier for them to work on the figure. Its majestic presence was further marred by a large chip off the mask that an investigator had removed to examine. A mass of undefined flesh showed through the opening, which made me strangely sad.

True, the suspect was clearly insane, but a secret part of me hated to see the work of any artist, even a mad one, taken apart and revealed to the world as a set of carefully assembled pieces.

Yet the last room remained untouched, and I was informed that the investigators took one look at it and went back to the rest of the house. They told me that it was too much to work on right away, and they needed time to make sense of everything else before they tackled his final "scene."

I walked up to the door and reached out to turn the handle as I saw the last bronze plaque a few inches from the knob. This one read **The King in Yellow.** I shrugged it off and opened the door, stepped inside, and closed it behind me. When I kept my eye on the door as it closed I noticed that the inside of the door was painted as if it was part of the wall, and not an exit.

Then I turned and beheld the room itself.

My breath stopped for just the barest moment, and the overwhelming feeling that took me over showed me exactly why the investigators were taking their time with this one. I've seen some horrible things in the thirty years that I've been a cop, but this blew them all away.

I had to give it to the man; he was a master of lighting. I didn't get to see the interesting lighting of the last room, but I can imagine it. As I understood it, even the first room had a tilted spot light that brightened at the door which brought so much terror to the two women. But the lighting in the last room was amazing. I couldn't see where it was coming from, but it wasn't bright or overwhelming in itself–instead it was just strong enough to give me a detailed view of everything in the room.

In the hard, stark light I saw that I was standing on what appeared to be a silky yellow flooring. All around me were the bodies of men and women in various stages of madness or terror.

I laughed a sick laugh to myself. A few minor touches, indeed.

Almost to a one their attention was drawn to the centre of the room. All except for one man who appeared to be gouging out his own eyes with his thumbs. And like the older woman in the first room, many of them had ragged tears on their faces and arms, which came from the bloodied nails of other bodies next to them.

It seemed that the ones which hadn't gone insane where they stood were trying to escape the figure in the middle, and it suddenly became clear why the door behind me was painted like a wall. On the other side of the room was what looked like a door, but after a closer glance it turned out to be painted onto the wall, complete with a fake handle attached to the flat surface. In their last moments these people were tricked into going for a fake doorway, and it looked as if they were all either too insane or too scared to notice that it wasn't real.

In their rush to get to the false door they had trampled and torn each other apart. Some of the bodies lay under the fancy shoes of the ones on top, their crushed faces bearing the same insanity and terror as their incidental murderers. Each of them was dressed in the same archaic clothing as the other figures in the rooms, in bright colours that were splashed with blood and gore from their dead neighbours.

The ones that had made it to the false door were the worst. The expressions they wore were unlike any of the others. It was as if they had felt a desperate hope at the last moment when they reached what they thought was their freedom, and when they found out that the door wasn't real, the hope broke apart and the shards of it splintered into a deeper insanity and terror than all the rest. Their eyes were wild and unbelieving, and their nails were torn ragged from scrambling at the wall, though the door was painted on so well that none of their efforts exposed anything beneath the perverted *Trompe l'Oeil*.

Strangely, the scramble towards the false doorway hadn't disturbed the yellow silk that flowed out from the centre, which turned out to be part of the robe of the centre figure. Not one wrinkle marred its liquid surface, though spatters and fans of blood decorated even the figure itself. I wasn't sure if these were the subtle fringes of red he mentioned, or if there were also real ones woven into the fabric itself.

The figure was as unblemished as its clothing. Up until I turned to it, I had been focused on the scene around the room, and hadn't fully understood what could cause such fear and madness. But once my eye caught the bright yellow thing in the middle, I glimpsed the reason why one would go mad being trapped in a room with it. For a moment I almost considered opening the real door behind me to a crack to remind me that I was free to leave, but I didn't want my officers seeing that.

As the suspect had led me to understand, the figure in the middle was that of a young boy. He wore a yellow robe whose bright colours reflected the sharp light, making him glow in the middle of the carnage and madness. It was tattered, yet it hung off of him like it was made specifically for his frame.

But the brightness of the whole thing seemed blasphemous. The author of such horror should be dressed in funeral black. Instead, he was a glowing image of youth and health. His hands were open wide in a welcoming embrace that mocked the fear of the dead around him.

I stepped closer to him, needing to see the expression on his face. Part of me needed some understanding of the whole thing; some explanation of the terror and the insanity that seemed to fill the very air of this room. But the look on his face only made it worse.

He was looking straight through me. His features were plain and unattractive; just a boy, with dull hair and inexpressive eyes. His mouth was bent in something like a smile which seemed to brighten up his whole face, but not with happiness or laughter.

I saw his hands stretched out as if he was beckoning me towards him, and I wanted to believe that if I went to him I would be blessed by him. Suddenly I felt a desperate longing that grew from deep within me, something inside me that I had never seen. I desired his love and compassion, but there was nothing of love or compassion in his face; just a knowing look of bleak eternity, like his empty grey eyes looked out onto a cold, unforgiving forever.

I felt that I was going mad, myself. I fell to my knees in front of him, and cried out for something like a message of hope. But the room was silent with the silence that comes with the closeness of so much death. I pulled at my hair and shook my head, trying to deny the facts in front of me.

My only thought was escape. I climbed clumsily to my feet and slipped a couple times on the yellow fabric beneath me, which never moved. I lunged at the hidden door and pushed it open, falling into the room beyond and nearly into the arms of one of my detectives. He looked at me with surprise, but with a hint of understanding.

I pushed past him and ran out of the second room, too. I made it outside the theatre and into the open air, which I gulped down in great swallows.

After I finally managed to calm myself down, and tried to forget what I had seen, I stumbled back to my cruiser and curled up on the seat until I felt stable enough to drive. Then I drove straight home and locked myself in with the familiarity of my family for the next couple of days, ignoring any calls that came in until I could face them again.

I left the investigation to my subordinates and washed my hands of it all, refusing to talk about it to anyone. Saying only that the scenes needed to be taken apart and studied away from the man's house.

To this day I think that what saved me that night was that I knew where the real door was. If I had been distracted by the fake door across the room for even a moment, I'm afraid that I would have trampled the bruised and mutilated corpses to get to the false exit, and have gone stark raving mad as I ripped my nails apart trying to escape through the painted doorway.

And I don't care what that madman says, our world will never be ready for the truths in those rooms, especially the last.

THE MASKED
Alexander Kreitner

You want to know why, don't you?

They always want to know why, as if mere words could enlighten them to a reasoning they couldn't already fathom.

But you want to know why a decorated captain of the police would turn his back on a respectable career to do what I have done. It must seem strange to you from where you sit, but once I had peered beneath the surface of this hollow life, there was no going back. The worst and most damaging thing of all would have been to be exposed to the truth and then attempt to walk away from it. By that exposure, of course, I mean the original Work that he had created.

I assume you know what I'm talking about. Have you seen pictures of it? I can see that you are familiar with it, but I assure you that still pictures and verbal descriptions of it would never do it justice. I had it explained to me by the author himself, yet I still had to visit it myself to truly understand. When they had brought him in to me for questioning, I thought about it much as you undoubtedly think of it now: merely as criminal insanity.

To my credit, I was still curious. I felt that I had to see what he had done to properly judge him and his case. Though I had to hurry before the forensic team had pulled apart too much of the original grandeur of the work. I travelled to the abandoned house which he had transformed into his theatre to view his interpretation of the Master's Work. I saw each tableau in its rightful place, though the vultures had already picked over the first two rooms by the time I had arrived. I was lucky enough to see the final room, the purest well of truth, virtually untouched. What I saw there, which had driven others mad, jarred me at a very basic level and began my transformation.

Of course, that's not how it felt at the time. Admittedly, I fled the scene in the most dignified manner I could and retreated to my vehicle to try to piece myself back together. When I had shaken off enough of it to drive, I travelled home and said nothing to my wife and children about what I had seen, but shortly afterward I took a leave from the police force to try to clear my head.

I had a desperate need to know exactly why I had felt such a longing when I had stood in front of the King in Yellow. His open arms attracted me in a way that seemed vulgar and degrading. I was drawn to and repelled from him simultaneously. I soon came to the conclusion that the only way to understand the interpretation was to track down and study the original Work. It was surprisingly difficult to find a copy of Castaigne's masterpiece even in our modern age of online commerce, but eventually I did.

What I found affected me greater than even the staging of it could have. The Work opened up vistas of knowledge that I had never dreamed existed. It was as if I was fulfilling a need I never knew I had as I pored over the book again and again, attempting with every repetition to fully understand what it was I was reading. Every time I reread how the King came to Carcosa, I felt the same pull deep inside that I had felt in the presence of the final room. It was only after dozens, maybe hundreds, of readings that something finally opened up and I had a glimpse of experiential truth.

All this time my marriage and my family seemed so distant from me and I knew I was beginning to lose them to neglect, but I could no longer find in myself any attachment to the identity of a husband and father. The routine of the mundane world depressed and sickened me, yet I kept up the pretence when I realized that I now had a greater purpose. I eventually returned to the police force, secure in the knowledge of what I had to do next.

THE MASKED

I passed the psychiatric evaluation without any problems. When you have witnessed the objective truth first-hand, another person's pale perspective of it is so easy to manipulate. Because I had found salvation in what this man–this "criminal"–had showed me, I knew that my first obligation was to save him in turn.

It took some time and subtle wrangling, but in a short while I was able to take advantage of a prisoner transfer of the man from our smaller, local jail to a high-security state prison. I installed myself as one of the guards for the transfer under the guise that I was taking final charge of moving the criminal outside of my jurisdiction, who had caused so much horror within it and to me. I was able to utilize the layman's apprehension of another's mental failings and use sympathy to leverage myself into the position and soon found myself in the front seat of the police van as it sped down a quiet highway.

It took less work to order the driver to pull over and ask him to join me as I opened the rear of the van and call the second guard out to me. Both were confused by my orders, but people are nothing if not obedient, and I gathered them together on the side of the road in the weeds and dust and shot both in the head.

The prisoner looked out at me with a dawning realization, as I had yet to this point shown any sympathy for his cause. He stepped out of the van on his own accord and I unbound him and handed him my gun and asked him to shoot me in the meat of the thigh to leave me with an alibi. He looked into my eyes and he saw truth mirrored back at them and he did not hesitate.

Though I wanted to flee with him and join him then and there, I knew that there was no way that I could disguise my compliance in his escape. It would be easier for us to work together if we were not both fugitives. And so I calculated that it would be better to be seen as incompetent than corrupted, so I waited in the dirt with a bleeding leg until the authorities arrived after a practiced and frantic call into my police radio.

I also waited, hidden behind a thin veil of patience, for a reasonable amount of time to pass before I would be suspected of collusion and quietly left the police under a heavy cloud of disgrace. I left my family, as well, with even less explanation and excuse and joined my partner in hiding to further our necessary work.

This act would seem to most as the final line I crossed from my old life to my new, from where there was no going back. I imagine this is how they will describe it. But I must emphasize that it was the plain, unattractive face of a young boy's corpse clad in the tattered garments of the King in Yellow that represented the ultimate threshold over which I had crossed. A threshold we have now offered up to the entire world.

***

Dr. Haster leaned back awkwardly in the uncomfortable chair that was bolted to the floor of the hospital's interview room and looked across the metal table into the masked face of the former police captain while he told his story. Haster had drawn up numerous profiles of notable psychotics and had made a name for himself as a profiler of the criminally insane. He reasoned that the high profile of this man's crime would work nicely into a celebrated paper, maybe even a successful book. And so the doctor eagerly observed his new subject.

The pale mask that covered his entire face was carved with such care and shined with a lustre that gave the illusion that it was made of liquid that flowed like water when he moved his head. His eyes stared out from the mask with a dark intensity, as if staring up out of two pits of shifting earth. The mask gave his voice a strange, hollow sound that issued from the narrow slit at the bottom of it, completely hiding his lips.

When the psychiatrist tilted his own head, he could see that the skin at the edges of the mask had a puffy, shiny look to it that indicated that the mask was melted or adhered to the patient's skin. It explained why they hadn't taken it off of him when he was brought in.

The man in the mask spoke in a very even, calm fashion uncommon to most paranoiacs. He explained his delusions with particular care, and his body movements were slight and economical. Over all, he exhibited a stillness of mind and body that was completely out of sorts with the clearly irrational actions he described.

The doctor looked down at a folder on the table, rather than continue to stare into his shifting face and burning eyes, as the man spoke. Haster glanced over the details of the tableaus that the man had investigated when he was a member of the police. Dr. Haster moved his eyes over the words as if he needed reminding, but he had already memorized everything from the documents. He felt it was best for the patient to imagine he was telling him something new, which might make him feel in control enough to offer more details.

The case that he referred to had been picked up and heavily sensationalized by the media. Luckily, the police had taken over and disassembled the three scenes in a controlled manner that stopped the press from sharing the grisly details with the public. Even Dr. Haster had very little indication of what they had looked like when the original killer had constructed them. He could only imagine the horror each room offered of once-living people in frozen scenes of madness and what chaos had ensued when the man had let in his closest neighbours to be driven insane, trapped together in the last room.

What the masked man sitting in front of him had concocted with that other disturbed individual, however, was significantly worse. Dr. Haster shuttered inwardly as, this time, there would not be the same stop-gaps enforced between this madness and the general public. He stared at the strange, shifting mask the man wore before interrupting the man's telling of his story with a question.

***

You ask me why I wear a mask, but I tell you that I wear no mask. You are the only one here who is disguised. I obliterated the last of mine already. What you call a mask is my true face that I crafted with a conscious awareness. This aware creation is the only thing that anyone could call real, whereas the mask you wear was given to you by others and reacts in time with others' whims. Mine reveals the truth beneath and yours can only deceive.

This is what I was shown when I experienced the physical manifestation of Castaigne's immortal Work. I stared into the face of that little boy who I came upon as a harbinger of Death. And what he showed me was the truth behind the mask I wore; the truth that there was nothing beneath it. While virtually everyone else has to wait for Death to come to them to show them this in their final moments, I was shown it ahead of my time, and have been given a chance to unmask myself and let my true self expand without the constraint of that façade.

This chance is what my companion and I wish to offer to the entire world, this opportunity to see the truth before one's time is up. Though it's true that many will not be able to withstand this revelation, much as the original audience he had invited to his theatre that went mad and destroyed themselves. The world will be forced to either adapt to this tearing off of their collective masks, or else it will be consumed in a pyre of madness and fear. If this is the result of the exposure to such unfiltered truth, then who is to say that this world is worth saving?

Yet I am getting ahead of myself.

As I was saying, I had escaped the confines of my false work and joined up with my companion in hiding to start my real Work. Though I had an experiential knowledge of the truth, I still did not fully understand it to be able to explain it to others. When I met him he brought me to see his collection of books from which, he explained, he had prepared himself to bring to the world his creation. He told me that I needed to purify myself if I was to be a pure vessel from which the truth could fully express itself.

I spent weeks in his library of mouldering, esoteric works, devouring each successive book that acted as a key to unlock yet another barrier within my mind. He had collected these tomes over the years and their scope was overwhelming. I read from books I had thought were myths or fictional creations, with strange names, often in other languages. The strangest thing was that the more I read, the more I could understand in the books, even the ones in languages I had never spoken, studied, or even heard of. He explained to me that the truth was its own language, and now that I had understood this objective language, I could understand any other subjective language with ease.

Then one day I looked up from a rather large work with a soft binding, suggesting a binding material that would have horrified me only a few months before, to find him standing across from me. He declared to me that I was now ready and he showed me the script that he had been working on. While I am no artist, certainly not of his calibre, I helped him with it in a more technical aspect, working to get the tone right. There is a certain octave or vibration that represents the truth and it takes a practiced ear to be able to hear it, or play it.

However, for all his genius, my companion is not a modern man. The one thing that I impressed upon him as a failing of his original work was its scope. It certainly had the impact he desired, but his narrow medium allowed the authorities to too quickly stamp out the fire that he had started. Of course it wasn't quick enough to keep from reaching me, so in retrospect it accomplished what it needed to at the time. But now, I insisted, we needed to work in a medium and construct our Work on a stage that was indestructible and was under no authority's control: the Internet.

Once we had our stage and we collected our tools, the next step was to take our script and start to audition. The problem was that, unlike his original piece, we couldn't trust to the air or the appearance of the actors, as they would have to play their parts in motion. Finding a pair of women to play the mother and daughter, Camilla and Cassilda, was relatively easy. Modern society is not lacking in cattiness, duplicity, or fear. So we very soon had our pair and they ran through their lines with a chilling perfection.

We realized that we would need two unique individuals for the Phantom of Truth and the King in Yellow. A few days searching the streets, interviewing likely or interested candidates, showed us that we weren't going to stumble upon anyone who could so easily portray the bringer and source of truth, respectively.

Then I had a realization. It was an epiphany that I am particularly proud of since, as I have said, I am not prone to creative inspiration. When it occurred to me, I fell to my knees in front of him, and I begged him to let me play the Phantom of Truth. While I knew I was not worthy of such a burden, it was a weight that I was willing to shoulder. Ever since I had witnessed his Work and had begun to pry open the edges of the barrier that stood between the reality beneath and the lie I had been telling for years, I'd had a growing itch to tear off my disguise. I knew it was selfish of me to ask, but I wanted my act of true self-honesty to reach out to the world and project what I felt so strongly deep inside.

He looked down upon me with tears in his eyes and lifted me up, promising me the part. He told me that I would be perfect and begged my forgiveness that he hadn't thought of it sooner. To think, he would beg me? I assured him that was nonsense; it was only the weight of our burden that had acted as a distraction. He would hear none of it. What's more, he said to me, to honour my devotion he would play the King in Yellow. I knew what that meant as we had discussed the particulars of each costuming and display ahead of time. I could only look at him with thinly disguised awe.

So we filmed it; all of it. Now Castaigne's great work has been uploaded to the Internet for everyone to witness, for all time. I know the authorities have tried to take it down, but as I predicted, once becoming digital it has become immortal. People are creatures of habit and reaction and they will share it back and forth between each other, spreading the truth far and wide and ushering in a new age of either madness or enlightenment.

I look in your eyes, doctor, and I see that you have not witnessed it.

Why not?

***

The man's words continued to echo in Dr. Haster's head as he finished speaking out loud. Haster felt a perverse instinct to look for the video online and see what this man had done to satisfy himself that it was as lunatic as it sounded. But the psychiatrist was worried that his desire to see the film grew from something deeper than incredulity.

As he stood up and thanked the masked man for his time, who now sat silent and staring, he remembered his first site of the folder in his hands. When he had studied it in preparation for the interview there were several photographs the police had taken of the man's companion when they had found what was left of the "production." The pictures showed the man, now a propped-up corpse, and the other "actors" as they reacted in terror and madness to his bright, yet somehow profane, costume.

The pictures had drawn him in so that he found himself studying them an hour later, having lost all track of time. He quickly put each photo through his office shredder, telling himself that it was inappropriate to put such explicit pictures in a hospital portfolio. But the words of the masked man still played in a loop within his own thoughts and he wondered at his own urge to view this *King In Yellow* with an eager fatalism that seemed alien to his usual professional detachment.

He took a final look at the seated patient and before the doctor turned his head away he saw the man reach up to touch his masked face and he could swear that the fluid-looking surface rippled at the touch of his finger. He shuddered openly and walked too quickly from the room and spoke curtly with the doctor on duty. The other doctor smirked as he made his excuses to leave and appreciation for the opportunity to interview his patient. He accepted the other man's handshake and tried to ignore his smugness at the hasty retreat of such an acclaimed expert in criminal psychology.

Dr. Haster straightened his back and strode away with as much dignity as possible, while the confused voices in his mind fought to bring him to his knees instead. As he passed the nurse's station, he heard one of orderlies address another.

"Hey, man. Alec says he found the video online that the kook down the hall made. We're going to get together tonight and check it out. You in?"

THE REST OF YOUR LIFE
Neal Wilgus

The interstate was traffic-jammed and I was drained, so, when I saw a sign reading *Carcosa Exit – One Mile*, I went ahead and turn-signalled. I'd never heard of Carcosa, but it must have a motel or two where I could crash for the night. Any dump would do.

I drove on the narrow bumpy road for an eternity before I saw the lights of Carcosa shimmering in the fog. The radio had blinked out and my headlights were only wishful thinking–only the moonlit fog giving enough light to keep me on the road. There was no other traffic.

Just past the Lake Hali turnoff, I began to discern a scattering of homes and stores, ghosts in the fog, and then, at last, I came to the downtown area–a few blocks of commercial buildings, some several storeys high, with streetlights to mark the way. Cars lined the streets and, at the far end of the area, a vehicle pulled around the corner and disappeared–I think it was a hearse. A convenience store, Hastur's Hardware, was still open and there seemed to be some activity going on at the Church of St. Barnabé.

Then, I spotted the Yellow Sign Motel with its *Vacancy* sign flashing and I put all else out of my mind and pulled up before the office. I could see no one at the desk, but I got out and went in, dog-tired and prepared to pay whatever they asked. The place was dimly lit and seemed almost deserted, but I rang the bell in desperation.

Still, no one appeared and, as I drummed my fingers on the counter, I noticed a few yellowing business cards on display. I picked one up and read:

```
YELLOW SIGN HOTEL
H.A. Robardin, Prop.
"The Rest of Your Life"
```

I tucked the car in my pocket and, a moment later, a thin figure appeared behind a curtain–an elderly, bald man who looked as if he'd not smiled in a lifetime.

"I need a room," I blurted out, impatient with the delay.

"We are open," he said, nodding. He wore a Pallid Mask.

"Can I just pay you now and go straight to the room?"

He nodded. "We are open."

He put a worn key on the counter and I pulled out some cash, not knowing nor caring how much it was. "I'll pay you now," I said.

"The room is open," he said, nodding.

The room was dingy–old and worn like Mr. Robardin. Dust covered all and I doubted the sheets had been changed in weeks, perhaps months, but then, the Yellow Sign obviously did little business, so perhaps it didn't matter. The place was dead silent and I doubted there were any other guests.

Strangely, once in bed, I found I couldn't sleep. Now, I began to notice how hot it was in the room and soon got up to look for a cooling system or a window to open. There was no cooler and the window wouldn't open, so I lay down and tried to sleep. *The Rest of Your Life*, the card had said.

Still, I couldn't sleep and, after tossing-turning for an hour–so it seemed–got up again and stepped to the door, peeking out at the fog-shrouded street. It seemed a bit cooler outside, so, making sure I had the key in my pocket, I stepped out and locked the door. It was cooler out, so I stepped out and locked the door, making sure I had the key in my pocket. It was fog-shrouded, but cooler out, I thought.

I walked past the office, but saw no one at the desk. The office was dimly lit and there was no one at the desk. I passed the office, but saw no one at the dimly-lit desk.

On the street, I passed the convenience store, Hastur's Hardware, which was still open, with one or two customers inside. Some kind of activity was going on at the Church of St. Barnabé–I could hear them chanting, "Have you found the Yellow Sign?" Far down the car-lined street, a vehicle pulled around the corner and disappeared–a hearse, I think.

Carcosa was such a small place, a village, a hamlet, that it would have been impossible to get lost there, yet, when I turned back towards the motel, I found I didn't recognise anything. Hastur's Hardware was not where I was sure it must be and, although I could hear the chant, the Church of St. Barnabé was not there either. I could hear them chanting, "Have you found the Yellow Sign?" but the church was not where I thought it should be, and neither was Hastur's Hardware. In the distance, a hearse turned the corner and disappeared.

At the next corner, under the streetlight, I saw a figure that wasn't completely menacing–a woman of indeterminate age, dressed all in black, smoking a cigarette. Carcosa was too small a place to get lost in, but I was unsure where I was, so I approached the woman under the streetlight, on the corner. She was dressed all in black and smoked a cigarette.

"Excuse me," I said. "I'm looking for my motel. Can you help me?"

"Have you found the Yellow Sign?" she asked, exhaling a cloud of smoke. She wore a Pallid Mask.

"That's it," I said. "The Yellow Sign Motel." I felt in my pocket for Mr. Robardin's card.

A woman of indeterminate age, smoking a cigarette, stood under the streetlight at the corner. "Have you found the Yellow Sign?" she asked. She was dressed all in black.

"Excuse me," I said. "Can you help me? I've lost my way and can't find my motel."

She exhaled a cloud of smoke, there at the corner, under the streetlight. "Have you found the Yellow Sign?" she asked. Down the car-lined street, a vehicle appeared from around the corner. Perhaps a hearse.

Carcosa was too small a place to be lost in, so I turned away from the cigarette-smoking woman dressed all in black and began to walk again. I heard a chanting from the Church of St. Barnabé in the distance, but still saw no sign of Hastur's Hardware. The hearse found a shadowed place to park. I felt in my pocket for Mr. Robardin's card.

It seemed cooler now on the street. In the distance, I saw a figure under a streetlight on the corner. The hearse was parked in a shadowed place and I heard the chanting in the distance.

It was cooler now and I walked faster, away from the figure under the streetlight, away from the shadowed hearse. I thought I saw Hastur's Hardware in the distance and began to jog down the street as the hearse moved out of the shadows and began to follow. Now I saw, once again, the flashing *Vacancy* at the Yellow Sign Motel and was relieved to see my car was parked in front of the office.

I passed the Church of St. Barnabé and heard them chanting, "Have you found the Yellow Sign?" There in the distance, beyond Hastur's Hardware, I saw the motel, with my car parked in front of the office. Under the streetlight at the corner, a woman dressed all in black exhaled a cloud of cigarette smoke and a hearse pulled out of the shadows.

"We are open," said the elderly, bald man behind the desk. The card in my pocket said he was Mr. Robardin, Prop.

"Have you found the Yellow Sign?" asked the woman dressed all in black. Carcosa was too small to get lost in, I reassured myself.

I was drained. "I need a room," I blurted out.

"We are open," he said. The hearse pulled to a stop in the shadows. At the Church of St. Barnabé, they chanted, "Have you found the Yellow sign?" Carcosa was too small to get lost in. I wore a Pallid Mask.

I found the card in my pocket. "The Rest of Your Life," it said.

THE LADY OF THE LAKE
Glynn Owen Barrass

After breaking into the artist's apartment, the last thing Cassandra Bane expected was an encounter with the surreal. Hired to find a rich man's missing daughter, she'd been prepared for many things, but not this.

The room, a large area roughly thirty-by-thirty feet square, had cream-coloured walls spotted with damp, the various rock band posters thumb-tacked across the walls making it resemble a student apartment or—more likely, with its worn green carpet covered in cigarette burns—a junkie's dive. The badly stained yellow couch stood against the east wall and the drug paraphernalia-covered coffee table at the room's centre reinforced this concept, as did the smell. The room bore the hovering miasma of old sweat, with the faint ghost of marijuana cigarettes. Illumination came from the large bay window at the west wall, the brown velvet curtains and rail lying on the floor beneath it, fallen or perhaps pulled down.

Adding to the room's trashed appearance, the white glossed door in the northwest corner had boot marks in its bottom. Another door beside the couch stood undamaged and ajar, leading to darkness. No Hi-Fi, no television, not even an old Playstation. She guessed things like that had probably been sold for smack.

None of this really concerned Cassey. The weird, life-sized wooden statues dotting the room were what had given her pause, urged her to turn around and walk away. This wasn't an option, however, so she stepped forward to examine those nearest the door she'd entered a few minutes earlier after picking the lock. There were three of the sculptures here, frozen mid-movement and facing the door as if running towards it. Male, naked wooden forms, with bald, almost triangular-shaped heads, they had the simplest of faces, just holes for eyes, nostrils, and slits for mouths. Each stood over eight feet tall, with overly long arms and legs in comparison to their stocky, wide-shouldered torsos. Weird, curled penises, pointed at the tips, hung between their skinny legs. The statues' hands bore gnarled, misshapen fingers, the only unity being that they each held more than five digits. Carved so they resembled trees in human form, the wood was a silvery grey colour, textured like bark. The statues had no bases, and one of them, at the centre of the three, stood precariously on one leg.

She touched it with her index finger, making it wobble slightly. Beyond the three, sprawled around the table, stood another two. Carved in positions of duress, their hands covered their faces. The one to the table's right was a female, with flaccid, scaly wooden breasts and a barely visible vagina.

Cassey examined the table, beneath which lay several leather belts and a piece of rubber flex. The wooden surface was covered in cup rings, burned spoons, wrinkled pieces of foil, and—of course—four dirty, used syringes.

The owner of the apartment, Ben Montoya, was a son of Chilean migrants. He was a junkie, obviously, and an artist? Information she'd gained from her client said he was a painter, not a sculptor.

"What creatures sculptors are," she said and stepped around the table, pausing before the final statue. Another female, this one was on its side, curled upon the carpet in a foetal position with its hands clutched against its chest. It lay a few feet before the north wall, an area clear of posters bearing a circular, sooty black stain, five feet in diameter.

The space beneath the stain held a dozen thick yellow candles. Placed haphazardly upon the carpet, some had burned to flat discs while others were only partially used. Blobs of wax spotted the area, some cracked and half-peeled away. Her eyes returned to the statue. Was that something other than wood tucked between its arms and breasts? Something else now grabbed her attention, something red.

A spatter of what looked like blood led from the area with the candles, leading to the ruins of curtain beneath the window. She followed with her eyes, then her feet, and, reaching the window, knelt, lifting one of the curtains. There was no visible blood upon the brown, and there certainly wasn't room for a corpse beneath the curtains. But... Cassey dropped the curtain, her eyes following the trail from the candles then back again.

Someone crawled, from there to the curtain. Dripping blood, they pulled the curtains and the rail down, and then...

Cassey examined the view beyond the window, seeing grey, rectangular apartment buildings and beyond these, the domed roof and golden spire of Sainte Cécile's Cathedral. The golden saint looked down on all, bearing mute witness to whatever sins were perpetrated in the apartment. She licked her lips, flexed her fingers, and stood, returning to the foetal carving. Crouching down, she placed her hands on the wooden woman's shoulder and thigh. The surface felt warm, roughly textured. The statue did hold something against its chest, for Cassey could see the green, frayed spine of a hardcover book.

Interesting, but probably bearing no clue to the whereabouts of her client's daughter. Cassey stood. There were other rooms to check, and considering the condition of this one, she wished she'd brought gloves.

She scowled at the statue. *If I come back for you, I'm going to need a hacksaw.* Then, she reluctantly headed towards the door beside the couch.

***

The other rooms were a bust. The single bedroom had smelled of sex, sweat, and marijuana, and revealed nothing of interest but an old school yearbook belonging to the client's daughter and a few of Montoya's unpaid bills. She'd taken them anyway, and placed them in a crumpled brown paper sack she found in the kitchen. That room, holding bare cupboards, a flyblown window, and a sink filled with dirty dishes, had provided one other useful item. Beneath the sink, in a cupboard reeking of mildew, a partially rusted hacksaw had lain among the other tools.

Back in the living room, Cassey stood before the prostrate statue and pondered where to start cutting. A minute earlier she'd wondered how the book had gotten there in the first place. Pulling at it brought no joy, and there were no signs of the arms being movable, or of them being glued or wedged in place.

With the hacksaw in her right hand, she chose a spot of slender arm just above the right elbow. She gripped the arm with her left hand, and began to saw.

Small clouds of dusty residue formed around the cut, the wood almost crumbling beneath the blade. Then, the sawing became easier as the blade touched pulp. Halfway down she removed the hacksaw, gripped the statue's wrist with one hand, placed her other on the elbow, and pulled. The arm snapped away with a satisfactory *crack* of breaking wood. *I've made a mess of this arm*, she thought, and placed the broken limb on the floor.

The book, still held between the left arm and the breasts, came loose easily. A small, slim volume, she took it in both hands and examined the worn green cover. It had an illustration within a black stamped rectangle, a lizard poking its long tongue toward the title above the box. Again stamped in black, the title read: *The King In Yellow*.

***

Cassey left the examination of the books until she was back at the office, placing them and the assorted bills on her black lacquered desk before shrugging out of her jacket and placing it behind her chair.

The little book was of no real interest, but Cassey flicked through the contents anyway. It contained a play set in a city called Carcosa, with foreign sounding names for the characters such as Aldones and Naotalba. *Carcosa? Is that French?* Less than a hundred pages long, it looked and smelled old, the yellowed, blotchy pages exuding an acidic smell. Turning to the title page she found it dated July 1895, published by a company called Pyramid Press. It had no author. *The King In Yellow, by Anon,* Cassey thought, and was about to put it down when she noticed something different about the page facing the title page. She turned it over, and discovered a small business card pasted to the inside of the cover.

The card was light blue with raised white graphics of corn stalks and flowers. The name at the top, printed in a brown handwriting style, read, *Daniel Wolsey,* with *MA, BA, Medieval Studies,* beneath. The bottom of the card held a phone number and an address in the Washington Park neighbourhood.

A lead? Possibly. Perhaps Wolsey has some clue to Reardon's whereabouts. With this in mind, she retrieved her cell phone from her jacket pocket and tried the number. It rang, and Cassey waited for a few minutes before severing the connection. Deciding to try a different tact, she placed the cell phone down and dragged her laptop from the edge of the desk. While the machine booted, she examined Montoya's bills, reading small but unpaid amounts for gas, electric, and cable. She flipped through the yearbook next, found a picture of Theresa Reardon not much younger than the one she'd received from her father, and with the laptop ready, logged on and performed a Google search for "Daniel Wolsey, Washington Park."

The screen displayed Wikipedia entries and articles about a man called Daniel W. Voorhees, a long dead senator. *Thanks, Google,* she thought. *Great help.*

The seventh entry down bore something of interest however, a *Times Union Online* article titled "Fire guts Italianate home in Troy." She clicked the link, and a photo of a three-story brownstone appeared, its smashed windows surrounded by soot, with ladders against the wall leading to the third floor. A group of firemen stood in the image's foreground, with the rear of a fire engine to their left.

The article read:

```
Firefighters fought a blaze yesterday at
the three-story brownstone at 349 Second
St. near the Washington Park neighbour-
hood. The home is owned by Daniel
Wolsey. Wolsey is president of the his-
torical society and active in community
affairs. Albany and Watervliet fire-
fighters helped to battle the blaze.
There were no casualties, as Wolsey
lives alone and was out at the time.
```

It was dated a week earlier, a day before Theresa Reardon's disappearance. *A coincidence? Possibly.* Cassey decided to ask the client about Wolsey during their next conversation, then checked the remaining Google entries. There was a LinkedIn profile, which gave her a tiny photo of a middle-aged man with long white hair, and a few links to a site called Alien UFOs, which she didn't bother checking.

She pushed the laptop away and removed a notebook from her desk drawer, flicking through to an empty page bookmarked with a pen. Here she wrote some notes on the case, including Wolsey's address, and decided to get some of her operatives to track him down and watch Montoya's apartment.

A few phone calls followed, one to a trusted operative named Abel Fujitsu, who she set upon the trail of Daniel Wolsey, and another to Reeves Investigations, a detective agency she sometimes contracted work out to, but that call went to answer phone.

Cassey cut the connection without leaving a message and checked her wristwatch. *Six-twenty, where has the day gone?* She retrieved her laptop and decided to examine her typed notes on other ongoing cases before heading home for the evening.

One case, about a husband's unfaithfulness, absorbed her attention for well over an hour, until she discovered the little book from Montoya's apartment was drawing her away from her work.

She gave it a glare, said, "I am not going to read you," and returned to her notes. A few minutes later she found her hand stroking the book's cover.

"No!" Cassey scolded herself. Lifting the slim volume up, she wheeled herself away from her desk and opened the top right drawer. She dropped the book inside unceremoniously, adding it to the used notepads, pens, and other stationary. Before shutting it she retrieved a crumpled, white and gold pack of Marlboro Lights.

Apart for the odd indiscretion, Cassey had given up smoking five months earlier. This was one of those indiscretions. She sat for a while with her legs on her desk, blowing smoke rings toward the ceiling and absorbing the nicotine rush. When the cigarette burned down to its filter, she tossed it into the waste bin she'd been using as an ashtray, followed by her lighter and the half-empty Marlboro packet.

I'm exhausted. Christ, what a day. Cassey leaned back, folding her arms across her chest. Feeling the need to close her eyes, she thought, *No, don't fall asleep here again; the office door isn't even locked.* Her lids became heavy however, like two little lead weights. *I'll just close them for a little while, then head—*

***

Through an unsettled sleep, she heard the bells in the city toll ten, eleven, then midnight. It was after the bell rang a quarter past that Cassey found herself waking properly, albeit sluggishly, and, rising from her desk, she walked to the west window. Raising the sash she leaned out, taking lungfuls of fresh air to try and clear her head for the drive home.

Three floors below, Twenty-Fifth Street stood deserted, with only a few windows illuminated in the Strathmore apartment building across the street. The trees along the sidewalk swayed in a wind that stroked her face gently, Cassey relaxing from the sensation until she noticed a dark shape moving in the shadows beneath the Strathmore's main entrance. It stepped forward, the streetlights partially illuminating a large man dressed in a brown hoody and baggy black jeans. His pudgy face deathly pale in the artificial light, he stared at her building, at her. Cassey squinted, seeing black curly hair, long sideburns... It was Ben Montoya.

She rushed to her desk, pulled on her jacket, and left her office without locking the door. She took the stairs to the first floor, panting from the exertion as she reached the bottom of the stairwell. It took a few fumbling attempts at the security code to open the building's entrance—her urgency to reach Montoya causing her to make mistakes while entering the code.

Then she was out, walking swiftly across the sidewalk, past her car, and across the street towards the Strathmore.

For a moment, her heart sank; it appeared he'd

gone, but then she sensed movement behind the bushes to the left of the entrance. She paused, remaining in the light from the streetlamps, and watched Montoya unfold from the shadows.

The man looked ill, his face damp, grey-looking, and just... too swollen, as if he was suffering some severe allergic reaction. *Or perhaps,* Cassey thought, nodding at her conclusion, *drugs withdrawal.* Montoya's eyes were tiny in the thick folds of his skin, almost black in the shadows. His hands were like his face: the fingers swollen, blobby members.

"Followed you, so long now," he said. His voice was oily, liquid, a guttural sound rolling from wet, diseased lungs. Like some damp, rubbery mask, his face barely moved as he spoke.

"Mister Montoya," said Cassey. She folded her arms around her chest, and not because of the growing, chill wind. "You look positively ghastly. In fact, I would say you need a doctor." *Or a mortician,* she thought.

Montoya shuffled forward a few steps. His swollen flesh glistening in the illumination as he moved, it was painful to watch.

"Where is she, Mister Montoya?" Cassey continued.

"Tessie? She lives near the lake now, Washington Park," he replied in that disgusting voice of his.

Cassey nodded, said, "And where are you living, Mister Montoya?"

Montoya shook spasmodically, Cassey experiencing a chill of horror as his lips issued a croaking rattle. The fear passed when she realized he was laughing.

The movement reached his hands, the fingers quivering like clusters of hungry grubs.

Then he stopped, stock-still. "You call this living, Cassandra Bane?"

Struck speechless at the mention of her name,

Cassey watched Montoya turn slowly on his heels. He walked away, clinging to the shadows along the side of the Strathmore. Despite his sluggish movements, by the time she pulled herself together, he was gone.

***

She lives near the lake now, Washington Park.
The words haunted her through a night of dubious rest, until, at six a.m., Cassey rose from her bed, tossed her crumpled sheets aside, and showered, dressing afterwards in a dark blue hoody and grey sweats with worn white jogging shoes on her feet.

As she was about to leave her apartment her cell phone rang. She removed it from her hoody, reading the name *Fujitsu, A* on the touchscreen. Putting it to her ear she answered with, "Abel, you're an early riser. I always liked that about you."

"Hey, I'm not the early riser, but the fire marshal is." Abel said in a strong, Italian Brooklyn accent.

"Fire marshal? This is about Wolsey, yeah?"

"Yeah, Cassey, this guy's an old friend o' mine. Says the fire at the apartment was arson. What d'ya think about that?"

Interesting development. "I think you've done a fine job, Abe. Thank you," Cassey replied.

"I'm still chasing this guy anyways," Abel said, then paused a moment. "Uh, Cassey, sorry ta get you up."

Cassey smiled. "Heh, I'm up and about already. Thanks again, Abe."

"Good ta know. See ya later, Cassey."

Abel severed the connection and Cassey tucked the cell phone back in her hoody.

A few minutes later she left her apartment building, entering a street cold enough to make her rub her hands together and wish she'd brought gloves.

Broeck Street was beautiful by day, but now the Rowhouse block she lived on felt too quiet, too shadowy. Cassey shrugged. This case had spooked her, and she wasn't easily scared. She looked to the sky and sighed. A dark shade of blue, it was lighter at the horizon, bearing a rich orange strip of dawn. *Daylight will make everything better*, she thought, and began walking.

Her left shoulder bore a black canvas bag. It held the little green book—her only real link to Tessie Reardon—and, for safety's sake, a stun gun.

No lights shone from the buildings surrounding her, the silence making the scene almost dreamlike in appearance. The trees lining the sidewalk reminded her of other things, with human shapes, and as she approached her green Lexus she experienced a strange vision of seeing copies of the book stuffed between the boughs.

A press of her keyring unlocking the car, she put the bag in the passenger seat before sitting down and fastening her belt. Starting the ignition, she drove downhill along the slope that Broeck Street afforded, turning right onto Clinton Avenue to pass between late Victorian-style houses and newer, ugly-looking square brick buildings.

The avenue held more silence, more solitude, until halfway down a yellow cab turned off Lark Street to pass her. *Lark, followed by Madison,* Cassey thought, considering the quickest route to the park. She slowed the car, backing up a little to turn onto Lark Street.

The streetlamps were illuminated along Lark Street, the mixture of business and residential buildings dark within, apart from the odd illuminated window. Cassey assumed the city rose earlier than this—she guessed she'd assumed wrong. Still quiet and dreamlike outside, the atmosphere beyond the car bore thin residues of morning fog, just ghosts really, departing skyward with the upcoming dawn.

At the intersection between Lark Street and Madison Avenue, she saw a tall, Italian-looking man leave a small bistro. Dressed in black, he wore a white apron and carried a large sandwich board in his hands. He stopped at the street corner, deposited the board there, and gave Cassey a smile and a wave. With his slicked black centre-parted hair and pencil thin moustache, the man looked positively Victorian, if not for the twists of tribal tattoos above his starched white collar.

She returned the wave absently, turned right on Madison, and passed more buildings for a minute or so until those to the right disappeared, replaced by an empty sidewalk beyond which stood the low, iron wrought fences and trees of Washington Park.

Cassey pulled over beside an electronic meter, went to leave the car, then paused in indecision. *Reardon is somewhere in there. Lots of homeless people there, too. Probably crazies, she's probably crazy now if the company she's been keeping is anything to go by...*

She scrutinized the park, the grassy areas of which were concealed beneath a thick sheet of morning mist. Tall elm trees lined the horizon, above which the sky had begun lightening towards pink. *Come back? No, get this over with, find the bitch.*

Two minutes later Cassey was walking along the fence, her hood pulled up and the rucksack strapped over her shoulders. She was about to head toward the gate, but realized she couldn't remember what time the park opened. This made her pause, look around, and seeing no one about, she slipped over the fence to land on the soft, mist-smothered grass. A quick jog later and she was in the trees. Having visited it since she was a child, Cassey was no stranger to the park, and turned left in the direction of the lake, hoping that the trees, and the pre-dawn half-light, would keep her concealed from any unwanted attention.

The air smelled fresh, invigorating, and helped dispel the cobwebs from her mind. Upon reaching a gravel path bisecting her own, Cassey paused and looked around.

No one here, she thought. Looking left she saw a section of Madison Avenue; her right, further down the tree-flanked path, the Biblical tableau of the King Memorial Fountain. A dark silhouette against a pink sky, Moses, atop his faux mountaintop, stood surrounded by preening acolytes.

With quick steps, she left the path and continued through the trees. A few long strides later and they parted at a wide path. The lake lay beyond a shore surrounded by elm trees, its surface as shrouded in mist as the banks surrounding it. Between the tops of the trees on the opposite shore, a small yellow orb was visible, Cassey experiencing a wave of vertigo as she realized the sun didn't rise in the west.

She turned sharply, but couldn't see the eastern horizon for the trees. She told herself the innocuous satellite must be a star, its light magnified by the atmosphere. Still, she walked towards the lake on unsteady legs, the cobwebs reforming as the path sloped towards mist-flanked trees.

Near the lake... *Where could Reardon be? What am I doing here alone on this dangerous, wild goose chase?*

As Cassey approached, dark shapes grew visible in the mist, making her pause and wonder until she discerned they were frayed, patched-up tents accompanied by small, jury-rigged shacks formed from rusted corrugated steel.

A shantytown? How can that be here and the authorities do nothing about it? But it explained where Reardon was living. *But where to start? First things first though...*

Cassie pulled the rucksack from her shoulders,

pushing her hand inside to feel around for the stun gun. She found the book—once, then again—and, grunting in frustration, performed a visual search. A few seconds later she had the stun gun in hand. She raised her head with a smile, a smile that disappeared as she saw a human shape stood in the shadows of the trees. Dressed in dark clothing, the figure remained motionless, like a statue carved from wood.

She moved the stun gun behind her back while making a show of struggling the rucksack over her shoulder.

The figure stepped forward. Cassey took a few steps back, almost tripping for her trouble.

"Are you here to confess your sins, dear?" A lisping male voice said, and the figure, escaping the shadows, became fully visible.

Long, wild grey hair, a high-browed middle-aged face thick with wrinkles, the man wore a stained, dusty black suit jacket, with a white vest underneath that revealed a pale, hairless, sunken chest. Beneath the jacket, he wore faded blue jogging bottoms, torn at the knees. She recognized his face. It was the owner of the book from Ben Montoya's apartment, the owner of the burned and gutted brownstone.

Daniel Wolsey.

Cassey gripped the stun gun tightly and said, "I am a Catholic, I like to confess, but not to the likes of you."

Wolsey smiled, nodded. "You are an unscrupulous woman, coming here to spy on us. So what, for one minute, makes you think *she* will be safer with you?"

Straight to the point, Cassey liked that.

"Because you burned up your apartment, and you're all living like bums in a park? Need I go on?"

The side of Wolsey's mouth twitched. "I had no reason to keep any of those books once I'd read *The King In Yellow*. And this place?" He raised his arms, resembling the preacher he pretended to be, "I've been collecting all the lost lambs that needed guidance after reading the book, like Theresa."

So she is here. Cassey surreptitiously moved her left arm forward, preparing to use the stun gun.

His following words froze her mid-movement.

"Oh, and you, of course. You've read it. Remember?"

A wave of vertigo hit her, as his words became a truth that could not be denied. Waking up last night, sometime before midnight, before that abomination of a man had appeared outside her window, she'd awoken with her hand inside the desk drawer.

She remembered it now: a play in two parts, a tale of tragedy, deceit, and murder, of pallid masks that failed to conceal the wearers' toxic evil. She recalled Hastur and Cassilda and how their poisonous, forbidden love had torn her heart, mind, and soul apart. She'd sobbed herself to sleep after finishing that dreadful little book, while outside, the fog had rolled against the office windowpanes, just as the cloud waves rolled and broke against the shores of Washington Park Lake.

Not upon us, O King, not upon us! Cassilda's words. They had echoed through the streets beyond her office building, accompanied by her and Camilla's agonized screams.

Blinking away fresh tears, Cassey found Wolsey's face mere inches from her own. His eyes were glazed, his grinning expression bearing the euphoria of an acolyte.

"Come home, little lamb," he said, and lunged for her as she collapsed into darkness.

***

A dreamless void followed. Though Cassey had sensations of movement, gentle lifting and petting, her body was stroked but not violated. She awoke to consciousness slowly, to the sound of a sweet female voice. The words were incomprehensible, and her eyes opened to see misty, unformed shapes of varying shades of grey. She found she was sat up, with damp softness beneath her and something hard and unyielding at her back. With difficulty, she concentrated on the words.

"—like Adam and Eve, but the whole world was our garden. Innocent, we *were* innocent, in our own way, despite the smack, the weed, etcetera, etcetera."

The nebulous view grew clearer, a shape before her forming a head and shoulders.

"But the book... that changed *everything*. You've read it too, yes? I can see it in your eyes."

Like an abused past uncovered on a psychiatrist's couch, new memories assaulted her mind. She recalled the innocence of the first act, then the awful scene on the balcony at the beginning of the second. Warped words filling her brain, she shuddered and hugged herself.

CAMILLA: You, sir, should unmask.
STRANGER: Indeed?
CASSILDA: Indeed, it's time. We all have laid aside disguise but you.
STRANGER: I wear no mask.
CAMILLA: (Terrified, aside to CASSILDA) No mask? No mask!

"My innocence was unmasked," the voice continued, "and I saw the ugly beautiful truth of a jaded place where all the misfits can belong. You understand me, yes, Cassey?"

Her vision finally cleared, and she found Theresa Reardon sat before her. Short blonde hair, spiky with grease, her pale face was thin and her eyes hollow, the silver studs surrounding her pursed lips almost as pale as her skin. Dressed in a thin, short-sleeved blouse patterned with roses and frayed denim shorts, her white flesh was goose pimpled, but she didn't seem concerned by the cold. Cassey saw barely healed slit marks on her wrists, jagged red welts that made her think of the scene at Montoya's apartment. The girl stared at her intently, awaiting a response.

Cassey had nothing to say. She stared back, tried to move, but found herself too weak to budge from what she now realized was a tree near the lake. A fumbling check of her hoody found her cell phone gone. She saw her rucksack a few feet away, on the grass to her left. The stun gun was nowhere in sight.

Theresa leaned forward, taking her limp hands in a sticky grip. "I took the serpent's advice, Cassey," she said in a conspiratorial manner. "I read the book, showed it to Ben." Up close, her breath smelled rank, stale with decay. "Not many have read it, not these days, anyway, according to Wolsey. He introduced it to all of us."

"Is..." her mouth clammy, the words fought against her before leaving her mouth. "Is Wolsey the serpent?" Cassey managed.

"Oh, he wishes," Theresa replied, and leant forward, her tongue flicking over Cassey's lips. Cassey didn't fight it, even when that tongue explored her mouth, their following embrace passionate and not unwelcome.

When someone came for Theresa, Cassey whined and tried to hold on to her. The man taking Theresa away—short, red-haired, and dressed like a bum—led the girl to a nearby tent, and moments later, sounds of furious copulation issued from within. Cassey put her head in her hands and cried from loneliness, only raising it when the ground beneath her started to vibrate, accompanied by a distant sound like nails across a chalkboard.

The sound issued from the lake, the nearby

shore of which she found lined with figures. Wolsey stood there, and Theresa, plus over a dozen others. All were from different walks of life, including business people in suits, bums, and hookers. The mist from the lake broke against their legs, all-embracing and enticing. Cassey tried to stand, to join them, but was still too feeble. Instead she watched, as twin suns rose from the lake, huge, glowing orbs permeating a cold, uncomfortable light. The screeching grew louder, joined by the crowd's collective cries.

Beyond the suns, on the lake's opposite shore, Cassey saw the Washington Park Lake House, or rather, the thing that had replaced it. The red-roofed Spanish revival structure was now a huge, towering edifice formed from brown, spiny coral; its fluted minarets leant forward at crazy angles. Looking at it made her head hurt, so she returned her gaze to the suns.

They continued rising, Cassey's gaze following them until they disappeared into the sky. Soon after the worshippers returned to their shantytown. Theresa appeared and sat with her for a while, talking in soothing, cooing words, until another man came for her.

This happened all day, the sounds of man-on-woman and man-on-man issuing constantly from the tents and structures. Throughout, Cassey found herself falling in and out of consciousness. Then a long stretch of void consumed her, her dreamless sleep filled with the screams and cries of rutting beasts. When she awoke, she found Theresa seated before her again, naked, her thin, pale body sheened with sweat and covered in bruise-coloured bite marks.

"It's time. Just look to the sky," Theresa said, pointing a slim arm toward the lake.

The twin suns, having returned, had almost set in the mist. They floated half visible, while the off-white sky above hung smothered in black stars, tiny flickering holes in the negative heavens. The sky invoked a strange optical effect on the world. The colours were diluted, drained of their former strength. The air felt charged, bearing an inaudible humming quality, as if she was surrounded by power lines.

"Time for what?" Cassey asked.

Theresa lowered her arm a little and said, "Them."

A further question died in Cassey's throat as she saw the row of figures standing upon the misty shore. The dark silhouettes, although humanoid, were far from human. She cringed inside, afraid of their approach, but to her relief they remained stock-still.

A strange thought occurred to her, and she turned to Theresa to express it. The girl lowered her arm, staring back with an expression of childish enthusiasm.

"They arrived with the suns, didn't they?"

Theresa nodded, said, "Carcosans, in the right light, can walk this world unhindered."

Cassey considered the wooden things in Montoya's apartment, frozen mid-movement. The curtains, pulled down, flooding the room with daylight.

"You killed them last time, didn't you, Theresa?" Cassey said.

Theresa nodded and lowered her head. A moment later she raised it and grinned. "But not this time," she said and rose to her feet.

Movement appeared around them, Cassey watching Theresa step towards the lake as others climbed from their tents and shacks. To her disdain, the beings from the lake loped forward to greet their human followers.

Viewed closer, the creatures were pale, almost milk white. Around nine feet tall with long, spindly legs, their overly long arms ended in twitching, many-fingered hands. Broad shouldered, their torsos terminated in slim waists, topped by heads resembling upside down triangles.

Cassey squealed in fright, pushing her body against the tree in trepidation.

One being took Theresa's hand and headed back towards the lake. The girl turned briefly, waved, and Cassey raised a limp hand in reciprocation. Another woman, dressed in baggy, dirty clothes, screamed at a being's touch and attempted to flee, her panicked flight terminated as it scooped her up and carried her wailing form away. A number of others screamed too, while some, like Theresa, went with the beings willingly.

Cassey watched the human exodus as if in a dream. She was brutally awoken when a warped shadow fell atop her. A low whine escaped her throat, cold ice filling her veins as she came face to face with a thing wrought from insanity and evil.

Its skin smooth and rubbery, the being smelled of sweat mixed with ammonia. Naught but gaping holes into darkness, its wide, slanted eyes stared into hers. The nostrils and mouth were similar to the eyes, the very simplicity of its face making it all the more horrifying. Unmade, uncouth... Cassey voided her bladder as its mouth opened into a wide grin, revealing brown, very human teeth.

The being said, "*To think that you are also a little ward of God!*" the sound more akin to radio interference than something produced by vocal cords.

It leaned forward, retrieving her rucksack with a large, spidery hand. A moment later and the being was gone. It loped away quickly before descending into the lake.

Her fear remained, accompanied by an overwhelming sense of loss over what could never be unseen or unread. Cold and wet, Cassey hugged herself, closing her eyes until, some unknown time later, she reopened them to find darkness had fallen across the world.

The twin suns were gone; the lake house had taken on its usual dimensions. The sky above was filled with regular, glittering white stars, constellations she knew by name. With some effort, using the tree for support, Cassey raised herself. She left the shantytown, then Washington State Park, and from the safety of her car, vowed never to return.

III:
...INTO THE HANDS OF A LIVING GOD

EXCERPTS FROM
TRAFFIC WITH AUTUMN:
An Experimental Narrative of the King In Yellow
Joseph S. Pulver, Sr.

(1)

Traffic With Autumn: Scene 2; Act 2

(Nearing twilight. A bitterly cold autumn. Two sisters, daughters of the King and Lady Cassilda–the eldest, the gazes of the court call her the saddest heart in the world, and her licentious younger sibling, sit together on a cast iron loveseat in a frost-burned garden of dry sluices and weathered trellises. They look out over a cheerless horizon of muddy fields.)

ANDROMEDA, THE ELDER SISTER: These musicless shadows clutch my heart.

EUROPA, THE YOUNGER SISTER: Drizzle and greyness offer no courtesy to this castle.

ANDROMEDA: Have you word?

EUROPA: There are tears on this woman's story. *(She turns in her seat and looks back at the dark windows of the castle.)* And from the day it began, intense eyes follow me.

ANDROMEDA: Intrigues, and lies, *and the poisoned curse of the witch,* embroidered on the frayed skirt of autumn. Toil and blood and no one *who cares for me.*

EUROPA: Nightmares, quicker now. Their carriage will not pause, they ride to drink us. *(She moves her unsandaled feet, the shorn wings of dead black moths, covering the parched-ground, flutter.)* If they would speak not—

ANDROMEDA: *(Looks at the tattered silk that covers her legs.) We are the slaves of repulsive monsters and spleen. Denied the peace we pine for... by... this distance.* I have spent too much time in this cauldron.

EUROPA: *(Gravely.)* I row... Yet, my desire to be free of this devil unleashed, serves me not... I look in the mirror and see I have only myself to blame.

EXCERPTS FROM *TRAFFIC WITH AUTUMN*

(2)

TRAFFIC WITH AUTUMN: SCENE 1; ACT 2

(Nearing twilight. A bitterly cold autumn. Two sisters—the eldest, the gazes of the court call her the saddest heart in the world, and her licentious younger sibling, sit together on a cast iron loveseat in a frost-burned garden of dry sluices and weathered trellises. They gaze out over a dour horizon of rotting fields.)

ANDROMEDA, THE ELDER SISTER: These musicless shadows clutch my heart. *The goodbye...* Every tremor and itch of Truth. *(Her hands come together and hold each other, as if a brick wall that could protect the flesh within.)* What haunts always haunts again.

EUROPA, THE YOUNGER SISTER: For you there is no healing. Strange things continue to bury you in woe.

ANDROMEDA: Tired is my soul. Having crawled through the unnatural, it is withered to the bone.

EUROPA: When the light came ashore and offered the ritual of flowers to your comely arms, you should have accepted the comfort of its hand.

ANDROMEDA: Will you again rave on the whole night?

EUROPA: You accuse me of being the revolution?

ANDROMEDA: You were the naysayer's sword.

(Andromeda rises and steps behind the cast iron loveseat, stands with her back to her sister.)

EUROPA: *(Without turning to face her sister.)* I was light... I am your mirror.

ANDROMEDA: Memory confines, reshapes our steps. All the days and nights... it is all that we can see. It destroys the art we are.

EUROPA: Your pathos could never stand The Light.

(Andromeda turns and looks down at her sister. She has begun weeping.)

ANDROMEDA: The Dynasty was at stake—it tried to silence my slight aria, I felt like a witch wrongly accused... The forge of its light would have burned me alive, Sister.

(There is the great sound of dooming bells in the distance.)

EUROPA: Its eternal knife still may.

EXCERPTS FROM *TRAFFIC WITH AUTUMN*

(3)

TRAFFIC WITH AUTUMN: SCENE 2; ACT 1

(A bitterly cold spring. Two sisters—a spinster virgin and her immodest younger sibling, sit together on a peeling, cast iron loveseat in a parched garden of dry sluices and weathered trellises crisscrossed with dead vines. They are looking out over a horizon painted by the torturer's hands.)

ANDROMEDA, THE ELDER SISTER: The bruising wind of broken spring arrives.

EUROPA, THE YOUNGER SISTER: And with it, the quiet elegance of the tombstones beckons to those with sore autumnal hearts.

ANDROMEDA: Will your good and true knight arrive with the night fogs?

EUROPA: If he can? The rain-drenched faraway is crossed by briars... and cursed with many venoms.

ANDROMEDA: Have you been to see the fortune teller?

(A small brown bird crashes upon the dry lawn at Andromeda's feet. Its tiny throat has been torn out. There is a maddened shriek in the darkening twilight sky above the startled sisters.)

(Europa screams. Andromeda kneels down and picks up the creature.)

ANDROMEDA: *(Sotto voce.)* Her fair larks will no longer adorn the infinite.

(Europa looks into the dead black eyes of the ravaged

creature and leaps from her seat, runs toward the palace of her father. Andromeda looks down at her bare feet and the litter of dead black moths that cover the flat stepping stones. There is a dryness in her throat. She begins to weep.)

(Many lands away. Hood of a rusty, old, big-block Dodge pickup. Two sisters sipping pop from glass bottles. The younger of the pair blows air into her straw, creating bubbles.)

EMMY: —dreamed I walked through his library. And get this, I was naked, not a stitch on.

ANDI: Was he there?

EMMY: Yes.

ANDI: Did he see you... *naked*?

EMMY: He sure got his eyes full. They were big, full of a man's hunger.

ANDI: So?

EMMY: Wouldn't you just like to know?

ANDI: I'd tell you. C'mon now, I told you *my* dream.

EMMY: You should get a man. You know how they look at you, all you got. You get one that likes it, he'll drive you around and buy you pop and candy. Jimmy Ray takes Becca Dunn to the movie-show all the time and he takes her to Sharp's and they sit at the counter and have lunch; think on that the next time a man looks at what you got. You like that Cinderella story, I know you'd like to be a queen, be pampered and all. Lot of women like it, and they know what they can get... Gives you the power over them.

ANDI: Or whuped-good you pick the wrong one. You better affect care, girl, or you'll end up with child. Think on what Daddy would do if he saw yore belly growin'.

EMMY: Daddy wooda lay his hands on me. Not ever.

ANDI: No, wooda have to, he'd give Mama the sign and have her and the women do what he wanted done. You know the power he's got. Haley's and Alar's won't cross him. John Law neither. Better just think on that and keep your womanly comforts to yerself.

EMMY: I believe you're just jealous that Spec Pesice's older brother, Duane, has eyes for me. I remember when you were upset when Donnie Lee was talkin' to me.

ANDI: Yer the one dreamin' of walkin' naked in Duane's library. Funny place to be naked.

(The next evening. Daddy sits on the porch, tellin' his stories. The girls like the one about the day he took Mama to the fair and saw jugglers and et cotton candy.)

DADDY: Got dark... Eight, maybe? All the lights came on quick as a finger-snap, more lights than you girls ever saw. Red and green blazin' on the rides. Twirlin' and goin' 'round so fast you'd be shaken and dizzy in a blink... Carnival had blue ones, Mama sure liked them, and orange was everyplace your eye gazed. Had food everyplace, too. Prize-winnin' pies and hand-squeezed lemonade. Hot dogs long 'nough to feed a litter of pups.

EMMY: Ice cream?

DADDY: 'Nough for every kid at the funfair to have one in each hand, and one melted all-over his shirt. Weuns goin' to have to take y'all to one... one of these days.

EMMY: When?

DADDY: Soon enough, Emmy. Maybe come summer, when it passes through 'gain.

EMMY: And did they have music for dancin'?

DADDY: Fiddles and mandolins, and a young banjo picker, powerful as Old Sam Earle's shine, put rattle in your head and get yore toes tappin'. Had the old boys and gals havin' a large time. Mama tried to get me to, but I wasn't of a mind to just then.

EMMY: What other things did you see, Daddy?

DADDY: Sights, and signs... for snake oil and rides, and 'bout every stripe of trickster can be imagined. Said, they had a girl in the sideshow could change into a fox, right before yore eyes. Had this furrin-man, name of Amazo. Said he could read your thoughts and see all the way inta your dreams, learn'd to in someplace in Europe where old sagas of strange goin's-on are fact. Had this woman in a red dress come down off the stage and pick a spectator. She handed 'im a hand-mirror, like the one yore Mama has on her nighttable. Told 'im to look into the glass, look deep. Up on that stage, Amazo stared into a twin of the mirror and went into a state, told 'im what he saw of their life and dreams. Was some lit right-outta there, like they was forked by Old Scratch himself.

EMMY: Were you fearful, Daddy?

DADDY: Ever see yore Daddy tremble?

EMMY: Ain't, sir.

(The moon has come up. It casts its cold, bright illuminations on Daddy. His hand rises from his kneecap and he points at Emmy.)

DADDY: Never will.

ANDI: Sounds kinda like one of them fairy-tale places in Mama's old book.

DADDY: Fairy-tale place to one soul might be the hard truth of yonder to 'nother... You take my meaning, girl?

ANDI: I do, Daddy.

(Mama opens the screen door halfway, she does not step outside. Looks at her daughters, opens the door fully.)

MAMA: Bedtime, girls. To-morrow's on the wind and there's preparations that will need our hands.

EMMY: Mama, Daddy was—

MAMA: Come now.

(The girls go inside the house and Mama closes the screen door. Daddy looks up at the far, cold moon. Grins.)

(4)

TRAFFIC WITH AUTUMN: SCENE 1; ACT 2

EUROPA: I see the Great Grey One.

ANDROMEDA: Here? Touching the night?

EUROPA: His words are worms, storms that flood my eyes.

ANDROMEDA: Do you hear the stillness of Nowhere ring?

EUROPA: His mouth speaks in a thousand languages.

(Andromeda rises and steps behind the cast iron loveseat. She slowly lifts her head and gazes out over a dour horizon of twilight-cloaked, muddy fields.)

ANDROMEDA: With morning light, should it arrive and leave any hearts as witness, there will come further mourning.

EUROPA: *(Still sitting, hands folded in her lap, on a cast iron loveseat, looking down at her bare feet and the litter of dead moths that cover the ground.)* Every bird will die in this bitterly cold autumn.

ANDROMEDA: The light of a poet will surely come ashore and offer comfort. This cannot be the end to heart-blood and tongues of longing.

ANDROMEDA: *(Placing her hand, simmered in madness and tears, on her sister's shoulder.)* I want blue and open doors, not arrowheads. Do you hear me?

EUROPA: In a thousand languages, he whispers to me, every bird will die.

EXCERPTS FROM *TRAFFIC WITH AUTUMN*

ANDROMEDA: *(As if she's been bitten by fire, as if she can shield her heart from arrowheads, her hand flies from her sister's shoulder to her breast.)* No bouquet of harmony. Bones... and rain again.

EUROPA: Everywhere: his greyness... *(It begins to drizzle.)* ...and rain.

(5)

itwas. twosisters. inaroom. ahideawayforcreatures whocannotsleep. oneinblackandred. oneinwhiteand whiteandwhite. facetofacepastandevertogether. both havetheirshoesoff. tworealitieslivinginonereality. both arethinking. rememberingitwas. sufferingtheoven oftime. dreamingitcouldhavebeen. shoutingnosilently. bothareedgy. nervousdestined—eventhemoonspeaks ofit. don'trusteachother. (asitwasthen. itisagain.) "no." "no." darkbrowneyeswatchtheshadowappear. move closer. (asitwasthen. itisagain.) doesoftbrowneyes watchtheshadowappear. movecloser. closer. (asitwasthen. itisagain.) "no." "no." theterriblestranger stretchingthehours. hereyesonhispath. hereyesonhis feathers. closer. thesongofhismeasurelesscloakreeks offar-offplaces. (asitwasthen.) slaveswoken. (itisagain.) "no." "no." far-offplacesemptyplacesrainingtakingroute andmidstandtakingbreath.

itis.now.curtainsopenwidethemoonafraidtospeak. (again.)twosisters.outsidethehideawayroomfleeingtear shiningontheirback.tworealitieslivinginonereality.face tofacepastofwretchedshapesanddryinggraveandever together.facetofacewithlastthingsruinedtruthdrytea cupsnearhome.thedancingshaowoftheterriblestranger (fromcoldafar)closercloser.twosisters(thedebrisofgreed andthepaintofcloakedlies)whocannotsleep.oneinragsof blackandred.oneinaweatheredfleetofwhiteandwhiteand white.hereyesonhispath."nosun."hereyesonhisfeathers. "nolight."memoriesbulge.teethareshown.ontheloomof yearningtwosisterssickoffate'spulsingcompassare silenced.notears.(thestarschangenot.)nolaments.(the blacknessbetweenthestarsoffersnotheyhavegone.)no graves.wholetheirshellsarehungonabarrentree.crows andravensbloom.

PAPER MASKS
R.C. Mulhare

"Every time I look at this paperwork, I feel like the very words are looking deep into me, scrutinizing me and judging me and finding me lacking," the young client said, watery grey eyes averted from her and from the paperwork that lay on the desktop. To look at her, sitting across the corner of the desk, would mean looking at the papers, fanned out atop the yellow manila envelope.

"I can see that it's hard for you, but it has to be done. You need to fill out these forms to state your case and explain your situation if we're to give you the assistance you need," Cass Archer, the young man's case worker, said, leaning across the corner of the desk, careful not to lean too close, lest he felt crowded.

"I know that in my head, but in my heart..." he paused, rubbing at his stubbled cheek with a still-childlike hand, clearly collecting the thoughts spiralling in his head. "It's like I'm wearing a mask, a mask with a normal face turned outwards for everyone to see, and they're fine with it. They suspect nothing, they can't see what I look like and it's just as well that they don't, because if they did, they would see how disordered and damaged I really am. And so... the mask has become my real face.

"But when I apply myself to this paperwork, the mask comes off—tears off, rather —and then everyone, including me, can see my face, how horrible it looks and is," he concluded, his gaze going to the shelves of books against a wall behind her, as if seeking solace in the titles. At least he looked in her direction, if not at her.

"And taking off the mask feels scary and reveals too much," she said, trying to speak his language.

He looked at her that time, nodding slowly, his

blue eyes trying to look hard and confident, for having made that admission, and failing at that expression: his eyes widened with renewed wariness, rather than narrowed.

"You know you don't have to fill out all of it at once: try doing a page or two, or a few each day till you've finished it," she said. "You still have time to finish it."

"I'd rather be done with it, to finish it quickly and be rid of it, be rid of the pain, so I can put my mask back on and leave it on," he said, looking away, sliding the pages back into the yellow envelope before shuffling it into the rucksack he carried.

"Whatever you think will work for you," Cass said, trying to sound soothing, but somehow the words sounded tired and hard even in her own mind. He must have sensed it as well: his shoulders rose toward his ears as he stood up from his chair to leave. He muttered some standard response about returning as he prepared to scuttle out of the cubicle farm that comprised much of the office space. She rose with him. "I can walk you out, if you like."

"I can handle that much of the path, I think," he murmured, not looking at her, as he took a yellow rain slicker from the coat rack and slipped it on, then scooped up his rucksack as he headed for the hall door.

On returning to her cubicle, she found a book lying on the seat of the chair which the client had occupied a moment before, a book bound in leather, brown turned nearly to black with age and handling, a design like a scorpion or three question marks joined at the point tooled into the cover, tinted with yellow enamel, still vibrant despite the age of the book. He must have left it behind, must have brought with him it to read while he waited to be interviewed. Picking it up, she hurried to the hall door, calling his name, going out onto the landing, looking down the stairs, then going down and out onto the grey and rainy sidewalk, the book clutched close to her to shield it from the mist. Looking up and down the street, past the storefronts and the autumn trees: no sign of him in either direction; he walked fast, that seemed clear. Returning to her cubicle, she slipped the book into a drawer of her desk, to keep it there till he returned for his next appointment.

Before she could close the drawer, Chong, her supervisor, approached, one eyebrow cocked. "Did something come up?"

"No, nothing really, except Castaigne left something behind," she said.

"He's prone to doing things like that," he noted. "I couldn't help overhearing you talking with him: you seem to have set up a good rapport with him."

"He's confused and bewildered by the forms we just sent him, but I think anyone would feel that way: some of those questions can be personal," she said.

"It's good that you established a connection with him, but take care that you don't get too involved in his case: there will be times when you have to ask him the hard questions," Chong said, his tone firm as his gaze.

"But we still have to keep in mind he's a person with a sense of space and the need to guard what's in that space," she said. "When he talked about masks, it made my heart ache a bit. Just for a bit."

"That's quite an image, masks. We've all got masks that we wear when we move out of the safety of our space, but we all need to take them off at some point. Keep reminding yourself that he needs you to help him remove that 'mask' when the time comes," he said. "We need to see what's behind the façades people put up, because we both know people do that to protect themselves–sometimes with good reasons, other times not, and that last group includes the fakers trying to get assistance they don't qualify for."

"Oh, there's no question there; I just hate to see

him suffer like this: he's such a sensitive soul."

Chong cocked an eye at the open drawer of the desk. "What's that book?"

"He left it behind: I tried to get it back to him, but he'd disappeared by the time I got outside. I'll make sure it gets back to him when he comes back with the paperwork," she said.

"One way he'll ensure he'll return: it doesn't look like the kind of book he'd leave behind without coming back for it," Chong said, with a wry smile, as he moved on to leave her to her work.

More clients, then her lunch break, taken at her desk. She caught herself opening the drawer to peer at the book, lifting the antiquarian covers, scanning its pages, reading some of the text, printed in an elegant, antique font. Its owner had expressed a fondness for poetry and plays, had spoken of writing verse of his own, but she had not imagined that he had such taste, had savored verses as elegant as the lines within.

The book fairly slipped itself into her briefcase and invited itself home with her; something this antique she could not in good conscience leave behind at the office, in case it got lost in the shuffle or shelved where it did not belong. She set it aside, focusing on her evening rituals: making tea, washing vegetables and cutting them up for a salad, but the book intrigued her. Once she had washed up, she took it out of the briefcase intending to flip through it, to see more of what the young man saw in it, to understand what he found in it. Exquisite verses, lush phrasing, no philistine scribbling these, she discovered as she pored over it, till the night sky started to turn pale blue rimmed in yellow. Crash to sleep, to awaken to alarm clock jangling, with just a few hours of rest to sustain her. Fuzzy-headed, staring down at a weight on the duvet, the book fallen open lying there. The book that had come home with her. Come home to her. The book that should go home to its rightful keeper. She got up and made sure that she returned the book to her briefcase, bringing it back to the office, to keep for its keeper, against his return to claim his treasure.

Morning routine, washing up, making coffee, dressing, putting on makeup.

(a mask painted onto one's face—where did that thought come from? Oh yes, the book, the masked stranger)

(No mask? No mask!) Couldn't be seen without a mask, or were these masks necessary? So many masks. So many rituals.

Driving to the office, navigating the damp roads, under the misty yellow sunlight. Traffic lights seemed to glow yellow today, she noted, as she dashed through them, running a gauntlet of horns and stares, whizzing past livid visages of consternation and annoyance seen in the windows of other cars.

Viv, receptionist and general office dogs body, gave Cass a concerned puckered frown as the young caseworker entered and signed in. "Did you sleep at all last night?" she asked. "You've got dark circles under your eyes."

(eyeholes like a mask)

What? Oh, sorry, no, I didn't: I got wrapped up reading a book, Cassie wanted to admit, but stopped herself.

"I slept just fine," Cass replied, voice even, her tone masking her real intent. So many masks. She hadn't thought, till recently, of how many masks people wear. The client, no, the boy, no, the dispossessed heir, had spoken rightly when he spoke of the mask he wore.

"You sure? You don't have to hide anything from me," Viv said, almost motherly.

"Oh, well, I was up late reading a book," Cass offered, wishing in that moment that she had not admitted this.

"Must have been a really good book," Viv said, as Cass headed for her cubicle.

Fuzzy-headed, thoughts in shreds of rags. *I need more coffee,* she thought, shaking it to cast aside the fuzz, veils that swaddled her thoughts. Veils, masks, visages, more masks, for what she really thought about.

(the whisperings of Hastur, kindly Hastur, the murmuring of the wind across Lake Hali)

No, she only needed her morning coffee, she told herself, as she went for the machine in the staff lounge, make a quick cup, bring it back to her stall in the cubicle farm.

Several cases, some appointed, some drifting in on the cold wind. Yellowing leaves sticking to the windows at the end of the cubicle farm. More clients bearing paperwork, hidden behind masks of names and dates and conditions and income verification, doctor's notes and medical records. Numbers and digits. Ciphers and sigils, mere pothooks from which to hang the shreds of one's persona for the vultures to pick clean, leaving the bones of identity. Faces all masks hiding the self within. More masks, her task to peel away. She caught herself wincing, the words of the young man from yesterday came back to her tired mind, cutting more deeply than they did the day before (the keeper of the book, the masked figure in yellow, no wonder she kept thinking about masks). More scripted verses to chant, to assist the initiates into their places in the mysteries. No sign of the dispossessed poet. She had not anticipated his return this soon: too many pages for him to fill out (truths to inscribe).

Glances of concern from her clients, looking toward her hands as they spoke and she jotted notes. When one had passed and before the next supplicant arrived, she looked to her papers: in the margins, she had scribbled strange sigils, slow spirals and question marks joined at the point. Where had she seen that? Ah yes, the cover of the book. Why had it gotten under her skin so, had twisted into her mind like a parasite?

(life/living/existence a parasite that gnaws on every one of us)

I shouldn't have stayed up so late reading that book, Cass thought, on her fourth cup of coffee in six hours. Why had she done something so unlike her? Ah yes, the poetry of the verses, the strangeness of the tale enacted within, the way the characters became actors in the theatre of her mind.

Office hours ending, and the curtain ringing down on the human comedy (tragedy). She rose from her desk to sign out and head home; Chong stepped into her path as she headed for the door.

"Cass, are you feeling all right? You look pale," he noted.

"I'm fine, I just need to remove my mask..." she stumbled. "I just need some rest: I think I'm coming down with something." (Why did she chatter so freely? Wasting words on trifles.)

He took this in silence, his dubious mask a face of concern. "If you don't feel better tomorrow, call me: I'll have someone cover your cases for you."

"Thanks, I just hope I won't need to," she replied. He stepped aside to let her pass.

She found the book still tucked into her briefcase once she returned home, as if it had secreted itself in there, dogging her every movement. She ordered herself to leave it there as she made herself a cup of chamomile tea

(with yellow flowers)

to calm her nerves. Made herself focus on making the tea: running water from the faucet into the kettle, setting it on the gas ring, taking a mug down from the cupboard, setting it on the draining board, taking down the box,

(yellow box, painting of a figure under a gnarled tree on the shore of a lake...)

(Lake Hali??)

taking out a teabag, placing it into the mug,

taking the just-steaming kettle off the gas ring to fill the mug, letting it steep, taking out the sodden teabag to toss it into the waste bin, sweetening the mug with honey, taking the mug with her into the living room.

To curl up again with the Book, reading it, whispering the lines as the mug of tea on the table at her elbow turned to chilly, yellow-tinged muck, like sand on a lake bottom.

Again, dropping to sleep as the sky turned yellow, though now it edged lowering grey clouds. Dreams this time, of lost Carcosa, twin moons sinking beneath the waves of Lake Hali, fearsome ceremonies in crumbling temples, sacrifices that made one shudder in ecstasy, chants whose melodies twined back on themselves, processions of mute, masked figures winding through the streets of the royal city. The throne of a feuding kingdom soon to be empty, the heirs to assume it, only one of whom could bear the crown. Through it all, glimpses of a gaunt figure in a tattered yellow robe. A blank mask of impassivity amidst the grotesque masks of the revelers dancing about it.

Awakening from these strange shadows, quivering with awe. Again, making the mad rush to prepare for work, this day putting on the tatters of the day before and eschewing the mask of makeup. She had to face her clients (subjects). She had to return the book to the young poet (had to see that he gained his rightful inheritance). Running the gauntlet of the streets, lined with autumn trees, dripping with rain and yellowing leaves.

As she entered the hall, Chong looked up at her with concern (mask hiding real intent). "Cass, you look terrible: you should have called me," he said.

"I will be fine: my subjects need me to tend to them," she said.

"Very well–Castaigne called in, said he'd finished the paperwork and he would bring it in today," he said, handing her an appointment list, his gaze dubious.

She felt her chin lift. "Send him to me the moment that he arrives."

The young poet arrived an hour later, the yellow dossier in hand, the formalities to prove his inheritance. He eyed the book laid upon her desk, relief showing behind his mask.

"Oh, you have my book: I thought I'd lost it, when I got home the other day and it wasn't in my rucksack."

"Yes, it has been awaiting you," she said, reaching out to his mask, her fingers stroking the sides warm from the life within. "As I have been awaiting you, Thale."

His mask gathered, puzzled, and he pulled back. "What did you just call me?"

"I called you by name. I wanted to tell you that you need not be afraid to remove your mask and show your true face."

"Well, I came here to hand in the paperwork: I finished it yesterday, though it left me feeling like I'd gotten skinned alive."

"That is to be expected, but sacrifice is to be made, to prove that you are worthy of your inheritance, worthy of the crown of Carcosa."

Trepidation contorted his mask. "My what? This is about my benefits: are you feeling all right, Miss Archer?" Proof positive of his worthiness: no worthy heir would rush into this with abandon or grasp at it wantonly, nor without some measure of fear. She would ease him free of that.

"I could not feel more all right, now that you removed my own mask," she said and, reaching to him again, set to work removing his.

Gasps from another part of the court, some of the courtiers rushed forward. Her vizier, the usurper with his mask of concern, running to her side, disrupting the ceremony, what must be done to make the rightful heir worthy to stand before the Yellow King. The heir's ecstatic cries, more guards interfering.

The crown would not pass as it must, the masks would remain in place.

FANTASTIC WORLDS
J.G. Ballard's Condensation of *The King In Yellow*
Cardinal Cox

Aldebaran

Aldebaran lies in the constellation of Taurus. Its magnitude is 1.06 and its distance from Earth is approximately 58.5 light years. It is a red giant, having incinerated its habitable worlds countless millennia ago.

Black Stars

Evening in Carcosa. Slaves prepare for the festivities by hanging haematic-red draperies. Cakes adorn the tables; marble icing hiding the maggots within. Tapers are lit. The anti-stars breathe an icy chill into the Castellan's heart.

Cassilda and Camilla

The pair cavort about the shadowy garden. Cassilda caresses the swollen fruit of a honeysuckle. For this production, Cassilda should wear a mid-calf-length fur coat of some silver-grey creature. The fur is thick and plush. Beneath this, she is wearing a black leather catsuit which laces-up. In her heels, she approaches six feet tall. When she smiles, you might notice a tooth is missing. By contrast, Camilla is nearer five feet and slight, her features sharp. Camilla's clothing is more peasant. Cassilda wears no makeup; Camilla has been given full crimson lips. The Queen's hair is brown, the servant's dark scarlet.

Demhe

A maw whose throat reaches to the stomach of the planet. Clouds fill the gaping cavity. A balloon surprisingly similar to those designed by the Montgolfier brothers is held above it by guy ropes. A weighted chain is lowered into the middle of the hole.

Emperors

Dynasty after dynasty, the lines of names of supplicants fill the walls of the palace. Each one written in blood, each one representing ultimately countless deaths. Each one a prayer to preternatural powers.

Flageolet

The horn-man in the canary suit put down his saxophone. The cat in the roll-neck tuned his double bass and the third, behind drums, wiped his skins to remove the sweat that had fallen from him.

"We've almost done playin' now," he said and turned to the others. "Five-four, F-sharp, middle-eight into B-minor."

A jaunty number tugged at the hearts of whores trying to rip-off their tricks, hustlers running scams and cops on the take. A wind blows Bay City.

Grand Guignol

Significantly, the theatre of terror opened its doors the same year that Slaughterhouse Jack led a razor trail around London. Originally, Guignol was the name of a puppet character from Lyons similar in many respects to the British Mr. Punch, that unnerving mirror to the nation's domestic arrangements. The plays produced were a jolly mixture of insanity and horror.

Hyades

An open cluster of stars in the constellation of Taurus; the nearest of its type to Earth. Its distance is only 130 light years away. Another cluster is the Pleiades, or Seven Sisters. They can, however, be ignored for the purposes of this story.

Incubus

She found him in a bar, catching his eye that filled with a predatory glint. They moved together, exchanging pleasantries, drinks, and touches. The detective followed them up to her room, regretting he'd returned to this side of the profession.

Jonquil

Cordelia huddled in her room, whispering a poem to a broken doll. No one came to disturb her. No one heard the doll's responses to Cordelia's chanting.

King In Yellow

Louis Castaigne is often heard to insist the play is a damnable thing that rots its readers' brains. He also believes that its author shot himself, or, if he didn't, that he should have. Critics have noted, as well as its supposed parallels to cholera, it also echoes syphilis.

Lake of Hali

The prophet and philosopher for whom this place is named is now all but forgotten. But clouds still break upon its nearest shores, while the more distant are lost in a geometry that falls somewhere between Mobius and the formula $z=z^2+C$. No fisherman harvests its waters, no gulls flap aloft, not even a Shantak. Parts of unrecognisable bodies break the surface. Dwell not upon what they might be...

Masquerade

A theme had been taken for the nocturnal revels, that of Poe's tale "Masque of the Red Death." Seven rooms had been appropriately decorated. A string quartet had been bricked-up in an alcove. Eunuchs of both cuts saw to the needs of the guests. All thrilled to the costume of one attendee, taking the Corman/Roeg film as its design source.

Noatalba

Tomes heavy with dust surrounded the priest. He moved from one to another, consulting the ancient parchments, his index finger moving beneath ancient pictograms dating from the earliest times of his civilisation. He stood. Searched for ink and clean paper. He wrote two short notes, one to Thale, the other to Uoht. Sealed them both with wax impressed with the sigil of his ring. Walked to the window where the moons could be seen passing between the towers. Jumped.

Orchestra

The fourteen members shuffled into the pit and desultorily they flicked through the music. The strings plucked and tuned up their instruments, woodwind and brass assembled and cleaned theirs. The conductor came out of the wings and clambered down. From a case, he pulled out fresh sheet music, written in a spidery hand. The title at the top read *The Devil in the Belfry*.

Paris

"Monsieur Dupin, I beg you, if not for the government, then for France."

"As I have explained, C. Auguste Dupin, myself, has retired."

"Sir, you are needed," the Minister continued.

"Who but you can help us? After the Rue Morgue, the disgrace of D–"

The other interrupted: "Don't mention his name!"

"As well as being the unsung hero of the siege."

"Too many people were unsung heroes, then..."

"Sir, even the Anarchists cannot defend this vile text; I implore you!"

"Minister, I am old, and if the world is going mad around me, why should I struggle to stop it? Good day to you..."

With that, he picked up his cane and arose from the park bench.

Quote

CAMILLA: You, sir, should unmask.
STRANGER: Indeed?

CASSILDA: Indeed, it's time. We have all laid aside disguise but you...
STRANGER: I wear no mask.
CAMILLA: *(Terrified, aside to Cassilda.)* No mask? No mask!
Act 1, Scene 2

Rhode Island

A piece of paper is blown by a breeze until a walking stick catches it and pins it to the cobbles. The top lines are visible and read *The Providence Players Present...* Behind the heavy muffler, a voice escapes wheezingly from the old man: "No, no, no..."

Shrine of Hastur

Once Haita the shepherd had visited here daily to thank his god; but, in turning his back on Hastur, it could be said that a pebble had fallen to dislodge a stone. This had nudged a rock that tipped the boulder that led to the landslide.

Towers Before the Moon

If they are indeed bone, then the creature they formed swam between the stars themselves. In Carcosa, they dwelt about the bases and, at night, never regarded what happened above their heads. In the surrounding mountains, however, the globes could be seen to have their orbits pass between the pitted, chalky structures. Some wondered, what would happen if the moons struck one of the towers? None knew the answers.

Uoht

Ran as fast as his fat form would allow, which meant he staggered and struggled for breath. He stopped at a junction in the sewers and looked for any marks upon the wall. There, the Yellow Sign. He shied away. Plunging into the alternate tunnel. Behind him, rats sniffed and chattered. Imagining what toilet he might have been flushed down to enter their world.

Vermillion Sands

In the desert, a touring troupe of actors starts to eat each other.

Worms

The high point of evolution was achieved early. Everything afterwards is just to make its existence more comfortable. Hermaphroditic, they can mate as they choose. They have no bones to break. If cut in half, they can regenerate. Once dead, all other plant and animal matter is their food.

Xenelasia

"Too late," they mumble. "Too late..."

Yhtill

A bundle of twigs in dirty golden tatters, it danced. Between the scalloped rags, something is glimpsed. No matter how terrible the presence this side, those clothes must always veil a ghastly truth beyond.

Ziggurat

Silent ruins. The Phantom of Truth has taken back the Pallid Mask. If you lean to the rocks, though, you might just catch a murmur: "It is a fearful thing to fall into the hands of the Living God."

BEFORE THE TATTERED KING
Genevieve L. Colter

It's dark here.

That's your initial thought as your eyes first open, seeing nothing. Nothing but inky blackness greets them, an oppressive darkness.

It's really *dark here. Dark, and* moist...

The feeling of that wet warmth makes you squirm. A humid, fetid, and musty breeze ruffles stickily through your hair, caressing your skin slimily. You shudder under it, and wish like hell for a shower to remove its filth as another thought crosses your confused mind.

Where... where am I?

You peer blindly around the endless black, which extends in all directions for what seems like miles. Every so often, a scrappy shadow of a ruined building or object jumps out at you–a tatter of cloth fluttering nervously in the wind, or a pile of rocky rubble–but just as quickly, it vanishes back into the blackness, never to be seen again twice. You strain your ears for a sound, but the only noise that greets them is the soft sound of water lapping on hidden shores, undercut only by the vague buffet of the noisome breeze blowing.

You don't even remember how you got here, let alone why or how you came. The last thing you recall is going on a walk on a foggy afternoon... and then nothing. Were you attacked? Are you lost? You must be, because you've never seen this location before in your life. You feel your gut twist in unexplained illness, as if anticipating some doom, and glance nervously at the dark in case something awful lurks, just out of sight. Just how damn far did you walk?

Where in the hell is this place?

As if in response, a flame suddenly bursts to life on either side of you, providing a pitiful amount of light to the gloom. You jump as you're startled by their arrival, then look up to see two more flames illuminate before your eyes, roughly equidistant from each other. Another two flames spark beyond those, then two more as you realize the flames are forming a path into the dark distance. To what, you are not sure, but each set that lights both grows your curiosity and your tension, as if afraid of what they will unveil. Something is wrong, incredibly wrong–and whatever is causing that wrongness, you know, lies waiting at the path's end. Even so, your curiosity begins to outweigh your nervousness, and you step forward as the flames continue lighting. You take another step, then another, a sick sense of morbid wonder tugging at the fringes of your confused and nervous mind as you walk. The walk seems to take hours, perhaps even ages, and with each flame that lights the way further, your gut begins to sink more and more, as if internally squirming in a need to turn back.

You ignore it, and keep walking.

The final flames light themselves falteringly, shuddering as they struggle to light before finally sparking, and that's when you see it. Him, that is–the figure in tattered yellow robes, settled in a throne of crumbling stone and rusting iron, hooded head down in silent, brooding thought. He is immensely tall, taller by far than anyone you have ever met, and that height alone is imposing, as if the gothic shadows cast upon him weren't enough already. The figure does not stir, but the flames do, shivering and flickering nervously at his dark presence, as if they were afraid to disturb him...

Your footsteps cease as the sinking feeling in your stomach becomes a full nervous fluttering. Your palms sweat and your heart rate picks up with your breathing, but you know not why. All you do know is that something about the seated figure frightens you so, so very much, so much so you don't dare say a word... If only you could comprehend *why*.

As the last echo of your previous footsteps dies, the mighty figure stirs, his ruined robes rustling in a way that sets your teeth on edge. His robed head lifts up, and you feel his eyes upon you, critical and commanding behind the cracked and peeling mask you now see that he is also wearing. Your breathing grows shallow as you watch several small tendrils, writhing little cephalopodic limbs, unfurl beardlike from beneath the mask's blank off-whiteness. You feel the need to backpedal and run, but something–perhaps the shock?–roots you to the spot. Something in his dark stare, or perhaps the sickening realization you have just had:

That thing is not *a human being...*

A voice, commanding and disturbingly calm, cuts the silence and lapping waves with the buffets of foul wind over them. It echoes from seemingly everywhere, as powerful as it is dark. It makes you tremble, that voice... *His* voice...

"And who be this that has come forth before me? Speak, traveler, lest ye be cast to the winds and forgotten!"

Your mouth is dry as you swallow hard, struggling to get the words out before you choke to death on them.

"I-I'm... sorry," you murmur shakily. "I-I... I woke up here, I d-don't know where I am, I..."

"Ye be alone?" His shrouded head inclines, the tentacles moving wetly over each other as he does so. "Allow me welcome ye, then, to my kingdom... What brings ye to the lost remnants of Carcosa, traveler? Have ye perhaps traveled too far?"

There is a vague amusement in his voice, a strange tone of mockery towards your plight–and you don't like one bit of it. And furthermore... why *are* you here, anyway? You wrack your mind, trying to recall the details of what happened–you were on a walk, that much you know, but after that... after that, nothing... It's all a blur, lost in a mental fog from which you can't extract it again.

"I-I... don't know," you admit, as much in horror as sheepishness as you stare at the ground–anything to escape his gaze! "I... I really don't *know...*"

"Ye waste my hours, then, traveler?" There is a grim tone of forewarning in the King's voice, his tentacles squirming in what seems like distaste or annoyance...

"N-no, sir!" You stammer, afraid–the last thing you want is this... creature, this ruler, upset with you. "I-I didn't mean to waste your time... I just want to go home, it's... it's all I want..."

"Lost then, are ye? Very good. Yes, most grand indeed..."

He chuckles, and the sound throws chills down your spine, electrifying every nerve ending in your body and setting all the hairs on your arms on end. It just hits you exactly what else is wrong with this bizarre ruler, what else is making your heart race with dread aside from the obvious...

Mad... He... this thing *is utterly, completely, inhumanly* insane...

"By a mortal's standards, perhaps," he responds, amused, and your mind recoils in shock at the realization that he can hear your thoughts. You almost whisper the words you speak next, afraid of the truth in them...

"You're... this... this isn't a..."

"A dream?" the King asks, his amusement mounting. "Nay, traveler, by no means... as ye may have noticed I am quite extant, and quite... *beyond* ye. I am something more powerful than ye could ever hope to become... I, traveler, am a living god."

He allows you just a few seconds' time to process this, basking merrily in the glow of your disbelieving dread, before speaking once more.

"Tell me, mortal traveler..." he leans in con-spiratorially, as if whispering a private joke to you. "Have ye yet been down to the lake, and seen the rising of the twin suns?"

"N-no," you squeak, squirming. What lake? What twin suns? You haven't seen a speck of light in this place except the flames around both him and you, and the only thing resembling a lake that you've seen or heard lately is the constant sound of lapping water, seemingly echoing from all sides and drowned out by your rapid heartbeat...

"No?" the King echoes, still with that vague tone of amusement. You feel he speaks to you as if to a child—no, less than a child...

"I-I told you... I told you already, I swear that I just *woke up* here..."

"Insolence!" he thunders, and his massive palm slams onto the armrest of the throne, the fingers writhing like so many dying worms as a shaking of dust tumbles from the crumbling stone. You jump with the percussive echo, trembling in fear of the King's wrath. "How darest thou speak out of turn? Do ye mock my authority, traveler?"

"I-I'm sorry, oh God, I'm sorry!" you beg, curling into yourself as if it might save you from what he might do next. "I swear! I-I won't do it again, I promise, just please, *please* don't hurt me..."

His hidden gaze looks you over dispassionately, as though you were an irritating insect, even as the anger begins to drain from it. In its place wells more amusement, as if pleased with your cowering. What seems like hours pass before the King speaks once again, his tone cool and calm once more.

"Very well, then," he responds darkly, his vision never once leaving your shaking frame. "Yours is an acceptable apology. But if it is truly meant, ye shall approach and meet my gaze without fear, so that mine eyes may truthfully see that your soul hides nothing…"

There is a soft rustling of fabric and a thick, wet slickness as the King stands, proceeding from his throne towards you. You look up in alarm as you hear this to see him sliding sickeningly forward on many larger tentacles, protruding from beneath his robe to serve as a means of locomotion. Finally, he comes to a rest just beyond the first set of flames closest to him, and extends a tentacle-fingered, cloth-covered hand.

"Come to me. I shall be the judge of your veracity, traveler. If ye speak the truth, ye have nothing to fear from me…"

Every fiber of your being screams no to his offer. Your soul screams no, shuddering in your chest with your heart. Your mind screams no, begging you to run as far and fast as possible. And yet, to your absolute horror, your feet disobey, taking one step closer to the King, then another…

"Good child… closer, yes, closer yet… I cannot yet smell ye…"

You whimper in fear as you approach still further, now within ten feet, now nine… You vainly beg your feet to run, but they do not yield, as if beholden to what the King wants. Your fear slowly grows to panic, threatening to consume you whole as your heart hammers in your chest and your mind reels with fear… Seven feet away, now six, until you are within five feet of his massive, imposing frame, far taller than any human being, your own body trembling as though you stood before a very angry bear and your eyes cast to the ground as if standing before an angry parent…

"Look at me, traveler," he hisses, and your eyes snap up to meet his gaze. "Good. Very good. Ye obey orders from superiors well, I see…"

You yelp as you feel a tentacle creep up your spine, ruffling your hair almost mockingly. Your fear… you know he can sense your fear of him. You know he is going to hurt you... you can feel it in his hidden eyes–assuming, you realize with sudden horror, he even *has* eyes...

"Such fear, such fear of me in your eyes," he murmurs, the tentacle brushing against your face in a fake gesture of sympathy. "I do believe that indicates your shameless guilt."

You are near the verge of tears from dread, watching as he lifts a hand, seven writhing tentacles serving as the fingers. You remain silent and horrified, almost frozen as he slowly reaches for your face and the broad palm covers your vision.

"Ye shall be shown the errors of your insolent ways," he says darkly. "For I see in your eyes a lying infidel, and infidels are not tolerated in my kingdom. Now kneel, foolish one, or I shall make ye kneel."

"G-god no, please," you whimper, snapping out of your frightened stupor and trying vainly to pull his hand from your face. As if in response, the tentacle fingers tighten their grip on you, wrapping around on themselves multiple times. "Please, *please* don't hurt me, Your Highness... *please...*"

"The time for such acts of mercy is long since passed," he responds gravely. "Especially for one such as ye. I will show ye none, and ye shall expect none..."

You cry out in pain as the tentacles constrict further, your entire field of vision now blocked by his massive hand.

"Now, infidel," he murmurs, his voice hard and uncaring of your pleading whimpers, "You will do as I command. *Kneel.*"

The blackness that covers your eyes gives way, just barely, broken by a single ember of dim yellowish light. You are confused and breathless momentarily as it slowly brightens like a sun peeking above the horizon, growing in size and intensity. Then, slowly, it begins to stretch, spiralling out fractally, forming into thin cracks of light from its center... cracks of bright, pure yellow light that... that... Oh God... Oh, *God*, no... That... that Sign... that writhing, awful, burning, horrid yellow *Sign*...

A flood of terror washes over you, consuming all thought, drowning you in a panic and awestruck dread to rival any wave. It speaks of a truth, that Sign, a horrible and inescapable, dark truth that no amount of amnesia could erase from your mind... Your face pales, your body feels alight with pain, your eyes and mind sear with agony as the symbol burns into them...

And you scream.

"*Oh God,* no! Stop! Stop it, please, it burns, end it! Please, I beg of you, *please!*"

But his grasp does not yield, and the Sign glows ever brighter, ever more painfully, and your mind wails in torment from its corrosive decay...

"I will not," the King replies, ignoring your constant cries for mercy. "I will not take it away. Ye shall gaze upon them, the suns of Carcosa, my crest... and despair. Let it sear into every memory so that it haunts your every waking moment and never leaves your eyes! This is your punishment, infidel-ye shall see naught else for all your days. May it always remind ye of your foolishness... and of *my* power..."

You thrash and scream until your throat grows raw. Every memory you have is burning, every thought you have is tainted now, stained yellow, burnt yellow. You can't think. *You can't think...* Your mind is dying, you can feel it dying, hear its shrieks of anguish... until finally, all you can manage is a mere whimper, an admission of defeat... and you kneel. You kneel before the King, half-collapsing in a feeble attempt to appease your ruler, your master. The Sign is pleased with your actions. You can tell. You can tell because it glows brighter, joyously, almost triumphantly...

It seems like an eternity before he finally releases you, and as he does so you curl into yourself, trembling with dread and awe. You've seen... you've seen... What *have* you seen?

"Do ye understand now, fool traveler?" he chides, looming deathlike over you. You can feel the slimy brush of his tentacles against your skin, and hear the soft rustling of fabric... You have no other response but to shakily nod, scarcely able to see past the deep and utter fear that clouds your vision... yellow... everything is yellow... anything, you'd give anything in the world to forget what you saw...

"Good. Very good. *Excellent...*"

The slick wetness of his tentacles fades away slowly as he leaves, but you barely hear it. One by one, the flames begin to die to blackness as he leaves you curled in horror on the floor, but you don't see.

The last of the flames begin to die, and the very final thing you see, just before the darkness consumes you and them both, is the Sign, the Yellow Sign, burned forever into your eyes, flickering away slowly with the very last remnants of the final flame.

THE STREETS OF ALAR
DJ Tyrer

The streets of Alar were thick with a sea fog that had rolled in from the sea lake of Demhe. An unseasonable chill held the city in its grasp, while the fog made the night-shadows seem all the darker. Shuffling figures passed through the streets like flitting shadows.

A gilded coach clattered past, forcing the figures to throw themselves out of the way. It proceeded towards the palace through the dark, narrow streets of the city, its wheels clattering across the cobbles. Within the carriage, Watch-Captain Destries slumped across the burgundy leather seat, his head lolling and eyes gazing blindly at opiate dreams of gargoyles and men wearing pallid masks.

It passed through the great palace gates and came to a halt in the yard. Servants helped the Captain out of the carriages just as the fog parted to reveal the moon. *Something* passed across the ivory globe and the men shivered, not solely from the cold.

***

The Baron de Calvadorr withdrew his rapier from the chest of the Comte d'Erlette, honour salved, and twirled his moustache with satisfaction. Blood pooled in curious shapes as he turned away to face a pageboy.

"Yes?" he asked, archly.

"Princess Thalé requests your presence, my lord."

"Indeed? Well, then my presence she shall receive! Lead on!" He flourished a bow and followed the page to the Princess' audience chamber.

Bowing deeply to her, he cast his gaze over the others in the room. Besides her advisers, there was a dozy-looking man in an archaic watch uniform. He had

215

seen Watch-Captain Destries around court; the man's pompous anachronism and dazed expression made him easily recognizable. An idiot, in the Baron's opinion.

"There has been a murder," one of the aides intoned. "A young woman."

"A noblewoman," said Thalé, icily. Her voice carried a quiet anger. The murder of peasants was one thing, but of nobles... quite another. Duelling was acceptable, but no one should kill a woman of noble blood; it was against all mores. "That is why you have been summoned, Baron: we desire for you to assist the Captain, here, in his investigations, ensure they are handled... with all due delicacy."

He nodded his understanding. Yes, you didn't want any embarrassing details leaking out. The Church of the Dragon was always agitating the plebs against their betters, and they could do without further ammunition; there was even speculation that the Primate had ordered his followers to support Aldones should its strained relations with Alar escalate to war. The Baron had nothing but contempt for the sect.

***

Together, Baron and Captain rode in the coach towards where the body of young Mareza Ladjeff had been dragged out of the river; then, they headed to the Watch-house, where her body had been laid out: it lay upon a wooden table with a thin sheet atop it. An assistant pulled back the covering to reveal her butchered corpse.

She had a cut lower on her abdomen, through which, the pathologist informed them, her heart had been removed.

"He reached up under her ribs," he said, "and pulled it free."

A large square of skin had been sliced from

across her bosom. Captain Destries cast a glazed and dispassionate eye across her corpse, the gaze of someone who had seen it all before and was not seeing it clearly now. The Baron put a kerchief to his lips and suppressed a gag.

"Please, cover her up," he said, looking away. "Why butcher her so?" he asked in a voice rich with nausea.

"Most odd," the Captain murmured, although it was not certain if it was the body or something else that he alone could see that made him wonder.

"An Invigilator will be here shortly," the assistant announced.

De Calvadorr raised an eyebrow.

"The Invigilator will use his power to see how she died," the assistant explained.

The Baron snorted.

***

"The symbol of Koth? What blasphemy is this?!"

"Calm down, Baron." Destries was the perfect example for him; too calm, in fact.

"That is what I saw..." gasped the Invigilator. In his trance, he had stuttered that Mareza had died in a dark room, surrounded by men in Kothite robes and with the symbol of Koth engraved in her flesh. The Baron, like many well-to-do Alarians, was initiated into the outer mysteries of the Church of Koth, and the suggestion of impropriety was offensive.

For over a century, the Church of Koth had dominated Alar under Royal patronage, providing an energy that the Temple of the First King just could not match—and a respectability the Church of the Dragon entirely lacked.

"It is obviously a conspiracy!" the Baron ranted. "An attempt to blacken the name of the Church!"

The other evidence was contradictory: half the witnesses indicated that she had indeed been interested in admission to the mysteries of Koth, whilst the other half painted a picture of an immoral life consorting with the lower orders in exchange for monies to finance an opium addiction. Neither portrait seemed entirely plausible.

"It fails to make sense," the Baron said to himself, as he played a game of cards. On the one hand, why would she be so secretive about her interest in the religion? On the other, why would she become so desperate for opium when it was freely available in courtly circles?

The one good lead they had was that the likeliest suspect for her murder was a bum known as Yanni the Skunk. If they could find him, they might find some answers–unfortunately, he was nowhere to be found. Still, that was the Watch's problem; he was having an evening relaxing in court.

***

Strange visions assailed his mind as he lay in a puddle of his own filth in the corner of a squalid opium den. Gargoyles with something of a bat and something of an insect about them wheeled through skies of yellow. Crazy towers climbed heavenward in defiance of all natural laws. And a shadowy figure hidden behind him whispered blasphemous words in his ear...

"Sir? Sir!" His adjutant had to shake him again to get his attention. "We have a sighting of Yanni the Skunk. He's at the Church of the Dragon in the Dafur slums."

"The Last King has come," Destries said, wistfully, a distant smile playing upon his lips.

"Sorry, sir?"

"Hmm? Yanni, you say?"

"Uh, yes, sir. At the Church of the Dragon, sir."

"Right; bring all the men who can be spared–I want him arrested."

***

Baron de Calvadorr was waiting at the Watch-station when three coaches clattered to a halt outside, returning Destries and his men, along with a comatose Yanni and a pair of priests.

"We caught him," said the Captain, the most lucid the Baron had seen him.

"It would seem he resisted arrest."

The Captain shrugged. "We will soon have some answers."

The usual procedure was a vigorous inter-rogation of the physical sort; had they not been priests of the Dragon, the Baron might have felt sorry for the two conscious men.

***

"And, that, milady," said the Baron, "is the result of our investigation," as he concluded his description of the Church of the Dragon's plot to incriminate the Church of Koth. New laws would soon be enacted to curtail the rights of the traitors, and he was more than happy at the result.

Captain Destries stood passively a few steps behind him, preoccupied with his own secret world. The frown on his face implied his visions were not necessarily pleasant ones.

"You have done well," nodded Princess Thalé. Her sister, who sat at her side, agreed with her, sharing a nod with the assembled priests of Koth.

Beneath his dark hood, the chief priest smiled a secret smile to himself as the city teetered on the edge of chaos.

DARK STARS & STEAM
DJ Tyrer

Dark stars hung in the sky above Alar like ebony pinpricks in the midnight blue arc of the heavens. Gazing upwards from where she reclined on a chaise longue that had been dragged out onto the balcony, Constance felt as if it were possible to imagine the city was at peace with itself and its neighbour; it wasn't.

The streets of Alar were under curfew by night for anyone not of the noble classes, and the city was at war with Aldones. Constance's uncle, the Baron de Calvadorr, had played a key role in the suppression of the Church of the Dragon that had sparked the violence that led to the curfew being introduced; she remembered the mobs pelting the house with eggs –and worse things–before the Household Cavalry had ridden them down and swept them away like the garbage they were. It was a shame that they had been unable to sweep the Aldonean armies aside with equal ease, only emplaced machineguns were not as amenable to cavalry charges as were rabble, no matter what she might wish.

"Milady," the word stirred her from her reverie and she turned to see her maid standing in the doorway to her bedroom.

"Yes, Odette?"

"This arrived for you, milady," Odette said, handing her an envelope.

Constance broke the seal, took out the card and read it.

"It is an invitation to the unveiling of the Land Behemoth," she commented, mainly to herself. The Land Behemoth had been the worst-kept secret in the city since the war with Aldones had ground to a bloody stalemate; a steam-powered war machine that, it was widely predicted, would grind the Aldonean army into dust. The armoured vehicle was to be officially unveiled in three days' time. Constance couldn't help but feel it might have been more effective to let their enemies have first sight of the Land Behemoth on the battlefield. Still, she would make the most of the soiree, nonetheless.

*****

Across the city, furtive figures moved slowly and purposefully through alleyways and across rooftops towards the Marigny Metalworks wherein the first production models of the Land Behemoth were located. Again, a secret known only to almost everyone in the city.

Guards patrolled in pairs accompanied by fierce hounds, but none entertained any thought of direct assault, merely the remote possibility of espionage or sabotage. They were wholly unprepared when the attack began with a fusillade of fire from out of the darkness.

"Hanse?" one guard exclaimed as his colleague collapsed to the ground beside him. A moment later, he was felled likewise.

An alarm began to ring, but it was already too late. The guards who had been out on patrol lay scattered in the grounds and those who came running to investigate were gunned down in turn. There was only a single strong point, a sandbagged machinegun emplacement beside the main entrance, but that was swiftly neutralised with grenades and gunfire.

The unthinkable had happened: the enemy had breached the top security factory in force. The remaining guards inside opted to survive rather than die gloriously for their city, allowing the Aldonean raiders to carry out their destructive activities unopposed. By the time the first troops arrived on the scene from their barracks, the raiders were gone and the first production model of the Land Behemoth was reduced to so much twisted and burnt wreckage.

***

Constance was awoken by an urgent knocking on her bedroom door.

"Uh? Who," she yawned, "is that?"

"Milady, it is I, Odette."

"Enter." She slithered into a sitting position as her maid entered. "What is it?"

"You have been summoned, milady, to court. Immediately." Odette paused a moment, then added, "Something terrible has happened, milady; there is smoke over the northern parts of the city and the messenger said there were explosions."

"Explosions?" she repeated as Odette helped her out of bed and began to assist her in dressing.

"Yes, milady; that's what he said."

"Was it an attack from the air?"

"He didn't say."

There had been numerous claims—never substantiated and mainly from the unreliable lower classes—of strange things seen flying across the night sky, and these had inspired an unspoken fear that they represented some Aldonean secret weapon that was not only spying upon Alar, but would one day rain down destruction upon the city.

Clothed in a light, casual gown of lemon yellow with a small, matching hat placed atop her piled-up blonde hair, Constance descended to the side entrance of the house where a steam carriage was waiting for her.

"All aboard, milady," the fireman said. His job was to keep the firebox well supplied with coal. In a city at war, running such a vehicle was a genuine luxury.

The compartment into which she climbed was

comfortable with red-leather seats and the same quilted across the walls, door interiors, and ceiling. There was a thick red carpet on the floor and the finishings, and two electric lamps—powered by a motor attached to the steam engine—were of gold.

With a groan and a hiss of steam, the steam carriage began to move. Even with the spring suspension and soft cushions, the journey was not a comfortable one, certainly no more than in a horse-drawn carriage, and the speed was slow until they reached the long straight of The Street of the Four Winds where it could pick up speed.

Arriving at the entrance to the palace, she dismounted to find the area abuzz with guards.

She was stopped, but a dismounted and agitated-seeming cavalry officer confirmed her identity and she was ushered inside by a flustered page until they reached a small side chamber. Constance was surprised, having imagined she was being taken to the throne room.

The page knocked and a voice bade them enter.

Within the room were Queen Thalé, Constance's uncle, the Baron de Calvadorr, Field Marshall Castaigne, and General Robardin. A map upon the table around which the four stood showed Alar and its dependent settlements; their enemy, Aldones; neutral Crespian; and the lake-sea of Demhe, although it was currently ignored and overlaid with the blueprint of a building.

"Ah, darling, you're here," her uncle observed, needlessly.

"Your Majesty," Constance bobbed a curtsey, "uncle, Field Marshall, General."

"Lady Constance," Queen Thalé nodded her head a fraction. "It is good of you to come."

"Your Majesty." She curtsied again.

"You have been called here," General Robardin told her, "to assist the investigation into tonight's attack upon the Marigny Metalworks."

"Attack?" she asked.

"Yes," her uncle confirmed and proceeded to outline the shocking events that had befallen the vital factory, concluding, "This is an unprecedented turn of events. Not only have they robbed us of a war-winning weapon, but who can say what new audacity they might stage next?"

Constance nodded. "How can I assist?"

"Your uncle," said the Queen, "tells us you are an intelligent and resourceful young woman. Whilst the military and the Watch will, of course, be conducting their own investigations into what happened tonight, I require someone to oversee what happens on my behalf. Once I might have asked your uncle to fulfil such duties, but he is no longer as spry as he once was, so I shall appoint you."

"Thank you, your Majesty." She hadn't expected anything like this! Constance had assisted her uncle a few times in minor ways, but nothing of any importance. She wasn't sure she would be of any real use to them. "So, uh, what do I do?"

"You keep Her Majesty apprised of what is going on," her uncle told her, "monitoring and keeping track of the investigation. You will have her full authority to go anywhere, ask anyone anything."

"A warrant is being prepared to that effect as we speak," Thalé added. Clearly, Constance was being given no option about taking the role.

"Very good, your Majesty."

The Queen gave a curt nod, then they all turned their attention away from her. Apparently, she was dismissed.

***

A short while later, she was at the Marigny Metalworks and listening to a Watchman describing the events in more detail.

"We have had the Invigilators examining the dead, but not a one has told us anything useful. Many died before they even knew they were under attack and those who did see anything were mostly restricted to shadowy figures and muzzle flashes. Even where they did see them, they were masked and wore no uniform."

"Were none of them killed?"

"The guards had little opportunity to fight back and we have recovered none of the attackers' corpses."

Had they possessed one of the raiders' bodies, the Invigilators could have wrested at least a few clues from the soul imprint.

"Any clues from inside?" she asked, thinking perhaps that something might offer an insight into their perpetrators.

The Watchman shook his head. "No. I mean, they think the explosives were probably made in Aldones, but..." he trailed off. That told them nothing they didn't already suspect: they needed to know if the attack had been carried out by Aldoneans or Alarian traitors; where they were based in the city; and whether they planned any further attacks.

Taking advantage of the authority invested in the warrant she carried, Constance wandered through the devastated factory, taking in the scenes of destruction so that she could answer any questions the Queen might have.

Just then, a breathless Watchman ran up to her and said, "We may have something..."

He led her over to a rather nervous-seeming man who proved to be a security guard at a nearby factory. A sot, he had been snoozing in his office with a bottle of gin, as was his wont—probably the attackers had ignored him or overlooked him for just that reason—when the noise had woken him. Constance was not surprised he had decided not to involve himself. He had, however, peeked out towards the end of the raid.

"I 'eard 'em, miss... uh, milady. I 'eard 'em, one of 'em, say 'Back to Gordo's.' That's what I 'eard, miss... uh, milady."

"Gordo's?" she echoed, turning to the Watchman."Is the Watch aware of such a place?" she asked. It seemed to be the only lead they had.

"Possibly, ma'am. There is a man named Gordo Bozz who was junior functionary of the Church of the Dragon before it was banned. He runs a sort of doss house in the Quarter; there are suspicions it might be a Church safe house."

"Has it been raided?"

The Watchman shook his head. "Not that I'm aware of, ma'am. Not enough evidence, nor enough resources. It's always down to resources, you see, ma'am; too much to do and not enough to do them with. We keep the occasional eye on the place, but that's about all."

"Well, I think the odds are that the people who attacked here are at this Gordo's place," she stated, pronouncing the name with distaste. "You should send some men there at once."

"That's for the Captain to decide."

***

Unfortunately, the Watch-Captain did not share her certainty, pointing out that the man was a drunk.

"But, I have the Queen's authority!" Constance cried, stamping her foot in a manner she realised immediately did her case no good.

"So you have—to observe, not to order," retorted the Watch-Captain, ending the conversation.

"Then, I shall go alone!" she declared as imperiously as she could, although the man was already walking away and deep in conversation with one of his subordinates. "The insufferable fool..." she muttered, looking around. Spotting an infantry Lieutenant, she explained where she was going and why, asking that support be sent as soon as possible if she did not promptly return.

***

A clanking, smoke-belching steam carriage was not the most inconspicuous mode of transport, so Constance disembarked on the edge of the Quarter, Alar's poorest neighbourhood, and travelled to the address the Watchman had given her on foot.

The building was old like much of the Quarter and in a particularly poor state, with flaking paint and winter shutters dangling loose from their fittings. A night mist was rolling in from Demhe, tendrils of damp air curling and questing through the streets, lending the scene a frightful and melancholy air. She thought she could make out a long-faded, white-washed dragon symbol beside the door.

Shrugging away her doubts and fears, she slipped down a side alley looking for a way to sneak inside. A small window devoid of both shutters and glass provided the means for her to squeeze through into the dirtiest room she had ever seen, a kitchen; the building was certainly insalubrious.

As she cautiously moved through the seemingly untenanted building, Constance became aware of the sounds of a large group of men in the basement, moving about and talking. Suddenly, she felt scared as she realised just how vulnerable she was, poking around on her own like this. She really should have requested a gun, she decided.

She was just about to turn and leave when she noticed a thin line of light running down the wall of the room she was in and realised that it was a narrow crack in the wall: a hidden door. Now, her senses of duty, of pride and of inquisitiveness warred against her senses of self-preservation and that rare quality termed common sense; until, at last, she decided to see where it led. Yes, it would be risky, but she was certain the troops she had requested would be along shortly.

Behind the secret door was a stairway down to the basement, well-lit with electric light. Descending, she found a small room with a rack of weapons—pistols and rifles—and two archways, one of which led into a small room stocked with open boxes that must have held explosives, and the other of which led into a large room in which stood two dozen men dressed in grey, some armed.

"Those of you who are Alarian will return to your daily lives; the rest of you will join me in an extraction by autogyro from Atheling Park."

The majority stripped off their camouflage clothing and turned to leave. Constance slipped into the room with the boxes, pausing only to take one of the pistols. She could do nothing against the traitors alone—if she was lucky, the troops were outside and would seize them—but she thought she might capture the Aldoneans after they were gone.

She listened as they climbed the stairs and hoped nobody would look into the room where she was. When she was certain they were all gone, she stepped through to the large room, pistol raised.

Something slammed into the side of her head and she fell to the floor, the pistol falling from her hand. Momentarily stunned and with stars—bright, unlike those in the skies above the city—dancing before her eyes, Constance had the impression of somebody looming over her.

"Ah, so we are uncovered," she heard the voice of the man who had spoken earlier, now with a chuckle in it. "Only, Alar sends a girl, not a guardsman. A pity..." He mock sighed. "A pity... And now, you die, as surely as the Dark Stars have doomed Alar to destruction."

Her vision cleared as she heard the sound of a

pistol being cocked and, from the corner of her eye, she had an unpleasantly clear view straight up the barrel of the gun that was pointed directly down at her head. The pistol she had held was out of reach. She was going to die.

Unless... Her thoughts turned to her hatpin. It was worth a try. She grabbed for it, pulled it free from her hat and stabbed it down into his foot as she rolled away from him. The man yelped and the gun boomed; her ears rang.

Constance stumbled to her feet and had the unfortunate realisation that, whilst the man was busy pulling the bloodied pin from his foot, his two companions had levelled their pistols at her.

Just then, there were the muffled sounds of doors being kicked in upstairs.

"The troops!" she gasped with relief.

"Come, we must leave," the man said, tossing the hatpin aside. He raised his pistol and slammed it into the side of her head. Everything went black.

***

Constance woke to find a guardsman shaking her.

"Ma'am, are you well?" he asked.

"Um, I'm not dead," she gasped in reply, sitting up and fighting to withstand the tide of nausea that washed over her.

As she slowly stood, she asked what had happened.

"We broke in, eventually found the door down to here, and discovered you and the weapons."

"And the Aldoneans?"

"Aldoneans? There was nobody here, save you. All long gone."

She shook her head and immediately regretted doing so. Pausing to gasp, she told him: "They were here and left as you broke in."

"We didn't see anyone," he replied, uncertainly.

"Nonetheless, that is what happened." She thought back to what the man had said, then exclaimed: "Oh! We must hurry! The Aldoneans are rendezvousing with an autogyro in Atheling Park! We must stop them!"

That got them moving.

***

The park was named for some mythological figure from the lore surrounding the cult of the First King. The old legends had been neglected as no longer relevant; Constance had read about them in some old schoolbook, but remembered little. Who needed ancient myths when the mysteries of the Church of Koth had served the city so well for a century and a half, and the advances of technology had offered so much? She herself had little time for superstitious belief.

Atheling Park, as if to affirm her certainty, had been the site of the Grand Exposition shortly before the war began, back when the myriad potentials of peacetime technology had been celebrated: new steam-powered vehicles, a thinking machine that some had said might herald a future technological deity, and a difference engine capable of contacting the dead with greater efficacy than any Invigilator. The majority of the glass-and-steel buildings that had housed the display were gone—the steel melted down to be reused in war—but the marshalling yards where steam locomotives had once sat for the admitting gaze of a fascinated public remained, as did a spur line. In fact, that spur line would make a good, albeit bumpy, landing place, a fact which the officer agreed when she suggested it to him.

"You stay back, milady," he told her as they

dismounted from the lead carriage that had borne them across the city.

She nodded, a little reluctantly, knowing he was right. She would only be a hindrance in the battle to come.

"Look after her," the officer told a young soldier who nodded and moved to stand beside her.

There was an old locomotive sitting in the marshalling yard, seemingly long forgotten. It was sturdy enough to provide effective cover and was conveniently situated so that she could observe events those few hundred yards down the track. Keeping as much out of sight behind a scattering of trees as possible, Constance and her protector headed towards the vehicle whilst the dozen soldiers fanned out to advance towards the rail line.

It was just as the soldier helped her up into the cab of the locomotive that they heard the chattering of a machinegun from somewhere beyond the spur line. Barely having time to react, the line of soldiers fell almost as one, mown down before they could respond. Once again, the raiders had overcome their opposition before the battle really even began.

The soldier swore in shock and disgust, but Constance found herself stunned into silence by the audacious act.

Then came the *whoosh-whoosh* of something approaching from the sky, and Constance thought she saw movement in the shadows down the spur line.

"The autogyro!" she exclaimed. "We have to stop them!"

"I can't see them for a clean shot," the soldier replied.

"Help me fire up this locomotive!"

"What?" he looked at her as if she were speaking gibberish.

"Help–me–fire–it–up!"

There was a smattering of coal in the ready

bucket, just enough, if they were lucky, to start the locomotive and get it a few hundred yards down the line. He started to shovel the coal into the firebox whilst she tried to work out how to start it: she had occasionally watched the driver of her steam carriage and thought she could remember the basics. She just hoped there were no major differences between the two vehicles.

Glancing out the window, she thought she could see the shape of the autogyro coming in to land. She began to worry: would the steam build quickly enough for them to move in time? Was there even any water left in the boiler? Were they just wasting their time?

Would it work?

It did! Just as the autogyro touched down, the pressure gauge began to creep upwards. Constance threw the lever forward and the locomotive began to move. It was slow, little more than a crawl, but it *was* moving. It began to pick up speed.

There were gunshots and bullets pinged against the front of the vehicle. She ducked down, as did the soldier; they didn't need to see what was happening: if the autogyro was still on the line, they would be successful regardless.

The locomotive lurched and something rained down upon it as it left the tracks and came to a sickening halt after a few tumbling moments. Constance found herself looking up at the dark stars, half in and half out of the vehicle, which now lay on its side. She lay there like that for several minutes, she thought, then slowly slithered over the side and dropped painfully down to the ground. She could see the soldier a short distance away, his head at an awkward angle. Not far past him was one of the Aldoneans with a chunk of metal sticking out from his check.

From out of the darkness stepped the leader of the raiders. There was no sign of his other man; she assumed—hoped—that meant he was dead.

"I really should have shot you back there," he said in a steady voice, pointing a pistol at her. "I totally underestimated you. You are no mere chit at all, are you?"

"I am Lady Constance de Calvadorr," she announced as haughtily as she could in the circumstances. She didn't think it prudent to admit she had surprised herself.

"Which means nothing to me. I am a servant of the First and Last King and the All-Devouring Dark Stars," he told her with fervour in his voice.

"You are mad," she told him in turn. She half-remembered that the Dark Stars were referenced in the mythos of the First King and were said, somehow, to presage the end of the world. Were the Aldoneans driven by some religious mania? What did the legend say? Once the stars were bright, now they grew dark. Trying to recall the legend, at least, took her mind away from the immediacy of death.

"Alar has abandoned the truth," the man went on, "but now, the truth returns to devour Alar and there shall be no escape. Soon. Soon..."

"I am not afraid of you."

He laughed. "Yet, you fear death."

"I do not!"

"You should! Death shall devour you and you shall cease to exist. I do not fear death!"

There was a single gunshot and he toppled to the ground before her. She stared down at the corpse and his final words replayed through her mind; she shivered. Was this a victory or a defeat?

From across the park came the sound of steam carriages and the clanging of Watch vehicles' bells growing closer, but Constance paid them no heed, just gazed up at the dark stars overhead, wondering if they truly heralded the city's final days...

DREAMS OF THE KING
DS Davidson

It was one of those dreams where you sort of know that it's a dream and, yet, it still seems to possess a certain solidity; it doesn't quite make sense, yet you, somehow, know what is coming and why. Rather like reality, actually—that never makes much sense, most of the time. Perhaps dream and reality are not so far apart. Perhaps in a dream you enter into some other dimension? Or, could it be that what we call reality is a dream and dreams are reality? I don't know, but this dream seemed to be more real than others, yet I had a hyper-awareness of its dream nature.

I was walking along a hallway that was dark and cobwebbed. Then it was as if I had turned a corner—I found myself standing in a room full of crates and cardboard boxes. I weaved around them; it was as if they had been stacked in a pattern. There was a meaning here—but what it *meant* I did not know. Passing through the warehouse, I stood upon a dockside, a quay of slimy black stone. A sea of cloud and mist broke against the dockside without force. Curls of breaker frothed upwards, spilling onto the stone, moistening the slimy surface. A dank tendril frothed towards me, caressed my leg like an over-friendly cat, then vanished, disintegrated apart and was gone. Like money at the bar. Then, the dockside was gone, too.

"Have you seen the Yellow Sign?" was the repeated refrain of reveller after reveller. I was pulled this way and that by the crowd as each asked me the same question.

"What are you talking about?" I responded. "What is the Yellow Sign?"

But, no one would answer me any more than I could answer their query. I closed my eyes, but blank eyes kept staring at me through the holes in the curiously pallid masks they wore.

"Leave me alone!" I cried, but they just asked, again, in sickening unity, "Have you seen the Yellow Sign?"

And then the thrusts ceased as I was cast aside, tossed through a doorway into another dark corridor. I walked for hours without getting anywhere, so paused and leant against a small bust of some dusty monarch as I caught my breath. I was going somewhere, but I knew not where nor how to reach it. But, what did I care? It was a dream! And yet... and yet, I felt an urgency deep within me: I had to get there! But, where?

Ah, yes! There it was. I could see an archway ahead of me. I was sure that I was where I was meant to be. I don't know why. Nor what it was. But, there you go. Why argue with a dream?

I stepped through and found myself standing in an office, a typewriter clacking away in one corner and a dripping tap in the other. Nobody was present. I stretched and looked around. It seemed to be a newspaper office, stacks of old 'papers were lying about, teetering towers of them. I pulled one out of a pile at random. The stack wobbled but remained upright. Reading the front page article, I saw that it was about the War. A photo showed refugees struggling along a road. Another showed a smiling man, a grinning man, a politician with a waxy complexion and faithless eyes. The headline above the picture proclaimed: **THE LAST KING HAS COME**.

"He has indeed."

I spun around at the sound of the voice. There was a thin man in a white shirt and black trousers leaning against the desk with the typewriter—with his pallid, perspiration-sheened skin and shiny-black hair, he could have passed for a black-and-white photograph. In one hand, he clasped a sheet of newsprint and, in the other, a dark hankie with which he mopped his brow.

"That would be Mr. Castaigne," he said. Maybe I looked confused, but then he clarified: "The picture. When he was discovered."

"I remember it well." I don't know why I said that; I didn't.

"I thought I knew your face. Well, you'd better be moving–he's waiting for you."

"Who?"

"The King, of course." He wiped his face again. Skin smeared with the hankie's pass, blurring his features until his face became a blank.

"Wake up!" His voice came from nowhere. "Wake up!"

A tinny ringing filled my ears. I pulled a pillow over my head, but it did not deaden the sound. I pulled the pillow away again and tried to prise open my heavy-lidded, encrusted eyes. It seemed as if I could hear my lashes tearing and snapping apart as I slowly tore my eyes open. Not that it made any appreciable difference–the room was dark and shadowed; I might as well have kept them shut. I knuckled them for a while, but all that did was make strange lights dance in front of my vision. Slowly, my eyes began to focus and make some sense of the gloom.

The hotel room was not terribly large: pokey is the word I would have used to describe it. The bed was flush up against one wall, the door a couple of feet away on the other. A basin, I think, on that wall, too; the tap dripping. A window was a similar short gap away from the foot of the bed: sickly orange light leaked in around the edges of a curtain that had been dark and grey in the light and was no prettier in the night.

I fumbled for the bedside lamp, but only succeeded in knocking it to the floor. Great! The alarm clock followed it, ending its ring. There was just enough orange glow bleeding in to enable me to stumble out of bed and to the light-switch beside the door. I had just felt the broken plastic fitting when an occupant of another room cried out: "No-no-no-no-no!" It sounded like night terrors. Well, I hoped that was all it was...

I flicked the switch just as the monotone cry ceased. The harsh glare of a cheap bulb made me wince after the darkness. Somewhere outside a mournful siren banshee-wailed into the night, then everything was silent again. I crossed to the window and yanked the grey curtain to one side. Through smeared, streaked glass, I could see a curling fog weaving its way past. It had not been foggy when I checked in, so could not have influenced my dream: it was like being beneath those rolling mist-waves.

I stood watching for a while as the mist curled about itself to form intricate patterns. I traced their flow on the murky window pane, drawing a strange pattern in the detritus of years of cigarette smoke and dirty air.

"Have I seen the Yellow Sign?" I asked myself, the words creeping out from somewhere in my dreams. "Have I?"

As I stood there, watching the fog swirl, I became aware of footsteps, off somewhere in the hotel's labyrinth of corridors, muffled by distance at first, but becoming clearer with an unpleasant inevitability. And still I stood there, staring at the fog. It was as if I was petrified and unable to move. I *wanted* to move, but I dared not. If I stood still, it would come to me—that I knew—but if I turned and fled... I would have to face it, pass it. Freeze or flee, neither offered a good prospect. And, so, I continued to stand still. Waiting.

The footsteps echoed closer and seemed, almost, to be behind me. I could almost feel its presence, feel its breath on my neck. My body was rigid with fear. I wasn't sure what *it* was, but I knew I didn't want to turn and see it... And then they stopped. Well, I hadn't heard the door open, so I guessed it hadn't actually entered the room, whatever my fear told me. It must have been just outside the door. To be honest, that was not much more comforting.

It hammered against the door and I sat up in bed. The old alarm clock was still ringing tinnily and someone was banging on the door of my room and calling "Wake up!" I reached for the lamp and knocked it to the floor. Great! Still there was enough light from the yellow sign on the wall outside for me to discover the light-switch and turn it on. Yellow sign? Why did I think that? The neon sign advertising this dump, the Lake Demhe Hotel, had been a lurid orange. It was my dream trickling through again... well, for the first time, I guess, into my waking reality. I was still a bit befuddled, but managed to switch the alarm clock off and open the door to the manager.

The manager was a thin man with shiny, sweaty skin. Perspiration marked his white shirt which, with his black trousers, made him seem almost like a photographic negative. Although his face was pinched and angular, it had a slightly waxy texture to it. He looked ill.

"You wanted to be woken in time," he said.

"In time? In time for what?"

"For your appointment—with the King."

"King?"

"Yes, the Last King; He has finally come."

That was when I realised that I was still dreaming. Unfortunately, it seems I still am... When am I going to wake? When will the King let me leave? When?

THE YELLOW DOOR
K.W. Taylor

The building was unremarkable save its doors. A block of connected brownstones, its unassuming façade's sole feature of beauty were the scalloped frames surrounding each door. Some tenants painted theirs a subtle mocha to complement the dark brick. Others had gotten more creative, cutting out sections of the wood and replacing them with mosaic tiles in a variety of colors. The doors themselves varied as well, but sleek, glossy black overwhelmed, as it allowed the frame decorations to stand out.

Number 1895 was different. No frame surrounded the door to this unit, and not even a shadow of one removed remained as a faded outline in the brick. The brick still looked original and otherwise unaltered, however, which hinted that perhaps no frame ever existed. The door itself was bright, matte yellow, the bright yellow of taxicabs and canaries and over-caffeinated soda. A cheerful color when seen in nature, sunshine dappling amongst trees or dandelions dotting a field of clover. On an overcast day in a part of Philadelphia without greenspace it felt false and disingenuous, like a smiley face on the sign of a discount department store staffed by employees forced to supplement meager incomes with food stamps. There was nothing cheerful about such faces, as there was nothing cheerful about this door's attempt at brightness. The paint provided a much less forgiving surface than the black doors around it, for the scars of urban detritus—litter, cigarette ash, puddle backwash, and sooty snow—showed up on the door's two bottom panels, streaks of filth shooting across the surface like the scars of claws against flesh.

On the sidewalk in front of number 1895, three people stood. The youngest, a woman with turquoise spectacles and a sleek bob of short hair, stared at the door for several long moments. Her companions were lost in conversation several feet ahead on the sidewalk, then noticed her absence and looked behind them.

"Wait, Becker, where's Jo?" the other woman asked. Slightly older than Jo, she wore a natty business suit. Becker, sporting a hipster salt-and-pepper beard, doubled back.

"Jo!" Becker called. "Did you drop something? Come on, we gotta go."

"What're you looking at?" the other woman asked.

"Karen, did you notice this?" Jo asked. "I'm going in."

Karen and Becker stared at Jo, their mouths agape in twin circles. Karen was the first to voice her objection, with Becker joining her quickly, their voices blending into an unintelligible muddle of sharp tones and nervous laughter. Becker stepped in front of Jo to block her path.

"No, you guys," Jo said. "I have to know what's in there."

"It's an apartment, then," Karen said. "I mean, the building is probably mixed usage, so if you open that door, you're wandering into somebody's house. I bet it's locked anyway, and there's no sign on the door."

"We're already late for the museum," Becker added. He pulled back the sleeve of his jacket to look at his watch. "Come on, everybody else is waiting for us."

Jo pointed at the door. "But look, there is a sign. Do you see it?" She darted around Becker and jogged a few feet closer. "Right here." She jabbed her index finger at the space between the two top panels.

Karen and Becker exchanged a look. "Do you—"

"No." Becker shook his head. "I don't know what she's—"

"*Right here,*" Jo said. "Come here. I'm not opening the door. I'm not even knocking. Just humor me and look, okay?"

The door opened a crack, and Jo squeaked and backed up. She murmured something but a hand darted out and grabbed her right wrist. As Jo screamed, the unseen resident tugged Jo inside and slammed the door shut behind.

Karen and Becker shouted Jo's name and ran to the door. Karen rattled the doorknob, now firmly locked, and Becker pounded on the dirty yellow wood. He let out a gasp after a moment and backed up.

"Whoa, she was right." He pointed to the spot Jo indicated earlier. "There *is* a sign there."

In the center of the wood a symbol was carved, its carefully hollowed edges tipped with gold leaf so faint it had been impossible to see from anywhere but much closer to the door. The symbol looked to have been made in seven smooth strokes, the topmost of which curved from a half circle down to a straight line, vaguely resembling a question mark. Below the vertical stem was a circle, with a larger circle—broken into three segments—surrounding it. The bottom half of the symbol resembled a pair of legs, one curling to the right of the inner circle into a tentacle-like shape, and the other a simpler, shorter stroke descending diagonally from the left of the inner circle.

"What does that mean?" Karen pulled her phone out of her blazer pocket and opened her camera application. When she tried to take a snapshot of the symbol, however, she was greeted with a message that her storage was too low. "What? I have like *nothing* on here," she muttered. She tried again to no avail. Giving up, Karen stared at the thing to commit it to memory. Beside her, she sensed Becker moving. She turned back to him. He was bent at the waist, hands on his knees. His back rose and fell in shaky, arrhythmic surges. Karen patted him on the back. "Are you okay?"

"Hyper..." Becker coughed and struggled to stand back up. "Hyper—I can't—"

Karen mimed slow breathing and tried to catch

Becker's gaze with hers. "Slowly. It's okay. I sometimes get panic attacks. You need to catch your breath. Slow, like you're sipping the air through a straw. In through your nose, out through your mouth. Count to five." As she ticked off one through five on her hand and modelled gentle breaths, she saw the sign pulse in her mind, glowing in greater and greater intensity with each number.

One. Pulse. Glow.

Karen longed to open the door. Someone was inside the building, someone needing help, someone small and weak and crying.

Three. Pulse. Glow.

Becker's breathing slowed. Karen forced herself back in the moment.

Four. Pulse. Glow.

They had to call the police.

Five. Pulse. Glow.

Karen had to look at the sign again. She had to. She had to see it. Its swirls and curves, so perfect, so important. "What does it mean?" She didn't realize she'd spoken aloud until Becker answered her.

"I don't know, but we gotta get her out of there." Becker slid his phone out of his jeans pocket. "My battery must've died." He pressed the top and center buttons repeatedly. "Nothing."

The symbol still pulsing in her mind, Karen managed to take out her own phone again. "Full battery and four dots. We have to call 911."

Becker tried the door again, and this time the knob spun in his hand. A click sounded from the other side.

"Maybe it's a case of mistaken identity?" Becker shrugged and gave Karen a weak smile. "The person thought Jo was a friend?"

"Then she'd be right out. You wouldn't be gasping for breath like you were about to die." Karen pressed the 9 key on her phone, but before she could finish dialing, Becker opened the door.

Pulse. Glow.

"Don't!"

Becker held out a hand, his palm facing Karen. "Just wait. It's okay." He slipped inside the building.

The door shut with a percussive clang, as if a gong sounded somewhere deep within the building.

Karen's body went limp. Her purse slid down her arm and onto the sidewalk. Her keys jingled against each other as it hit. She willed her knees to lock to keep herself upright, and she gripped her phone hard in her hand. Should she finish calling the police?

She looked up and down the sidewalk. The night was growing chilly, the hint of late fall tangible in the air, the sort of smell presaging overworked chimneys and the first snow of the season. She longed to be safe and warm at the museum with the others, listening to music and poetry and tossing back cheap beer.

In her hand, her phone buzzed—a text. The contact card read "Caitlyn Tanner." *Where are you?*

Karen slid her thumb across the screen and typed. *Emergency. Don't freak anybody out, but I gotta call the cops. Will update soon.*

SEND

She immediately regretted it, as all it might serve to do was alarm Caitlyn. Still, if Karen, too, disappeared, at least there would be a record. At least the police could find her last location, if they looked for the source of the text. She checked her phone's display and was dismayed to see the GPS arrow wasn't on. Could they still find her?

Another text to Caitlyn. *We're on Carcosa.* The phone kept trying to autocorrect the word to "carcass," and she backspaced and tried again. *1895 Carcosa Street.*

SEND

No cops. Not yet. This could be a prank.

But he was hyperventilating. And the sign, it's

crawling inside your brain. Is that a prank?

Becker and Jo were not serious people. They loved horror and mystery and being weird for weirdness' sake. This entire situation was probably that, writ large, and not funny. Well-acted, to be sure, but still. They were messing with her.

Karen thought of her kids, thought of texting them, too, but... no. They would worry.

"Okay, very funny, you two. Get out here," Karen called. "Joke's over. Who set this up?"

Silence.

She spun around and looked out at the street. Though there were cars parked along both sides, though the traffic lights still went through their rotation, there was no longer any traffic. She scanned the sidewalk and could see no other pedestrians, either.

Caitlyn didn't text back.

Karen held her breath and listened.

The wind had stopped.

All she heard was the faint hum of her own body, the hum of silence, the hum of her ears straining for a sound, any sound, and getting nothing back.

Karen was no longer cold. She shoved one sleeve of her jacket up over her wrist. No breeze touched her skin.

Blood rushed in her ears.

I've already waited way too long. I have to get help.

With shaky hands, Karen dialed 911.

***

Inside the building, the clockmaker wound a hand crank. With each revolution of the crank, a giant marble orb spun in an ebony globe frame. The orb was milky white with swirls of pale yellow shot through it at irregular intervals, and as the orb passed across an opening in the frame, it paused and stuttered, and the clockmaker released his grip on the hand crank. After a brief moment, a circle appeared on the orb surface visible in the frame's opening, then numbers, and finally the hands of a clock.

Four wooden flaps were attached to the table beneath the hand crank via door hinges. Once the clock face was fully visible in its frame, one of the flaps banged open, and the clockmaker trailed bony fingers across the surface of the word carved there.

`Kitchen`

The clockmaker nodded and pressed a button on the top of the hand crank. A tiny marble, this one a quarter of the size of the large one, exited a slot near the base of the globe frame and ran down a wooden ramp. The clockmaker did not see where it went, but under his chair and behind him came the sound of rolling, rolling, rolling, and a ping.

He closed his eyes. In his mind, he saw the marble falling down a metal shaft to rest in a cup resembling the well of a nutcracker. A lever lifted the cup a few inches and shoved it through a tiny set of wooden double doors, where it came to rest.

If one were to observe the marble now, they would think it a simple clock face in a wooden clock, a Swiss style likely to feature a small yellow bird *cuckoo-*ing on the hour. No one would suspect the face wasn't always there, was in fact sent there by a man who lived in the walls.

But now that the face was installed, the man could see the room from all directions and anyone who entered it.

As the word carved in the table indicated, it was indeed a kitchen, but dark, windowless, and bore the marks of decades-old grease fires smudged along the wall behind the stove. There were no counters, only a high, wood-surfaced worktable, its top sliced with knife marks and darkened with food stains. The icebox—a 1950s model—looked like the most modern appliance in the room, but its silence revealed its inoperability. The clockmaker smirked as his gaze fell upon it, and he wondered how loudly someone would scream if they dared open the door and spied its contents.

He opened his eyes again and turned the crank. This time, a second marble exited to the foyer.

The clocks seldom ventured in that direction unless there was reason to. "Lovely," the clockmaker whispered. "We have guests."

He rose, his chair creaking behind him, and walked to a crumbling side table in the corner. There, a black candlestick telephone stood upright. Its mouthpiece, receiver, and dial connected via a frayed, fabric-covered cord to a wooden rectangular box. A set of two tarnished silver bells were affixed to the front. Before the clockmaker could pick the receiver off the hook, the bells clanged in a broken, rattling peal.

"Yes."

The clockmaker would never get used to the voice on the other end—the voice of nothing, of void, of tatters and madness—yet he kept the receiver pressed hard to his ear to listen, even as blood trickled in thicker and thicker rivulets down his cheek.

"Thank you," he said. "I will."

He hung up and gasped. The clockmaker's left eardrum came alight with a prickly sensation. His vision swam. More blood oozed out onto his face and the side of his neck, and he grasped the back of his chair to keep from passing out. He swallowed hard and steeled his body against the pain until it subsided.

Still bleeding from his ear, the clockmaker pulled his frock coat closer around his slender frame. In so doing, a button popped off into his hand. He withdrew a handkerchief from his pocket—yellowing around the outer edges and thin as a piece of fine parchment—and wrapped the button up in it.

"This will make a beautiful eye," he said.

He tucked the small package back into his

pocket and made his way to the foyer.

***

Jo rubbed her wrist. "Watch it!" she called. She scrambled backward, hoping to escape the grip of her unseen assailant, but when she looked around the room, she was alone.

It was dark, but she could tell a mirror hung on one wall, as in its reflection she could see a lamp glowing, soft and gold, though its shape was indistinct and its light barely reached beyond the mirror. She looked at the floor and saw dark, smooth, clean slate tile beneath her shoes.

"Hello?" she called. She looked up, willing her eyes to adjust and hoping she could pick out more detail or, if she were lucky, a light switch.

"Hello."

She shrieked when her greeting was answered and pressed herself against the door. Behind her back, she scrabbled at the knob.

"I'm afraid it's locked from the outside." The man who emerged from the shadows was tall and slim with light hair combed back from his forehead. When he smiled, he revealed slightly crooked, slightly sharp, teeth. He stepped toward Jo and, towering over her, snapped on a light via a switch placed far too high for her to reach herself. As he brushed near her, Jo caught a whiff of mingled tobacco and leather.

The room came alight via two hanging lamps descending from the ceiling. Encased in green and blue stained glass, they turned the small front room into a dreamy maritime seascape, with dappled aqua patterns playing against the white walls.

The man was pale. In this light, now, his hair looked less blond and more truly yellow, and she spied tiny spiked tufts along the sides resembling the points of a crown. He wore a long black coat and dark blue jeans. Jo couldn't gauge his age. He was older than her own thirty years, but whether he was a world-weary forty or an extremely well-preserved sixty, she couldn't tell. He pulled a black cylinder from the inside of his coat and twisted it in a semi-circle.

"Does this bother you?" he asked, waving it at her. "They say it's harmless, the vapor, but some people find it's still an annoyance." He had a strange accent, not quite British, not quite American.

Jo had the sudden, irrational urge to ask him if he was Canadian, but reminded herself she was perhaps in some small measure of danger.

The man took a drag on the device, and a plume of weak smoke wafted from his mouth. Jo had expected the tip to glow blue or orange, as she'd seen other electronic cigarettes do, but this one gleamed a bright, flashlight yellow before dimming. "So, does it?"

Jo blinked. "What?"

"Bother you?"

She shook her head. "No, no, it doesn't. I'm sorry. I think I came in here by mistake. May I leave, please? You said the door was locked—"

"Did you?" the man interrupted. He tucked the cigarette away in his pocket. "Did you come here by mistake?" He stepped closer.

The doorknob pressed into Jo's back.

"Please let me go."

"You can go," the man said, "if you tell me the truth." He lifted his chin, closed his eyes, and inhaled. When he opened his eyes again, he smiled. "You have it with you."

Jo's mouth crumpled into a horrified and confused frown. "What?" She wanted to curse him out, push him away in disgust, and yank the door open to her freedom, but her hands wouldn't work, her feet wouldn't move, and the longer she considered whether or not she was disgusted, the more drowsy and confused she felt.

She blinked hard against exhaustion and clenched her hands into tight fists. "I don't know what you're talking about," she managed, but her words came out slurred and slow.

"You only just purchased it, however," he murmured. He took another whiff of the air around her. "It's new. Very new." His smile broadened into a grin, and his teeth flashed again, looking more pointed, vaguely lupine. "You haven't read it yet."

At first, Jo misinterpreted his words. "Red? What's red?" She pawed at her scarf, a russet piece of gauzy fabric. The urge to sleep swelled over her like a wave crashing. She slumped into the corner beside the door.

"*Read*," the man repeated. He held out a hand to her, and Jo took it, despite not wanting to. His skin was rough and weather-beaten. He pulled her up to standing and moved closer still. "You haven't read it yet."

Then he was touching her jacket pocket, and before Jo could protest, he pulled a thin paperback from it.

"Oh. That." Jo recognized the book as one she'd picked up earlier in the day, when she and Becker and Karen weren't yet running late—*Becker! Karen! Help!*—and had some afternoon to spare.

The shop had drawn her in, of course, because of the big, beautiful cat stretched out in its display window—a sleek Burmese with bright amber eyes lazing contentedly and displaying a hint of fang, as if smiling at passersby. She could hear its purrs as soon as she entered the shop.

"Oo, I gotta find some Gibson," Karen said, clapping her hands together and searching for the science fiction section.

"Don't you have all his stuff already?" Jo asked.

Becker didn't seek out new discoveries but, ever the practical sort, chatted up the clerk and asked if he could put a flyer for their event in the window. "And here, I have some business cards, too. Do you ever do consignment sales for chapbooks?"

Jo didn't hear the clerk's reply. She'd found a staircase nearly hidden behind a precarious stack of old RPG magazines. SUSPEND YOUR DISBELIEF HERE! read a Sharpie-scrawled sign taped to the wall. A shaky arrow pointed up to the second level.

Jo shrugged and made a mental gesture of picturing herself depositing a small box on the floor. *My disbelief, I shall take my leave of you.* She nodded at the imaginary spot and climbed.

I'm such a goofball.

Now the man held the book out to her, and though she knew—she *knew*—she'd found it on that second floor of the used bookstore, but she couldn't remember her time there, what drew her to the book, or even paying for it or leaving the store. From the time she stepped onto the bottom step to the time she passed through the door and rejoined Becker and Karen outside, Jo could remember nothing.

She looked at the book cover. There were no words on it, no title or author. The cover itself was bent and creased as if the book's contents had been frequently pored over, the cover itself immaterial and its preservation ignored. The image on the front was done in a mid-1960s style reminiscent of a hand-illustrated movie poster in colored pencil and watercolor. She half thought it looked like it was advertising a production of *My Fair Lady*, but she looked closer.

Brownstone. Doors, elaborately framed. Sidewalk. Caged trees lining the street.

And the door in the center of the image was bright, blinding yellow.

Jo reached out to it, meaning to pluck it from the man's hand, but instead her fingertips reached for the door in the picture itself. She felt a tingle, a burning sensation, and finally a yank and pull at her wrist before everything went dark.

When she opened her eyes again, Jo stood in front of a battered icebox. With a trembling hand, she opened the door.

***

In the recesses of the house, a third wooden flap creaked, revealing a third word.

`Parlor`

The clockmaker pressed a button on the top of the hand crank, and another marble wound its way through machinery and chutes. Rheumy eyes fluttered behind papery lids. The parlor's widows ran floor-to-ceiling, but light was obstructed from entering the room by heavy drapes. Once rich, burgundy velvet, years of neglect had rendered the drapes a hazy gray weighed down by thick piles of dust. The room's only light came from the last dregs of a fire smoldering in the hearth, nearly burnt down to glowing embers. Every few seconds, a small blue flame would sputter on a remnant of log and come back to life to reveal chipped marble tiles and golden walls covered in paintings of stern-looking aristocrats.

The clockmaker's gaze fell on a black-and-white framed photograph near the entrance to the room. A young woman in Victorian dress, her hair piled high, as if she were a Charles Dana Gibson model. Yet the eyes of the image had been scratched out, gouged to white meaty paper pulp. The clockmaker opened his eyes. A tear threatened to roll down his cheek, but he brushed it away and cleared his throat. He patted his pocket and breathed a sigh of relief to feel the button still there.

"I just need a second one," he said.

He rose and straightened his lapels, knowing the foyer would be opening again shortly for another guest.

***

Becker strode into what he first took to be a swath of spider webs. He spun at them with windmill arms, only to discover he wasn't batting at arachnid silk but fabric. He stopped and raised his hands closer to his face. Reams of pale silk pooled through his fingers, smooth as running water. He pushed it aside and heard the distinctive snickety-snick of curtain rings spinning against a rod. Becker craned his neck, but overhead all was dark. He could see smooth gold curtain reaching up, up, up to the ceiling—*or sky?*—dozens of feet above him, until the cascades of cloth disappeared into shadows, darker and dimmer and fading into the black.

But now that he had some of the curtain out of his way, he could slip through the folds and into a room. When he looked back behind him to orient himself to the exit, however, he could no longer see the door. It had to be behind the curtain, of course, so he batted reams of it back again, yet each armful yielded more and more curtain.

Footsteps.

Becker's heart sped up, and he spun around. "Hello there."

It was Jo, only it wasn't. It was a woman in a long skirt and frilly white blouse, dark hair piled up in a bun. She held a hurricane lamp, which she placed on a side table once she entered the room. Behind her was more gold curtain. A few feet of it twitched, revealing a small gap through which she must have come. With the glow of the lamp, Becker could now see the room was circular, every inch of wall covered by silk. In addition to the side table, there were two red armchairs with high, winged backs. Low footstools sat in front of both, the tops covered in matching red fabric. The floor was glossy black wood, polished to a reflective shine. Becker caught his shadowy, smudgy image there, his eyes registering panic even in such an imperfect mirror.

Though the woman couldn't have been Jo, she still resembled her enough to give Becker pause—she had the same expressive, wide eyes, and the same friendly, bright grin. But Jo had been gone mere seconds; there would have been no way for her to don a wig and complete change of clothes. Unless this was all an elaborate ruse, this couldn't have been his friend.

Could it?

"Jo?" Becker ventured. "Are... you're not Jo Brightman, are you?"

The woman frowned. "No." She laughed, a throaty sound identical to Jo's hearty chuckle. "Do I know you, sir? How did you gain entry?"

Becker jerked a thumb behind him. "I, ah, my... did..." Words wouldn't come, and he couldn't explain the series of events without sounding insane. The woman sized him up and seemed to grow impatient.

"Do you have the wrong house, sir?"

"Probably, yes. Yes, I'm sure I do."

The woman took a step forward. "You look positively rattled, sir," she said. She held out a hand toward the chairs. "Do you want to have a seat? Perhaps collect yourself?"

Becker looked at the chair closest to him. The red against the gold in the lamplight looked royal, old-fashioned, like something out of a medieval castle. He had an image of a tapestry shot through with gold and red thread depicting a coronation. A king sat on a throne as a robed figure stood above him holding a crown, the same bright golden yellow as the curtains.

If I sit there, I will be at his service.

The phrase danced unbidden through Becker's mind, and he shook his head to clear it.

"What's your name, sir?" The woman pressed a hand against her throat. "I'm Anna Ouro. You've somehow ended up in our home, and—"

"Our?" Becker eyed the chair again. His knees were weak, his legs tired from the long walk from the... where had they been coming from? And where were they going?

The museum. We're going to the museum.

"Yes, my husband Robert and I live here." She straightened up and looked to her left, as if listening for something. "He's resting, I believe, but if he hears someone at the door he's likely to be roused."

"I'm sorry to have disturbed you." Becker stroked the back of the chair, his fingertips running along the curves of one tall wing.

"Please, sit," Anna repeated. "Let me get you a cup of tea." She reached behind herself and pulled a section of curtain aside. "In fact, come into the parlor. It's much more comfortable there, and I have a fire burning."

Behind Anna was a cheery room. A fire did indeed burn within, casting dancing flames across a low settee with wooden legs carved into lion paws. A dog slept on a rag rug in front of the fire.

Becker followed Anna through the curtain and smiled at the sight of the dog, a rangy Irish setter with its snout resting on its front paws. "Beautiful dog. What's its name?"

"Camilla," Anna replied. She looked around the room. "Her sister's around here somewhere. Cassilda?"

Another ginger snout appeared behind the settee. The second dog gave a short bark in reply to her mistress and padded across the floor to sniff Becker's hand.

"Hey, girl." Becker gave the dog's ear a scratch. "Those are pretty names," he said. "Where did you—"

But Anna was gone. He turned around. "Mrs. Ouro?" he called. He patted at the gold curtain at the room's entrance, but when he drew a few inches back, he was met with a brick wall.

Becker turned around again, but the parlor was

darker, the dogs gone, and the fire almost out. He sank down on the settee and pulled his phone out, its screen dark and useless.

"Nobody has a charger here, do they?" He laughed, first with genuine amusement and then with swiftly mounting hysteria.

***

The clockmaker's telephone rang before he'd returned to his room, but he plucked the earpiece up before the bells stopped sounding. "I'm sorry! I'm so sorry. I'm here." He caught his breath and listened to the sound of knives scraping against each other. "Yes, yes, your highness. Yes. There will be enough actors tonight."

The knives moved apart with a clang, and the clockmaker realized they were not knives, but swords.

"Sir, I still have work to do. You can't... I serve you, sir, of course. Without you, I'm nothing."

One sword sailed from a hand to land in its target, and the phone line went dead.

The clockmaker gasped and dropped the earpiece. Blood bubbled up from his mouth. He clutched at his abdomen, and more blood gushed from the new wound across his stomach. He collapsed against his chair and crumpled into the seat. He felt a rending and tearing at his back, and realized the worst wound of them all had split every organ below his ribcage.

"Am I to be released?"

And the clockmaker saw him, a figure in tattered robes, his face covered by bandages. The figure floated from the threshold to the clockmaker and reached out a bony, pale hand. When the clockmaker felt his master's touch on his stomach wound, his body went limp. The clockmaker felt a great release, as of a heavy burden being taken from him.

"Thank you, your highness," the clockmaker

murmured. The king withdrew his hand, and at once his robes seemed to knit themselves into repair, turning from a washed-out, nondescript light hue to gleaming, golden silk. The bandages dropped from his face, and the clockmaker at last received his reward—a moment to gaze upon the king's true face.

Tentacles slid from behind reams of silk. Though the creature's mouth was but a lipless, gaping slit in ridged and mottled gray flesh, it warped and moved into an expression of joy and mirth.

You have served me well as my avatar. The clockmaker heard the words in his head, though the creature did not speak aloud. You may rest. I have summoned new actors, new servants, and one will emerge to take your place.

"But I made the clock."

And it is good. It is perfect. It requires no making now, only watching.

The marble spun in the globe frame on its own, unbidden by the hand crank. When it came to rest, a flap opened in front of the clockmaker.

`Theatre`

"Oh, thank goodness," the clockmaker murmured. The king disappeared, leaving his yellow sign carved into the table's surface, a twin of the sign carved into the building's front door. The clockmaker closed his eyes for the last time. As he took a shaky breath, his arm fell against the table, dislodging a cuff button. The clockmaker heard it roll and scuttle against the floor before coming to rest.

The second eye.

He smiled as he died.

***

"911, what's your emergency?"

"I think I've witnessed a kidnapping," Karen said. She couldn't take her eyes off the yellow door. As she stared at it, the compulsion to enter grew stronger. She longed to pull her gaze from it, but feared losing sight of her friends if they should manage to escape.

"Okay, can you describe what happened?"

Karen swallowed. She willed the words to coalesce in her mind to explain the afternoon's events, but everything felt like sludge.

"Two people..." she managed before trailing off. "Door."

"Ma'am, are you in physical danger yourself? What is your location?"

Karen looked around. She knew the address mere moments earlier, but it eluded her. She looked up and down the street. The moon hung overhead, full and hazy with a yellow aura, gauzy and filmy, circling it. A dog howled, low at first, then growing in intensity. A second dog joined it, their voices a few steps apart, forming an accidental harmony. Karen dropped her phone and followed the sound.

"Hello? Ma'am?"

The operator's voice grew fainter and fainter the closer Karen drew to the dogs' howling. She rounded a corner behind the block of brownstones.

A few doors down, she spotted them—two russet-colored dogs, their heads thrown back, baying at the moon.

Or, no, not at the moon.

Between them, a small figure squirmed. Karen stepped closer. A black fence, wrought iron and tipped with pointed spires, separated the dogs' yard from the sidewalk. When she approached, the dogs stopped howling and padded over to the fence. They dropped to their haunches and panted at her, mouths open as if smiling.

"Hey, fellas, what's going on?" Karen looked behind the dogs to see what they'd been howling over.

A whimper in the tall grass. Karen leaned over the fence. "Hello?" she called.

"Help me." A child's face poked through the dark green blades. "Help, please."

"Are you okay?" Karen eyed the fence and tried to determine if she could scale it. The child crawled closer. In its hand it clutched a stuffed animal. Karen saw the child's face was streaked with something dark—mud, perhaps, or was it blood?

No, it's just dirty, out here in the yard.

A tiny, shaking hand held up a scruffy teddy bear. A cloud passed by the moon, and silvery light streamed into the yard. Karen leaned forward.

The bear had no eyes.

"Hey, I'm going to get you help, okay?" Karen's voice shook.

One of the dogs trotted to the side of the fence and nudged at it. Karen looked to that section and saw it was a gate, its latch empty. She reached through the bars and patted the dog. "Good job. Thanks." She lifted the gate latch, and it opened with a loud creak. "Hey, I can get help," she called to the child. "Are you hurt?"

She scanned the yard. The child was nowhere in sight. "Hello?"

The back door of the house opened. Nothing was visible inside but inky darkness.

"Becker? Jo?"

The wind picked up. Karen felt her hair dance around her ears. One of the dogs nudged her hand with its nose, leaving her skin cold and moist.

I shouldn't go in. I shouldn't. Caitlyn knows where we are.

The address finally came to her, but when she patted her pocket, it registered that her phone was gone.

"Guys?"

"You should unmask."

Karen jumped. "What? Who's there?"

"Indeed, it's time."

The voices were close. Karen looked around.

The dogs were gone, and in their place stood Becker and Jo, now wearing long, black robes belted around the waist with rope.

"We have all laid aside disguise but you," Jo said.

"You should unmask," Becker repeated.

"Un... what?" Karen shook her head. "What are you talking about?" She moved to Jo and grasped her by the shoulders. "Jo, snap out of it. What's going on?"

"You wear no mask?" Becker said.

Jo wriggled out of Karen's grip. "No mask?" She trembled and looked at Becker. "No mask!"

Becker dropped to his knees and stared up at the moon. The cowl of his robe fell away from his face. "Not upon us!" he cried. "Not upon us, oh, king!"

Karen spun back around to Jo. "What is—"

From every corner of the small garden sprang the sound of applause. Becker stood back up and clasped hands with Jo. Lights came on, temporarily blinding Karen. She blinked hard, and once her vision adjusted, she saw they were no longer out in a backyard but on a small stage. A circle of three rows of seats sat in a tiny auditorium. Though the applause was thunderous, there was only one audience member.

A man sat in the middle of the second row, clapping slowly over and over as Becker and Jo took bow after bow. His face was in shadow, but he was lean, tall, and his hair stood high, in spiky, crown-like tufts. Backlit, it glowed bright, amphetamine yellow.

"Bravo!" he called. He threw something at the stage, something Karen at first took to be a rose until it hit the floorboards with a sickening wet flop.

She looked at her feet and saw a beating human heart. It pumped and a plume of blood squirted from it. Karen felt a stinging pang in her own chest. She clutched above her left breast and dropped to the floor, pain shooting agony down her arm.

The theatre walls faded. Karen cried out and

squeezed her eyes shut as another wave of pain seized her body. She rolled to her knees and crawled. Gravel bit into the skin of her palms. She opened her eyes to find herself out on the sidewalk in front of the building.

I can't look. It won't still be there. It's gone.

Karen fell to her side, and darkness gripped her for several long moments. She awoke again when a clear mask descended upon her nose and mouth, and she felt a blessed swell of oxygen flow through her lungs. "Hang on, Mrs. Miller. We're almost to the hospital."

"Karen, we're here." Karen couldn't place the voice. A hand grasped hers and clung to it. Another hand stroked her hair.

"Don't try to move. Rest."

"Becker?" It didn't sound like Becker, but Karen couldn't tell who was with her anymore.

It's not real, any of it. I'm having a heart attack. I must've collapsed on the sidewalk outside the building. Everything else was a dream. Oxygen deprivation. Dying.

Karen felt a rush of relief. Hallucinations were logical, if trippy. Medical emergencies could be caught in time. She would be okay.

I need you healthy before you come to me, a new voice said, a languid baritone, a feline purr rumbling under the words. Let them tend you. Come back strong.

The voice wasn't Becker's. Its words tickled and scraped around her brain, sliding amongst synapses and filling all her available senses. Karen imagined bony fingertips lifting her chin, a face in shadow examining her. Something wriggled in the shadows, undulating like a charm-hypnotized serpent swaying to the low, reedy strains of the song of the pungi. She felt a trickle of blood run from both ears and slide, salty and cold, down her cheeks.

The last thing Karen felt before falling into

deep, dreamless sleep was the oxygen mask lifting from her face.

***

White. Fuzzy and white. Rectangles and light, pale and indistinct.

"Everyone was very worried about you."

Karen turned. "Caitlyn." She smiled. "Am I gonna live?"

Caitlyn laughed. "To fight another day," she replied. She waved her phone. "Thank you for telling me where you were. When you didn't show, I called an ambulance. Glad I did." She leaned forward and squeezed Karen's hand. "They caught it right in time."

"Heart attack?"

Caitlyn shook her head. "No, not even," she said. "Your doctor thinks it was a panic attack, but if you'd gotten further stressed, who knows?"

Karen exhaled. "Wow, I'm lucky."

"Well." Caitlyn looked away. "I mean, mostly."

"Mostly?"

Caitlyn leaned forward. The ends of her braids brushed the raised side of Karen's hospital bed, and Karen stared at the braids, as they swung in gentle half-circles. She watched them, almost hypnotized, as Caitlyn uttered the words Karen dreaded but didn't dare ask herself.

"Nobody can find Jo or Becker."

Karen pulled her gaze from Caitlyn's hair to the table beside her bed. A fuzzy yellow teddy bear sat there. "Who left that for me?"

Caitlyn turned and swept it from the table. "I'm not sure." She held it out to Karen. "It's cute, though."

With the toy closer, Karen could tell it had black buttons sewn to its head where its eyes should be.

"Those do make beautiful eyes," Karen murmured. She stroked the buttons and grinned, realizing there was a job opening available for her.

"Why are you smiling?" Caitlyn asked. "I mean, sure, you're going to be okay, but our friends are still missing."

"They're not missing." Information flooded through Karen. The marble clocks. They would show her Becker and Jo and where everyone who'd ever been trapped in the house had gone. "We just need to know how to look."

EASY COME, EASY GO
Steve Sneyd

John's attention was fully occupied juggling the two full glasses, trying not to spill any as he weaved his way between chairs and tables back towards the corner where Cassie was waiting. He didn't even notice Soldier's solid figure completely filling the gap between the next two tables, blocking his way, until he was right on top of him. Best say how he'd enjoyed the man's set before the interval–even though, really, it was a sort of fancy multi-instrumental thing he didn't really go for; fancy for the sake of it, to him, not that he ever knew what to say about music; best handle he'd been able to get on it, imagine free jazz played alternately on a guitar and on an accordion and on a horse's jawbone, or maybe a sheep's, with mumbled scat, like a sort of male Lotte Lenya–but had to say something really, something brief but positive and then get straight past. He didn't want to get involved in a conversation, not with the drinks to carry, and, anyhow, he didn't want to leave Cassie on her own too long–that fragile, helpless look always seemed to attract idiots to come and pester her and he could do without that to deal with again tonight. Anyhow, no real reason to get involved in a chat with the guy, not as if Soldier was a friend, just one of those people you keep seeing around over so many years it makes them acquaintances of sorts, even though you'd never really say you knew them much more than to say, "Hello."

All this flashed through his mind in a fraction of a second, it seemed–his mouth was already opening to speak, but before he could say anything, the face in front of him seemed to shoot forward like a snake's, right up to his, the cold voice hissing straight into his face, "You're too old for Cassie, too cold for her, Mr. Iceman, Mr. Emotional Illiterate. You'll do her harm–leave her alone, you've been told, or you'll be sorted out."

John could feel the rage-glitter come across his eyes, a sort of instant migraine or cataract cracking-windowpane, but, unlike the few previous occasions in his life when it had hit him in that total way, somehow, against the odds, he managed to hold himself back from losing it, losing control, smashing in the face in front of him.

As if from outside himself, looking down from the ceiling, he saw the glass in his right hand start to move, stop abruptly, swaying, so a few drops splashed out onto Soldier's Sun Ra Saturn Tour t-shirt. Then, somehow, John managed a noncommittal nod, a tap of the left-hand glass against his own nose, which sprayed a few more drops, universal symbol for *keep your nose out.*

At the same time, as he moved forward, some automatic program of a lifetime in his mind, which tried to make him say, "Excuse me," was blocked like the urge to vomit. Somehow, he wasn't surprised that the human obstacle moved aside, and Soldier swung away with contemptuous swish of grey pony-tail. Again, habit tried to make John say something—"Cheers," perhaps—and again was blocked as he fought for self-control, for calm. Only a few more steps to go now, and he didn't want his face to show anything by the time he got back to his seat by Cassie.

Feeling as exhausted as if he'd climbed a huge cliff, he put the glasses down on the table, shoving empties aside to make room, slumped down beside her.

"You've gone all white," she said. "Are you okay?"

Of all the times for her to notice something about him! Of all the times... It was so unnatural for her to do that, the one thing he could always be sure with her, all through the few months he'd been with her, it'd been the same—she never paid any attention to things about other people, him or anyone else, that any usual person would. That was one of the great things about her, really, part of what made her so special, okay, it *could* be annoying at times, but most of the time, it made her amazingly peaceful and relaxing to be with, having your mind left in peace to go its own way unquestioned, undisturbed.

She was always so busy reliving being back in her own place, whatever place she used to live in and couldn't and wouldn't get back to, even to visit. It was weird, really, if you thought about it, which John tried hard not to–what was the point when he obviously wasn't going to get any answers?–you couldn't even get sense from her how or why or when she came from, so he'd long since given up asking. She just went on about these pictures that seemed to fill her mind, realer than anything around her in the here-and-now–talk about not living in the moment–it was as if back there was all the quality time she'd ever had and, yet, at the same time, it frightened her witless thinking about it and, yet, she couldn't stop going back, like when you've got a hole in your tooth and your tongue always ends up poking at it, the dark water and body was with you, not even noticing when you went in her. In a way, he wished he could help her switch the whole thing off, but he soon learned he couldn't, couldn't help nor distract her from somewhere outside her own head, to listening to it all going on round and round in her thoughts, and, he had to admit to himself, it was a bit like playing a favourite record over and over, some sort of concept album–you could get addicted to it, and, knowing he didn't need to find anything to say when she was on that track, as she usually was, it made her wonderfully unstressful, somehow, to be with in a relationship.

Only *dammit*, something had made her notice now, so he'd have to say something, when all he wanted was to be quiet for a while, till the last of that almost-overpowering anger ebbed away. He just felt drained by it now, past speaking, and it'd given him instant gut-rot pains, too, he could feel them now–he was noticing things properly again. Have to say something, though, he thought again, but all he could manage was a mumbled "Yeah," and then, as he gulped at the Doom Bar bitter–typical daft real ale name, where did they get 'em?–yeah, he remembered reading it on the beermat, now a soaked dark pool on the table, some sandbank that sank loads of ships in Cornwall somewhere, Wadebridge... Typical weird brewery sense of humour, that... Maybe that's how Cassie got here, he thought irreverently, wrecked in a ship and lost her memory... An idea came to him: "Maybe it's this stuff: odd, musty taste," though it's probably me, he thought, aftertaste of rage in the mouth. "Could be a bit off, or maybe its stale air in here, make anyone a bit dizzy, so many in this one small room, and the air-conditioning not on because the noise'd've spoiled the music, I suppose. You're lucky if it's not affecting you, too."

John felt bitter, then an odd little glow of satisfaction–if he'd managed all that in the way of plausible answer, must've got himself under control again, *excellent anger management, there,* he imagined an instructor saying, and felt himself grin slightly. Cassie didn't respond, presumably satisfied with his answer and heading back into her own memory world, so he let himself glance around.

Soldier was over on the other side of the room now, back with his usual fan club, not looking John's way... Interfering know-all bastard, thinking because he was a local hero-type musician it gave him the right to tell other folk what to do... Still, John thought uneasily, he had to wonder if there was any truth in what the damn mad said: "See ourselves as others see us," all that. Ah, to hell with it, what did it matter what the stupid bighead thought or said? He was only a muso, not a relationship counsellor, what the hell did he know? It wasn't as if Cassie herself had told Soldier to say it, John felt one hundred percent sure of that... Anyhow, how could he be harming Cassie, when he was sure he was no more for her than anything else in this town, which meant totally unreal compared to wherever the damn place was she acted like she really lived in... And why the hell couldn't they just go there, for a weekend or something, even if it was abroad somewhere–you could get anywhere now with these cheap flights, John was sure he could find the cash for a long weekend wherever the hell it was, get it out of her system, compare the facts with these dreams she had of it, probably turn out to be some real dump when you got there, worse even than this rustbelt town. He didn't want to doubt her, but how could she not know where it was or how to get to it? That only happened in those neurotic fairy stories or on TV, whatever, not in *real* life–it wasn't as if she'd been a tiny kid when she left. She was full-grown, that much he did know for sure.

He realised she'd said something, a sort of shrill whisper, not a bit like her usual low, soft tone. He focused back on her, excused inattention with the excuse of something he'd just noticed going on: "Couldn't hear you for the racket that barmaid's making collecting glasses... Say again?"

"Did he say anything about me?"

He knew who she meant, but instinctively stalled: "Who?"

"Soldier–did he say anything about me?"

"No," John said automatically.

"What did he say to you, then?"

"Not much."

"I want to know!"

The curiosity about something like this was as out-of-character for her as noticing his rage pallor a few minutes ago. But then, there was something else he'd been trying not to think about–not that it bothered him, really, never had... But it was a fact, and it obviously explained Soldier feeling he'd a right to stick his beak in, and now Cassie asking questions... He knew, because everyone knew, that back a while, Cassie'd been with Soldier–for a long time, too, from what people said, several years, anyhow. In fact, from the stories John'd heard–always plenty of people glad to try to stir up trouble, telling you about the past of anyone you were seen with–Soldier'd been the first to have her when she first turned up round here. All that mystery-woman-out-of-nowhere business had got her known right from the start, perhaps that's why Soldier'd picked her out, suited his image to have someone by his side everyone was curious about, like he was the only one had solved the puzzle–not that he had, John was sure. Maybe frustration at that was why he'd let her go. Yeah, thinking about it, okay, the years blur, but must be a good long time now since they were together; he'd never known Cassie mention him, not that she ever talked about anyone in *this* town, anyhow. But maybe neither'd really cut the mind ties, that could happen... Although, if he himself and Cassie split, he doubted she'd even notice, let alone remember him a week later–none of which speculating was getting her question answered...

"Tell you after the next lot finish," he said, "must be about to start: look, there's someone getting up to the front, must be them," relieved to have a good excuse to stall for time to think out what, if anything, he should let her know about what'd been said to him. A massive figure slowly ascended the temporary low stage at the end of the room–now then, what was this act supposed to be? He glanced at the already beer-stained programme flyer: **Under The Rainbow – Mixed Media Night** – etc, etc, etc... There was "living in the past," real '60s that, mixed media–who was next... **Soldier Premiers Composition Death's Lovehandles**–Soldier... Talk about an obvious nickname, out of date, too. He'd bet it had been twenty years since, according to the usual tale, he'd been a regular army band muso, still, you had to admit it's a name that stuck in your mind, clever really... Wonder what his real name was? Never heard anyone call him anything else. *Pretentious sod!* he thought, and then, with conscious effort, pushed the anger aside before it could take a grip again; forget it, nothing worse than brooding on it, that really would be giving Soldier a victory, taking it seriously. Now then, he'd been on right before the interval that'd just finished–when *that'd* happened–*forget it!* he told himself firmly. So, next on should be... Huh, typical, no info: trust the organisers trying to sound intriguing when it just meant they hadn't filled a gap when they hit the deadline to do the prog; wonder who they'd come up with... He tapped his finger on the place to draw Cassie's attention to it, prepared to make a joke, but she was staring fixedly past him at the performer. So John looked too, for the first time taking the figure in properly, turning now to face the audience.

Odd, really... Funny, hadn't noticed him coming into the room before he'd gone up to the stage, or in the room before then, either, come to that–must've put his stage gear on outside, in the bog, whatever, but would've thought he'd've spotted someone so conspicuous, unusual, though there'd been the Soldier business, of course: after all, that'd been enough to give anyone tunnel-vision.

Yet, this one wasn't easy to miss. Even among this fringe arty-wannabe lot, he stood out a mile: huge in size, though the loose outfit probably made him look bulkier even than he, presumably, was... Weird, too, the costume–kind of a cloak suit'd be best way to describe it, what you could see of it for tatty, ragged yellow strips hanging down all over its surface. Perhaps he'd been tearing up old *Yellow Pages* and gluing 'em on, sort of thing that sort of clever act did, make themselves look different on the cheap... Odd face, too, oversimplified looking, like a kid's drawing of a man, just blobs for eyes, nose, mouth, no real sense of detail, badly-applied or too-much theatre makeup, presumably, and the improvised spotlight setup making it even harder to see clearly with its crude glare–could be that making the face look so weirdly, sickly, yellowy too, reflecting up off the clobber.

For what seemed like ages, the figure simply stood and stared out at the audience... Muttered conversations ended, silence became total. John glanced again at the flyer–**Mystery Guest**–huh, that told you sweet-fanny-all! He glanced again at Cassie–then stared in shock. She was the one who didn't look so good now. A huge drop of sweat hung at the corner of her mouth, by the lip-piercing. Lucky it's rust-proof metal, he thought irrelevantly. He put an arm around her, felt her tense and rigid as metal herself.

"Are *you* okay?" he whispered.

She ignored his question, sitting stiffly as if paralysed. Then sound came from her lips, sound repeated so softly he had to put his ear nearly to her mouth to hear her say: "Home... He came here, too..."

No point in asking her what she meant, she wouldn't be able to explain, he was sure–she never would, nor could. He squeezed her, trying to be comforting, although her back remained like a stiff board.

Still, the figure on the stage did nothing but stare, a gaze that seemed to pierce straight into John's eyes. He's doing that trick of looking at the Fire Exit sign at the back, that way everyone in the whole audience thinks you're looking at them personally, real pseud's crap trick... Typical, organisers booked what must be the worst mime artist ever.

But trying to mock didn't work, didn't help him shake off the penetrating impact of the figure. He made himself look away, look at Cassie, still rigid next to him. She looked worse now, awful, face squeezed somehow–he couldn't think how else to describe it–like an invisible sculptor squashing it together. She'd a slim, even narrowish face, anyhow, the bunched dark hair always seeming to compress it into the smallest space possible, like a little lake between high, black banks, but now it looked sharp and thin like a razorblade, and her neck muscles were so knotted with tension they seemed to stand out in lumps, her back knotted, too, against his arm. And her mouth was twisted inwards, as if it were biting itself to force back a scream. Better get her out of here quick, before she lost it, had a fit or something.

"Come on, let's go, I've had enough of this." She didn't respond at all. He tried again: "Cassie, Cass, come on, let's get out of here, *now!*"

Nothing, still no response. He was about to stand up, pull her up from her seat. But somehow, he couldn't move either, even his arm out from behind her, or his other arm to lever himself up. That was when he started to feel totally claustrophobic. His chest felt painfully tight, as if it were shrinking inwards–oh, chest pains–but with a heart attack, you taste metal, don't you, and he couldn't.

There was a kind of instant relief, then, in recognising a familiar sensation, even though it was one he'd only ever experienced a tiny handful of times: near crushed once way back, stood at a footie on a steeply-pitched stand and the crowd started swaying, pushing you against a crush barrier; then on a crowded London underground rush hour platform when he thought he'd be pushed off under a train; worst of all, on a tiny rural minibus-thing he'd got stuck between two hugely-fat women coming back from market day in town with masses of shopping, and he'd had to dive out at the next stop, middle-of-nowhere, gasping for air–it was like that, a real whammo of an anxiety state. Never mind Cassie if she wouldn't shift, he'd have to get out of here himself, right away–he'd have to.

But still, he couldn't seem to move at all anyhow–his legs wouldn't obey, glued to the floor, somehow.

And still, the figure on the stage remained unmoving, utterly still, his eyes never seeming to move from John.

Then, abruptly, across the room, there was a sudden, loud distraction. Who was it? Could've known, Soldier, having to be centre-of-attention again. Shouting at the top of his voice: "Bastard's trying to make a fool of us! Get him off the stage! Come on!" Then the musician leapt to his feet, pushed those around him out of the way, surged forward to within touching distance of the figure looming above him. Then he stopped utterly still in his tracks, as if suddenly aware that no one had followed his lead, that he stood utterly alone, just a foot or so from the forest of yellow, strips as unmoving as their wearer. Stopped, and then, suddenly, clutching at his chest, toppled forward to the floor.

It took a few seconds, as if everyone at first thought it was part of the act, a stooge planted in the audience to enthral the audience–and then action verging on panic set in, people shouting for the Ambulance Service on their mobiles, folk grappling at the slumped figure: "Put him on his side!" "Recovery position!"–"Heart massage!"–"Get his tongue free!"–"I can do Heimlich, get out of the way!" A babble of crosscutting voices.

Suddenly, John found it was possible to move again. He looked at Cassie: she was still staring fixedly, but now at empty space, no figure now on the stage. Gone as undetectably as he'd come while everyone's eyes were on Soldier's fall.

He pulled at her, somehow got her to her feet. "Come on! We need some air."

"He..."

"Nothing we can do, love, only get in the way... I

heard somebody say an ambulance is on its way, and there's someone who knows first aid with him now, doing what can be done... Come on, let's get out and make some room in here." Instinctively, he lifted his drink, gulped the last, always taught don't waste it—only in crime films do they always leave half their drink—dropped it back on the nearest flat surface without even looking to see if it had landed safely. All the while, he was push-pulling her—limp, now, rather than rigid—towards the fire-door, much nearer than going through the main bar area, and anyway, he didn't want people looking at her, the state she was in, not fair, idiots always saying "What's up with her?" and all that.

She was scarcely walking, her feet dragging on the ground, muttering unstoppably, as if compulsively, but so softly he couldn't make any sense of it. Still moving her forward as best he could, he bent his head and just managed to make out words.

"It was supposed to be you, to get rid of what was keeping me here, but I managed to change things, I got him to take Soldier, instead. It's all my fault!" And then a kind of silent, dry sobbing.

"You'll be alright in a minute," he said, pushing the fire door bar, hoping like mad that it'd open, it should, but half these damn places kept 'em locked, law or no law. But it opened okay, if creakily, and they were out into the pub yard. He started to try suggesting other places to go for the rest of the evening, anywhere but here, wanting to get somewhere where she could sit down, and he could find out what that'd all been about. But she obviously wasn't listening. Her face was fixed again, staring. He followed the direction of her eyes.

The long pub yard sloped, sure, always had, up towards the arch on the main road. But now, somehow, it seemed to tilt straight up to the sky, like a cliff. And right up there, where the arch now seemed to be filled with stars, even hung among stars, sat behind a huge hunter's moon, in fact–and *that* was crazy, it was a filthy, cloudy night, anyhow, and even at the best of times, with all the streetlights and security lights and ad signs and whatever, there was always such a glow you never saw the stars at all from town, and here they were glittering in millions, none of this made sense, none of it–right at the top, the yellow figure stood, hung, floated–John couldn't make out which, as if his eyes were being pulled, distorted, till nothing was where or what it should be.

The figure beckoned.

Cassie muttered again. Again, John bent his head, struggled to make out her words: "Got to go home."

He pulled at her arm, tried to hold onto her, but all at once she seemed to have immense strength, incredible for such a small woman, little more than child-size, really, throwing his grip off as if it were nothing, easy as tearing paper. She began to move away, up the yard, like a compelled person, a sleepwalker, up against gravity, up above him, towards the down-staring figure that seemed to grow even taller as he watched helplessly, to begin to even blot out that impossible, star-filled arch of sky.

John tried desperately to move after Cassie, but it was like having nails through his feet–he couldn't move, just stood as if paralysed, as she slowly drew nearer to the vast figure. He tried, at least, to shout after her: "Come back, Cassie! Come back! Everything will be alright, you'll see!" but words wouldn't come out, as if a hand was choking tight around his throat.

"Mine... Time to come home now, Cassilda," he didn't so much hear the words as feel them sliced into air, not meant for him, only her, but overheard somehow, by some extra inside ear John didn't know he had, that perhaps, somehow, she'd made him grow.

And then he seemed to see the cloak of yellow open like a gate and take her in, then reclose around her, swallow her completely. She was gone utterly from view, and then there was nothing there at all, the swell of yellow vanished, too, and the dark arch was left bare of anything but its own arc of blackness that had taken them.

Then perspective was back to normal–the ground was in its proper place under the old, dull glow of town night sky, and, slowly, so slowly, an ambulance inched through the gap of the arch and down the yard. Instinctively, John backed against the wall to let it pass downwards towards the pub's main door, knowing perfectly, as if the words were written on the vehicle's side so he could read them as it crawled by, that it was much too late... Soldier was dead.

And Cassie was gone. Nothing made sense anymore.

And then, suddenly, something in him shrugged acceptingly. Nothing to be done about any of it, after all. No one'd believe him if he told 'em what'd happened, so he'd have to keep it to himself. Learn to live with it. Well, Soldier'd called him Mr. Iceman. Maybe he'd been right. So, what would Mr. Iceman do under the circumstances? Go for another drink, he supposed. Not here, though–anywhere but here.

As he walked out onto the road, not even trying to think which way to turn, leaving it to his feet to decide which way to go, which pub it'd be, he felt an odd, wry grin touch his mouth: well, she'd got what she wanted. They always said *never go back*. For Cassie, at least, he hoped that warning was wrong, that things'd be good, perfect... Better than this dump, anyhow. Well, that hope was just all he had left of her now, he thought. Then, he found he was heading left, towards The Wayfarer's Arms.

THE COLOUR OF DEATH
Dirk Holland

"All things have a beginning and an end," he read, "and that beginning is in the blazing womb that men have named Azazoth and that end is in the frozen death that bears the name of Hastur."

"Not your common-or-garden occultism," commented Reynolds. De Payens nodded his agreement. The words had been written some two centuries past and, yet, seemed to be referring to the scientific theories of the Big Bang and the heat death of the Universe. Elsewhere in the tome, Azazoth seemed to be identified with the nuclear reaction and Hastur with entropy, concepts seemingly out of place in such a text.

De Payens flicked a few more pages and continued to read: "And, The Last King is come to The City and to claim His Throne, bringing an end to The Eternal War that has engulfed the Dark Stars above The City for a million years: And the crustacean races of Aldebaran and the winged races of the Hyades bowed to The King in His triumph: And The King alone was victorious as all the Universe grew still: And even the Byakhee ceased to flap for all had become still and dead and silent as the grave."

"You know what this means?" asked Reynolds. "It's describing an interstellar war: a war between aliens... recorded in an early 19th century text. How can they have known of it? How could they be aware?"

***

De Payens had died a few days after that conversation. The text that had been in his possession had disappeared. Their masters had been displeased at that and demanded answers. Investigators had no answers to give.

Reynolds had his suspicions, but kept them to

himself. He had read in the texts of a secret Brotherhood whose colour was the colour of death: a secret empire that stretched across the world and fought an unending conflict against the crustaceans of Aldebaran. The text also revealed that they concealed the secrets revealed therein. "The Brotherhood are recognised by a secret sign and, yet, never are revealed nor the natures of their masters and foes."

He had begun to see the colour yellow everywhere, from the colour of the sunflowers at the florists he walked past every day to the cars of that colour that suddenly seemed to predominate the streets about him. Yellowed teeth grinned in the mouth of a dosser, who demanded cash, yellowed nicotine fingers reaching out towards him. Turning away, the yellow scarf of a young lady whipped across his face. Shrieking, Reynolds stumbled away through the crowds of yellow-suited passersby.

The colour of death seemed to envelope him.

***

Reynolds had been found dead: suicide was the verdict returned. He had clambered into a yellow dumpster and seemingly immolated himself, dying in a blaze of yellow flame. His masters were not best pleased.

A bouquet of yellow roses was sent to his funeral. No one ever knew who sent them.

CHAMBERSWORLD
Five Snapshots by Steve Sneyd

I
blithe four dance brick road
don't won't see same yellow how
king ahead soils away

II
as benbow black spot
no escape fate such each moves
seeks to return to
rejoin symbiote living
robe's ragdangle slurpsuckle

III
clock-back brown letter
wodge unopened tries fails to
frighten more'n how
book hid there drowns all ticktock
by sweet flyhum song "Read Me"

IV
twin walls upthrust fat
towers: off highest peers past
moon at Other Earth

V
white face black holes pierce;
sealed-gash mouth maybe sewn-up
asylum-seeker's
protest but instead let's hope
is fun hockey mask comes off

ACES AND KINGS
David M. Hoenig

"...'And he will go on before the Lord in the spirit and power of Elijah, to turn the hearts of the parents to their children and the disobedient to the wisdom of the righteous—to make ready a people prepared for the Lord.'" Jedediah Stowe closed his book and looked at the townsfolk assembled before him around the freshly filled grave on Bone Hill. They mostly shuffled a bit and looked at their feet in response. "Luke wrote them words as out of the mouth of the Angel Gabriel to Zecharia," he went on in a firm voice which carried in the still of the place. "But mark me well: they is as true today as ever they was when they was spoke in the Holy Temple in Jerusalem!"

"Alright, Preacher. You had your say," said a tall, lanky man with his hat in his hands and the calm air of command. "Best we all be getting back into town afore it gets too late."

Jedediah held his book to his chest with his left hand, just underneath the hanging pendant of the man-Jesus, and pointed with his right at the man who had interrupted him. "But you forget, Sheriff Cosy, what Zecharia prophesied when he were filled with the spirit of the Lord! 'He has raised up a horn of salvation' he says, 'salvation from our enemies and from the hand of all who hate us—to show mercy to our ancestors and to remember His holy covenant, the oath He swore to our father Abraham!'"

The people in the cemetery muttered uneasily. Over their sound, Cosy spoke musingly. "We'll have no more talk about 'salvation from our enemies' this night, Jedediah: it's getting late and it's well past dark. Just say the words to usher poor Jesse Anderson on his way and let's finish with this."

The preacher's jaw clenched tightly enough that muscles bunched in his cheek. He turned back to the waiting folk who were now looking up at the sky, at him, and everywhere all at once. "Lord," he barked suddenly, snapping several to guilty attention. "We commend the spirit of this here Jesse Anderson to Thee. Shower him in Thy love, and see him to his eternal reward as Thy loyal servant. Amen."

A rustle of "Amens" followed, and then everyone began to break up into singles and small groups who started back down the hill, whispering to one another.

Jedediah moved to stand near the sheriff as people filed out of the cemetery. "Didn't think you was afraid of the dark, Eric," he said sullenly.

"Only babes and idiots ain't afraid of it, Jedediah." The sheriff looked away as he put his hat back on. They stood side by side, watching folk leave until just the two of them were standing by the grave. When he spoke again, it was in an angrier voice. "And only an idiot would try to use a man's death to rile up his flock into some kind of foolish mood!" he hissed. "All it'll do is earn poor Jesse here a bunch of company and not much else!"

Jedediah pitched his voice to that of the sheriff's. "It ain't enough that the world's gone mad? I mean, take this here Bible," and he thumped the book in his hands. "'And God said, Let there be lights in the firmament of the heaven to divide the day from the night; and let them be for signs, and for seasons, and for days, and years; And let them be for lights in the firmament of the heaven to give light upon the earth: and it was so. And God made two great lights; the greater light to rule the day, and the lesser light to rule the night: He made the stars also,'" he quoted hotly. "It don't be saying nothing about *two* suns in the sky, do it?!"

"You know it don't..." Cosy began, and struck a match.

"Nor nothing about *moons*!" Jedediah interrupted, stressing the plural. "Nor black stars which shine with unholy light in the heavenly firmament!"

"And?"

"'And?' You can honestly stand there and tell me we ain't damned to some oblivion, or some kind of Hell on Earth?"

"Ain't hot enough for Hell, Preacher," Cosy said, and lit his pipe and drew on it. He turned to follow the rest down Bone Hill.

"'And you, my child, will be called a prophet of the Most High; for you will go on before the Lord to prepare the way for Him, to give His people the knowledge of salvation through the forgiveness of their sins,'" the preacher quoted, calling after him. "You hear that, 'Cozy' Eric Cosy? The Lord commands His prophet onto the path to prepare the way for Him by giving His people the knowledge of salvation! That's me, Sheriff. I am the one to lead the Lord's folk to salvation and to the Holy Land!"

Cosy stopped, shifted the pipe to the corner of his mouth and turned his head back up Bone Hill to see the wild-haired preacher backlit by two gibbous moons. "Ain't no salvation in the town of Kingdom Come, Jedediah! Ain't nothing holy 'bout this here crazy land, what with the city of the Yeller King a day's ride thataway." He jerked his thumb over his left shoulder. "And while you're easily full of enough shit to be a preacher, you sure as hell ain't no prophet. Best you get on back to town afore the dancing masks make it out this far, unless you'll be wanting to ask the Lord personal-like about why there's double the suns and seven times the moons he set in the sky, ya bastard." He resumed his methodical way down, satisfied when he heard Jedediah's quick, scurrying steps pass him on the slope about twenty yards to his left.

***

At the bottom of Bone Hill, Cosy turned right, and went past the sign at the edge of town which read:

<pre>
KINGDOM COME,
WYOMING
</pre>

He grimaced and shook his head, pipe in the corner of his mouth. *Weren't Wyoming anymore,* he thought. *If it ever was.* But the oldest written documents kept at the courthouse were pretty clear on the subject, he was forced to admit. Back in his grandfather's day it must've been: he'd seen the yellowed newspapers from that era, even read them. Once a part of Wyoming and the "US of A," everything had changed one fateful day in 1878.

Just how the Shift happened had been the subject of much speculation ever since, recorded by the town's inhabitants. *And almost certainly a shit-ton of Hell-fire and Damnation preaching.* About the only sure thing had been the solar eclipse of July 29th of that year, and multiple reports about a "hot wind which knifed through the streets during the time of darkness, setting the Mercantile's front porch ablaze."

Newspapers from Laramie had even reported the presence of celebrities in Rawlins about twenty miles south of Kingdom Come, who'd arrived ten days in advance of the event: "Professor Thomas Edison and the Draper party of scientists..."

Cosy's thoughts were interrupted. "Evening, Sheriff," said an older man from his right. Thomas Reynolds was sweeping off the porch of his shop, dressed in his usual brown vest over a white shirt.

"Evening, Tom," Cosy acknowledged with a wave.

"How was Jesse's send-off?"

"The usual, pretty much."

"Leastways his family's all gone already. I just feel bad for the girl," Tom said.

"Yep," he said around the stem of his pipe. "It's a damn shame about that." Cosy walked over and Tom came down the stairs to meet him. "Smoke?" he asked.

"Don't mind if I do, thanks," the man said, leaning companionably against the wooden railing there.

The sheriff took out a slip of paper and handed it over, then spread a pinch of his tobacco on it. Tom lifted it to his mouth and licked it smoothly, folding it over and sticking the end in his mouth. Cosy took his pipe out of his mouth and held the smoldering bowl out, and the older man lit his cigarette from it and took a long inhale.

"You know anything about what Jesse was up to t'other night, eh, Tom?" the sheriff asked. "What it was made him risk riding out, 'specially out where the masks gather and do their crazy?'

"Nope. But you know how some of the young'uns get, right? All kinds of twitchy and itchy, and they don't know for themselves how dangerous it is out there."

"Just seems a waste, is all," Cosy said. "Fayette Reese is a pretty thing, ready to bear. They made a good pair."

"True that. Go back in both families to the Shift and beyond, and there was never any mixing. Would've been good for a whole bunch of healthy young'uns. Damn shame. Was she there for the burying?"

"No. Fine thing, too, considering that Jedediah brought out a bit of his fire and brimstone to toss around instead of sticking to the Lordly goodbyes he ought to. Who knows what foolishness would have come to pass then?'

They smoked in companionable silence for a few minutes. Then the sheriff spoke around his pipe. "Say, Tom?"

"Yep?"

"How's the numbers looking lately?"

The older man put his left hand into the pocket of his vest and tapped out ash to the ground as he thought about it a moment. "We're holding our own on wheat and corn, mostly, and the town ladies are canning and jarring all the fruit and vegetables we're not eating now... I'd say we're ahead on those. But the cattle are tossing more strangeness among the calves, and there was a foal born with his skull still open just the other day."

"How far behind are we?" Cosy tried not to show too much concern.

"It's more misses than hits these last few. And the damn animals know they're throwing strange seed too, Eric."

"How d'you mean?"

"Well, that foal I mentioned? It was trying to stand up and the mare kept her distance from it, eyes wide. Then the stallion came over, reared up and came down with his hooves and crushed its head in. Like it knew how wrong it was."

Cosy nodded, expression grim. "More of the same."

"More of the same," Tom agreed. "You heading to Jesse's wake?"

"Yep."

"You going to celebrate that young man's life, or try to keep trouble to a minimum?"

"A little of both, I guess."

There was a long shared look between them, as if there was much more which could be said, only what was the point of saying it? "Well. Luck, Sheriff."

"Have a good night, Tom, and thanks," Cosy said, and tapped out his spent pipe against the heel of his boot. He put it away in his poke, and went on into town as Thomas Reynolds went back to sweeping his porch.

***

The Running Shadows Rest was already on the raucous side when Cosy reached it, spilling light, music, and loud voices out into the street through the worn batwings. He stopped and listened for a moment, picking out much of the usual: curses, squeals, laughter. Something didn't sound right, however, and he had to consider it for a moment, one foot on the saloon's lowest step.

Then he had it–the piano sounded rushed, almost frantic, like it was trying to keep up with the forced hilarity of the party but was falling behind. *Golden Rudy must be messed up tonight. Not sure I blame him that much.* He went up the stairs, spurs clicking against the old wood, and the sound mashed him in the face as he peered over the batwings before entering. It had a chewy flavor to it, like stale beer and smoke and desperation, if those things all together had some kind of flavor, anyway. He could see much of the usual late night crowd, plus a few range-riders who'd worked with Jesse Anderson out on the plains.

There was a momentary hitch in the music when he entered, and the room fell silent as dozens of conversations all came to a pause at the same time as people looked his way. All but one.

"...And we should be ridin' out tonight and slaughterin' them masks!" shrilled a young woman's voice to a circle of young men. "Takin' my Jesse should be a killin' offense!" she finished, and realized only then how her voice had carried. Fayette Reese's head jerked a little in surprise, but she looked around defiantly at the saloon crowd.

Cosy watched the young men in her circle eyeing her with excitement and anger in their faces, drinking in her words along with the whiskey in their glasses. "Hell yeah!" Virge Phillips yelled from within that group. "Let's kill us some masks, 'stead of them taking us!" Other voices joined in. A quick look around the rest of the room showed most folk looking down, or at each other, or anywhere they could which wasn't at Fayette and her boys.

His heart sank somewhat when he met the gaze of the Stranger, standing on the upper landing and leaning against the banister rail, watching the scene below. He cleared his throat loudly and addressed the room. "That's enough of that kind of talk, Virge. And that goes for you too, Miles Mullery, and you, Amos Benedict. We're here today to celebrate the life of a young man departed afore his time, not work up plans to get more of this town's lifeblood soaked into the ground!"

Low-voiced mutters of agreement answered him from around the saloon's main room. He glanced up at the Stranger who had not altered his position at all, except to raise his hands to soundlessly clap. A flicker of movement caught his attention, and he saw Fayette glance up to the balcony to see who he'd been looking at, and then her flushed face went stark white. Cosy was moving her way before he even realized what he was doing.

He got there just as she grabbed for the revolver on Miles' right thigh, and he clapped his hand onto hers, holding it there. Miles jerked back, shocked at the sudden contact, and the gun slipped out of the holster and clattered to the floor.

"Don't you dare touch me, Cozy Eric!" Fayette hissed at him.

"Now, just calm down a second, Miss Reese..." he began.

The girl brought her other hand around with the speed of a striking snake, and shrieked as she raked her nails across his cheek. He let go of her hand and lurched backwards, stumbling into someone who grabbed him and kept him from falling.

"Gotcha, Sheriff," said a familiar voice from behind him.

A quick glance showed the homely, gap-toothed, and freckled face of one of his deputies, Sullivan Overcash. Cosy got his balance back, and stepped deliberately forward back into the group of riders around the girl. Fayette Reese backed away a step, and he put his foot down firmly on the gun on the floor before putting his hand up to his face. His fingers came away bloody. "Now that is quite enough of that."

"It isn't quite enough of anything, you bastard!" she cried at him, and then her face flushed red again and the tears began to fall to the dusty floorboards below.

"Deputy Chatterton?" Cosy called out in the direction of the bar without taking his eyes off the hot-headed group in front of him. He felt the crowd around him shift, almost uneasily, though he didn't look away from the weeping girl for an instant. Someone pressed a cloth into his hand.

"There you go, Sheriff," said Overcash from his left side.

"Thanks, Sully."

He held it to his cheek and saw the boys around Fayette back off from a woman with chestnut brown hair under a tan Stetson, wearing a tan duster over a chambray shirt, and soft, black leather pants which looked to have been poured onto her legs. She had a double tie-down rig with pearl-handled Colts.

"Alright now," Deputy Chatterton said to the group around the girl as she shouldered her way in. They gave ground. She grabbed Fayette around the upper arm. "Let's go take this upstairs, girlie, and have us a little set-to."

"But Allie..." the girl began hotly.

"Don't you dare 'But Allie!' me, Fayette Reese: I ain't in the fucking mind for that shit." She flicked the barest glance up to the balcony before stepping in against the girl. "You already done said too fucking much as it is."

She pushed the girl in front of her towards the

stairs. Virge Phillips looked like he wanted to move to her, but Cosy reached out and tapped him on the shoulder. "Let her go, Virge, she'll be fine with Allie." The boy looked at him. "'Sides," Cosy continued. "We got man-work down here."

"What's that, Sheriff?" asked Miles Mullery in a surly way.

Cosy bent down and picked up the young man's shooter, flipped it around and offered it to him by the grip. "We'd best be drinking and wishing Jesse a safe trip to Paradise."

"But Sheriff!" Miles protested.

"Later for that," Cosy whispered to him. "I want to talk to all you boys tonight, only not right now." He gave a minute shake of his head towards the upper landing. "Who's got a tale to tell about our boy?" he said in a more normal volume.

Sully Overcash stepped up. "I remember this one time when Jesse D. was maybe ten, and he done stole his father's mustang and took it for a joyride." He looked around, an infectious grin on his face. "Only he never shortened the stirrups, so he was riding with one foot in and couldn't get his other foot in, and the horse tossed him into that huge cactus out the back end of town..."

Cosy clapped him on the shoulder and motioned to Happy Pete behind the bar, who was only too glad to bring out a tray of glasses and a fresh bottle of hooch. He left the group as someone else began a story, and made his way over to the piano where Rudolf Golden Eichelbeck sat at his instrument with a nervy, distracted expression on his face. The saloon slowly got noisy again, and the toasts to Jesse Anderson began, even without the music.

"Rudy?" he asked, laying a hand on the pianist's shoulder.

The blond-haired man jerked, eyes wide like frightened wounds in his pale face. "Wha...? Oh, dear

God, it's you, Sheriff."

"You alright? What's got into you tonight?"

"It's him." A slow pan of the head, filled with obvious dread, to fix on the Stranger above.

"He's here lotsa nights, Rudy. I ain't ever seen you so spooked."

"It's his mask."

Cosy looked up at the visitor they called the Stranger. "He ain't wearing a mask, fella."

"That's what he said."

"So?"

Rudolph Eichelbeck put his face in his hands, and his back began to shake as he sobbed his distress, quiet-like.

"Shee-it." Cosy put his hand on Eichelbeck's back and sat down next to him. "I need you, fella."

The pianist turned his head to look at the sheriff. His eyes were now red and wet, and still very wide. "For what?"

"I need me Golden Rudy to start tickling them ivories like only he can. We got us a bunch of hot, young tempers what need cooling down, and the drink's just gonna push that off a bit unless they blow off the head of steam they're building up. Start playing something happy, for pity's sake, okay? Something light, like."

Eichelbeck wiped his eyes and sniffled. "My heart isn't in it, Sheriff, but I'll try. For you."

Cosy put a warm smile on his face, nearly fatherly, and he hugged the pianist around his shoulder. "I know you will, Golden Rudy. No fear." He met the Stranger's steady gaze, saw his look acknowledged, and stood up from the piano bench. He walked to the stairs at his slow, measured pace, then up to the landing at the top. The music started up again, and a rousing cheer brought the noise level inside the saloon back up to something like normal as he approached the Stranger. He took in the pale face, the glittering green eyes with almost no white showing, and the milky hair hanging limply and loose to frame his angular features.

Up close, tonight the Stranger wore something similar to a preacher's frock coat, but it was done up of more than a dozen mismatched patches of leather, from smooth, to scaled, to furred. It was almost dizzying, catching the eye the exact same way that a dead varmint squirming with maggots might. Or maybe that was the yellow symbol hanging from a chain mid-way down the coat. "Whyn't you and me take a walk outside?" Cosy asked him, sour saliva flooding his mouth.

"All things have their time," the Stranger said agreeably, and held out his open hand, palm up, as if inviting the sheriff to lead.

***

Outside on the streets, Cosy and the Stranger walked side by side beneath the starry sky. The only moon up now had sunk below the crest of Bone Hill, and the heavens were clear, bright, and hard-edged.

"So, I don't want you to think that those young'uns back there was doing anything but voicing some frustration and grief," Cosy said.

"Cassilda gave voice to song when last came the Yellow King to Carcosa," the Stranger said, companionably enough.

"I ain't rightly sure what you mean, but I take it you're no stranger to the rash impetuousness of those without the years to know better."

The Stranger gave nothing in reply but a smile, his teeth white in the darkness.

"You've been coming to us since the Shift, and my father, Lord rest him, wrote that you never really came out and said anything head on. He thought we had to take things you said in the context of where you're from," Cosy said. "But none of us have ever been to your Carcosa, eh? All we see are you here, and them masks out there."

"Camilla's agonized scream yet haunts the docks of the city, recurring even as the twin suns daily seek their tortured beds in the Lake of Hali," came the reply. "And yet the masks came off then. At least, off all who mattered, when the scalloped, tattered cloak brushed the rocks of the docks of fair Carcosa, and yellow was all that mattered to the scattered."

"Ah, yes!" Cosy exclaimed, finding at least a thread to try and follow. "I been meaning to ask you about them masks you mentioned. Why do they come out so far from your city at night?"

"Midnight sounds from the spires of the fog-wrapped city, carrying even over the rapture of Devotions to Hastur, finally echoing in the cloudy depths of Demhe."

"Riiiight," Cosy muttered. "I don't think we're on the same page here."

"We are not even on the same planet," echoed the Stranger.

The sheriff stopped, expression of shock on his face, even as his companion continued walking a few steps ahead. "Did you just actually answer my question?"

The Stranger also stopped, then turned back to regard Cosy with a considered look on his pallid features. "The King cannot rest until he has seized the minds of men and controlled even their unborn thoughts. And though he may scorn the diadem, Yhtill will no longer be hidden beneath the wings of the King's raiment."

"Right, that's what I thought you meant." Cosy rubbed his eyes. "Goodnight there, Stranger. Go with whatever god you call yours." He turned back towards the saloon.

The Stranger said nothing. Had Cosy glanced

back at him over his shoulder, it wouldn't have been obvious if he was even aware of the sheriff walking away.

***

Back at the Running Shadows, the noise filtering to the streets was less, like the angry young'un crowd might've passed out already and left just the dead-drunk drinkers and the equally serious gamblers to keep the party going. Rudy'd either gone to bed or taken a break, and the piano was silent. Cosy looked up at the sky, calculating how much of the night was done, how soon the twin suns would stagger their un-Biblical way into the firmament. *Shee-it, Eric, get ahold of yourself! You know that preacher's only got one set of words to use, he just twists 'em to make his hold over folk stronger. Don't be so fucking skittish all of a sudden; there's work to be done!* He checked the horizon out the front end of town past Bone Hill, and saw the quick moving sixth-moon skirting the horizon.

More'n half way to morning already. He went up the stairs and into the Rest.

And into a scene that would haunt him 'til the day he died.

He jerked to a stop just inside the batwings. At first his mind couldn't make sense of it all, like he was seeing the scene in the saloon reflected over his shoulder through the spiderweb-cracked mirror behind the bar. "Fuck," he breathed.

The place was mostly empty, as if the usual crowd of sinners had been blown away by the sinning going on right then. Cosy's gut clenched when he saw Sullivan Overcash pinned to the bar front by a large Bowie knife stuck through each palm, his head slumped forward over another one brutally jutting out from the center of his chest. Pools of blood like there'd be no end to 'em were under him, under his outstretched arms, and his eyes were wide open, showing the horror he'd died under. "Sully!" Cosy cried, like he was feeling the knife in his own chest. "What've you hot-headed bastards done?" he demanded, his hand dropping like lightning to his own rig.

Standing to one side, bottles in their off-hands, big irons in their rights, were Virge Phillips and Amos Benedict, and fast as Cosy was, they already had them pointed blank at his chest before he'd cleared leather. "Evenin', Sheriff," said Virge in a manic tone.

"Fuck yeah, evenin', ya sorry bastard," Amos added with a lopsided grin.

"Hand away from your Colt, unless you be wantin' what Overcash got!" Virge warned.

Cosy slowly extended the fingers of his right hand outward so he wasn't gripping anything, then raised both hands over his head. His eyes were shiny with unshed tears for Sully, and yet his tired and bludgeoned mind only then took in another bit of horror over near the piano. What had looked like a lumpy bundle of leather on the floor was moving, and as he focused on it, he realized it was two people, one on top of the other. Miles Mullery had Allie Chatterton down on her face and knees, Stetson gone, face twisted to the door side. She was gagged, her nose bloody and with blackened eyes. He saw her hands roped behind her back, and Muller was moving up and down, hips thrusting... "Oh, dear Lord, NO!" he cried and took an involuntary half step forward.

He cringed as the bullet from one of the guns went just wide of his right ear and blew splinters off the batwing behind him. "Nah, nah, Sheriff," Virge said with a majestic grin. "Gotta let Miles have his fun afore we do what we must."

Cosy looked once more at Allie, anxious, and then he saw the expression on her face: she wasn't broken, she was fucking furious. And if she wasn't broken yet, then he couldn't break, not even with Sully gone. He felt a coldness descend over him, and he turned back to the rogue range-riders. "What's that shit you got to do, you murdering curs?" he demanded in a low, tight voice.

"We got to go pay them masks back!" Virge said. "Seeing as you ain't got the balls to, Sheriff."

"Well, *we* do," said Miles with a mean laugh as he stood up and stuffed himself back in his pants. He stuck his booted foot up on Allie's hip and shoved her over onto her side. Cosy saw that her gaze still promised a vengeance surer than the Lord's.

"I told you I was coming back to talk..." he began.

"Time for talkin's done, Sheriff!" yelled Amos, his voice breaking. "We got our marching orders now!"

"And who's given them orders, Amos?" He saw the young man look uncertainly at Virge, and that was when he saw the shiny thing on Amos' chest catch the light and glint. "What's that on your chest, boy?" he asked. His quick eyes, knowing what to look for now, saw them on Miles and Virge, too.

The young men glanced at each other, all three of them, but before they could say anything a powerful voice rang out from the upper landing, words crashing to the floor of the saloon with the dull finality of a falling body. "'The Devil led him up to a high place and showed him in an instant all the kingdoms of the world. And he said to him, "I will give you all their authority and splendor; it has been given to me, and I can give it to anyone I want to. If you worship me, it will all be yours."' That's what ole Nick said to the man-Jesus, Sheriff, and do you know what that son of the Lord did then?"

Jedediah Stowe stood on the landing, his book held in one hand just under something which hung around his neck. Something which glinted in the light, and which was not the crucified figure which usually sat its questionable place there. To his right, under his arm, stood Fayette Reese, looking at the Preacher with adoration. Cosy took in the mussed look of her hair, the disheveled clothing, and the puffiness of her lips and his stomach turned. For the second time that horrible night, he felt bitter saliva flood his mouth and he spat it out onto the floor in disgust.

"The man-Jesus told that fallen angel to keep his offer to his own damn self, Sheriff! He told him to take that load of horseshit and shove it up his damned ass!" he cried out. "Can you believe what that son of the Lord did, Cozy Eric?" and the preacher threw his head back and cackled laughter at the ceiling.

"I believe it, Jedediah," Cosy said. "But what—"

"HE... WAS... DEAD... *WROOOOONG!*" came the bellowed response.

Cosy's jaw dropped.

"What's the matter, Sheriff?" Virge taunted. "You still ain't figured out the game here, have you?"

"Boo fuckin' hoo, Sheriff!" called Miles, who now sauntered over to the bar and went around back to pull a new bottle down from the wall.

"What...?" Cosy began, but had to stop to moisten his lips with his tongue. As he did so, he saw Allie rocking slightly on her side, tied arms behind her... near her spurs! He covered his surprise, and played for time. "So what's the game, Jedediah?" he called upstairs, and moved to his right, slowly, hands still in the air to pull their attention further away from Allie Chatterton and whatever she might be about. "Looks to me like you done been throwin' over one Lord for another, mayhap," he said.

The preacher started down the stairs like he owned the Running Shadows, young Fayette on his arm radiant in her own fanaticism, and she, too, had the Stranger's golden sign on a chain around her neck. "And why would I not, eh, Sheriff? What has that good ole Lord done for us but to abandon His precious flock? Have we not been cast, as Matthew said, 'into the fiery furnace, where there will be weeping and gnashing of teeth'? Are we not already in Hell, Cozy Eric Cosy!"

"And if we were?"

"AND IF WE WERE, SHOULD WE NOT RATHER REIGN IN HELL THAN SERVE IN HEAVEN?" boomed the Preacher as he crossed the floor of the saloon towards Cosy, to a chorus of "Amen!" and "Say it, Preacher!"

"You honestly think we are meant to reign here, Jedediah?" the sheriff asked.

"I most certainly do, Eric. Me and my young friends, because they've seen the light and the darkness, and they don't wanna die like your deputies. Or like you, fool that you are."

At that moment, an enraged Allie Chatterton blew a righteous and messy hole through Amos Benedict, and Cosy dropped to his knees and fell left, hand slapping hell-bent for the leather tied down on his right thigh. The Running Shadows dissolved into chaos as the range-riders and the law of Kingdom Come both shot to kill.

Cosy's first bullet hit Virge Phillips in the left shoulder, knocking off his aim and spinning him to that side. He heard Allie screaming her wordless rage as she strode forward and fired again. He saw her shot shatter the bottle that Miles Mullery was holding, and he dropped down, out of sight behind the bar. Fayette Reese shrieked and jumped at Allie, grabbing her gun hand and spinning her about.

Virge still had his big iron out, and was down on his knees but still shooting. Cosy rolled to his left, firing again as the range-rider's slugs tore chips out of the floor where he'd lain. The sheriff caught sight of Jedediah staring blankly down at a wound in his chest, before falling backwards like a great axed tree. Nearby, Fayette still grappled with Allie and both women grunted and yelled. Still pulling the trigger, he finally saw the last bullets of his load-out snap Virge's head back and lay him down.

Then Miles popped back up above the bar top with Happy Pete's big scatter gun in his hands, and it boomed out with a roar louder even than the preacher's had been. Cosy ducked his head and shoulders instinctively even as he reloaded, then looked up in time to see Fayette and Allie fall together, fresh blood splattered on them both. With a yell, he brought his own gun up even as the last of the range-riders swivelled towards him, and then both blasts sounded almost together.

Miles Mullery crashed back into the mirror behind the bar with a cry of pain and a black, smoking hole where his right eye had been. He sank behind the bar.

Cosy scanned the room quickly, ignoring the blood dripping from his shredded ear and the badly damaged left hand door of the batwings behind him. Everyone else in the saloon was down. Neither of the two range-riders he could see were moving, but Jedediah was on his back gasping for breath like a landed fish, his life's blood pooled beneath him. And in the middle of his chest, Cosy saw the yellow sign of that Stranger sitting like it was happy with the night's work, and then the preacher finally lay still.

He ran to Allie and saw her eyes spring open just as she tried to sit up, and groaned instead. "I gotcha, Allie," he said as he dropped to her side. "Dear Lord, are you...?" and he saw then that Fayette Reese had taken the brunt of the scatter gun's load as she hung on Allie's right arm, shielding her from the worst of it. Fayette was very dead. Allie's left arm had been perforated by some shot, but looked to be minimal compared to what she might have taken. He looked up into her face, saw the gag hanging limp around her chin and the bruising around her eyes, and his own anger bloomed hot and red in his chest.

"Shit, Eric," she said, her face pinched.

"It's done."

"It ain't done!" she cried. "I've got that Mullery fuck to kill, and...!"

"They're all dead, Allie. You and me, we put paid to 'em and it's done."

Her lips quivered and she closed her eyes, then her fist made a hollow booming noise when she slammed it down into the floor.

"Don't you dare cry on me, Allie Chatterton," he said. "We ain't got time for that now, and you're tougher than anyone I've ever met, and that includes m'self."

"But they, what Miles did to me...!"

"What he did he'll pay for in Hell, Allie—he's gone. They all are, the whole sick lot of 'em. And I need you. This bunch is done, sure, but that Stranger's still out there! Look what he done, inciting these to all of this!" Cosy was breathing hard as he tore strips from the least messy parts of what was left of Fayette's dress.

"I heard what they said, Eric," she said in a shaky voice. Anger still smoldered in her eyes, the debt owed her by Miles Mullery clearly far from paid in her estimation. She made no sound of protest as he began binding her arm, just gritted her teeth. Then: "But why would that Stranger set them on to go kill them masks out on the plains at night? They're from the same city by the lake—they serve the same King, right?"

"I thought the same as you, Allie, but now I got to wonder... You ever heard that story 'bout that English feller, Robin Hood?"

"Why exactly in the fuck are you bringing that up at a time like now?"

"Hear me out for a God-blessed moment, deputy! It's like that, mayhap... See, the rightful King had to go off to do something or other out of the country, so he set his cousin to do his necessaries while he's away. But then the cousin thinks he's the special one, so he starts maneuvering to make a King out of himself, and—"

"Eric Cosy!" she interrupted exasperatedly. "You're saying that the Stranger's making a play against the Yeller King and using our folk to do it."

"Uh. Well... yeah. Like that."

"Well, shit and just say so then! Man-Jesus, but who knew you'd be such a talker?" She reached for one of the discarded shreds of cloth, then bunched it up and held it against his bleeding ear. "To be honest, though," she said, a weak smile on her face as she saw him wince, then he took the cloth himself. "Best you be a talker, I guess: you're gonna be a shit listener with only one ear." And sitting there in that room full of death, she began to laugh.

Cosy joined her, his guts finally unclenching. And then he heard something shift from over to their left and both of them brought up their guns, aimed in that direction...

"Sh... Sheriff?"

"My God! Golden Rudy, that you?" he said, letting his gun hand fall as he saw the blond Rudolph Eichelbeck stand up from behind a collapsed table, hunched over, hands under opposite armpits. "You alright, fella?"

"Yessir, mostly like."

"Okay, well, I'm gonna need you to round up some townsfolk, even's late as it is. Maybe start with Tom Reynolds out by the front end of town, and—"

"But, Sheriff!" Rudy interrupted, walking over slowly, his shoulders hunched with his misery. "I can't! See, I heard the preacher talking to that Stranger before you came back in, and..."

"Wait," Cosy interrupted. "That's flat impossible, Rudy. I'd walked the Stranger out towards the back end of town and left him there when I came back this'a'way. He couldn't have been here talking to Jedediah when you say he was 'cause he was behind me."

"Not the regular Stranger, but the other Stranger."

"What other Stranger?"

"You remember, don't you? I told you earlier, Sheriff. The one with the mask."

"But the Stranger didn't have a mask on."

"He did! I swear! It was pale, and he looked sick, and he was here and I could see him drinking the sin like a heat shimmer off the preacher, Fayette, and those boys. Then he took off his mask, and handed out them chains to each of them, he did!"

Cosy spared a glance at Allie who looked as stunned as he did, then he turned back to Rudy. "What happened next?"

"Then he looked at me, without the mask on, and it was horrible. Horrible!" Tears stood out in the young man's eyes, spilling over the lashes and running down his cheeks. "And I had no choice, I didn't want to die!" he wept. "Not in his sight, not from him!"

Cosy took him by the shoulders. "Didn't have no choice of what, Rudy? You're not making any sense, fella!"

"I had to take one of them signs from him, too!"

"What? Why, Rudy?"

"Because if I didn't, then I'd be dead, sure as everyone else!" he sobbed.

"Everyone else who?"

"Every man, woman, and child in Kingdom Come," Rudy said in a near-whisper.

"Fuck me sideways," Allie breathed.

"That's impossible, Rudy. They can't all be..."

"They are, they are!" the young man wailed.

"You mean," Cosy said, and had to swallow and start over again. "You mean it's just us as is left alive?"

"NO!" Rudy cried as he suddenly pulled his hands from his armpits. He viciously drove the knives they held at both Allie and Cosy. "IT'S JUST ME NOW,

IS ALL! IT'S JUST ME IT'S JUST ME IT'SJUSTME…!"

***

Outside the Running Shadows Rest, the Stranger smiled as he heard just one, lone voice crying out in the wilderness.

Then came a single gunshot, and he walked away.

And it was good.

ACKNOWLEDGEMENTS

"Not On the Recommended Reading List," "An Investigation Into The King In Yellow," "Hastur and the King In Yellow," "Play Fragment," "Yellow Triptych," "Dreams of the Yellow King," "The Swelling," "The Unmasking," "The Rest of Your Life," "Fantastic Worlds," "The Streets of Alar," "Dreams of the King," "Easy Come, Easy Go," "The Colour of Death," and "Chambersworld" originally appeared in the 2007 edition of *The King In Yellow* anthology from Atlantean Publishing.

"Future Imperfect" originally appeared in the 2014 anthology *In the Court of the Yellow King* from Celaeno Press.

"Dark Stars & Steam" originally appeared in the 2015 anthology *The Steam Chronicles* from Zimbell House Publishing, LLC.

All other stories are original to this anthology.

All editions herein are ©2016 by their respective authors.

Title page art by Betty Rocksteady.

ABOUT THE EDITORS

Editor at Atlantean Publishing for twenty years, **DJ Tyrer** has worked in education and retail, and has been published in magazines such as *Cyaegha* and *Tigershark*, in anthologies *Chilling Horror Stories* (Flame Tree) and *Sorcery and Sancitity: A Homage to Arthur Machen* (Hieroglyphics Press), and has a novella available, *The Yellow House* (Dunhams Manor).
http://djtyrer.blogspot.co.uk/

Joseph Bouthiette Jr. is co-editor of Carrion Blue 555 and Scrimshaw Obscura, and the mastermind behind this collaborative project. He owes thanks to Ovid's Withering for inspiring his contribution to this volume.

Atlantean Publishing is a British small press, run by DJ Tyrer, that has been going for 20 years and is based in Southend-on-Sea, Essex, UK. It produces five 'zines—*Awen, Bard, Garbaj, Monomyth* and *The Supplement*—and publishes a variety of fiction and poetry booklets and broadsides.

Mythos related products include the poetry broadside series *Xothic Sathlattae* and *Yellow Leaves* and the following booklets:

Another Fine Mess, or The King In Yellow in Black and White by DJ Tyrer
Beyond the Wall of Death: Lovecraft @125
Codex Yokai by Cardinal Cox
Mythos Fragments
The Art Mephitic and Other Poems
The Phantom of Truth by DJ Tyrer and Glynn Owen Barrass

Guidelines and a complete listing of all Atlantean products can be found on the wiki at http://atlanteanpublishing.wikia.com/wiki/

Further information on the Yellow Mythos may be discovered at http://kinginyellow.wikia.com/wiki/

CATALOGUE BLUE 555

CB555-01: 555 Vol. 1: None So Worthy
CB555-02: The Book of Adventures
CB555-03: Mr. Malin and the Night
CB555-04: Haiku Fuck You
CB555-05: 555 Vol. 2: This Head, These Limbs
CB555-06: The Book of Adventures 2
CB555-07: A Terrible Thing

Forthcoming:
CB555-08: 555 Vol. 3: Questions & Cancers
CB555-09: Savage Anesthesia
CB555-10: Plague Gods